Shaun Meeks is the author of the Dillon the Monster Dick series as well as Shutdown, Down on the Farm, and Maymon. He has published over 50 short stories, the most recent appearing in *Zippered Flesh 3*, *The Best of the Horror Zine*, *Dark Moon Digest*, *Rogue Nation*, *All That Remain*, *Monsters Among Us*, *Insidious Assassins*, *Fresh Fear*, and *Zombies Gone Wild*. His short stories have been collected in *Dark Reaches*, *Brother's Ilk* (with James Meeks), *At the Gates of Madness*, and the upcoming *Salt on the Wounds*. He is currently working on the fourth novel in the Dillon series, two standalone novels (*Gone Crazy…Be Back Soon*, and *The Desolate*), as well as a collection of southern horror (*Blood on the Ground: Six Shots of Southern Discomfort*).

Shaun currently lives in Toronto, Ontario with his partner, Mina, and their micro-yeti, Lily, where they are always planning their next adventure.

To find out more or to contact Shaun, please visit:
www.shaunmeeks.com,
www.facebook.com/shaunmeeks, or
www.twitter.com/ShaunMeeks

T0116831

Shaun Meeks' Dillon the Monster Dick series published by IFWG Publishing International

The Gate at Lake Drive (Book 1, 2015)
Earthbound and Down (Book 2, 2017)
Altered Gate (Book 3, 2019)

Book 3:
Dillon the Monster Dick series

ALTERED GATE

by
Shaun Meeks

Altered Gate

All Rights Reserved

ISBN-13: 978-0-9945229-7-9

Copyright ©2019 Shaun Meeks

V1.0

Printed in Palatino Linotype and Arno Pro.

IFWG Publishing International
Melbourne

www.ifwgpublishing.com

Acknowledgements

As always, this book wouldn't be possible without the help and guidance of so many people. My work with Toronto Police Services helped me learn about, and sometimes twist, police procedure. This book, as many others, is full of liberties I've taken. I'd love to name the officers who've helped me over the years when I worked in the downtown corps, but to respect them and their wishes, I won't. They know who they are.

I also want to thank my kids who live in Niagara Falls and provided me with some background on areas they thought would be great in my book. I've been going there for years, but it was nice to hear what places they thought were creepy, or they'd just love to see in a book. Of course, I took a lot of liberties with the geography in Niagara Falls and in Toronto as well. The best part of writing fiction is reforming landscapes and cities to suit the needs of the story.

As usual, I also want to thank my partner, Mina, for everything she does for me. She's my springboard for ideas and helped me realize if something was a good choice and worth pursuing, or if I should dash it and try another road. I love and appreciate how she never shies away from the truth, which I think makes for a better story.

I also want to thank everyone in the Toronto Burlesque community who I've had the pleasure of meeting over the years. You people shine so hard. I know there are times in these books where things might be read between the lines, as though I may be talking about this performer or that producer, but I assure you, I'm not. Everything in this is fiction. There is real drama behind the sequins curtain, but none of that is what I'm playing with. This is all drama created to push the story forward. I don't want anyone to get their ostrich feathers ruffled. I need to stir this pot this particular way to cook up what I have in store for the future.

To the editors who've helped me fine-tune this book, and my writing as a whole, I give a huge thanks. I've always looked forward to the feedback, even if it makes me feel like I'm still at a grade three level when it comes to grammar. But with great editing comes a greater understanding of what I need to change, so thanks to all of the editors at IFWG who did their best to make me appear as though I can flawlessly string thoughts together.

And to all the readers of the Dillon series, thank you. Seeing how many people are enjoying the books so far makes me want to keep writing them. There are still four more to come after this one, plus some short stories, so I hope you're looking forward to going down this road as much as I'm looking forward to paving it.

This book is dedicated to the memory of Gordon "Elvis" Symonds. Co-worker, friend, and someone I genuinely looked up to. He had a way of affecting people in such a positive way. Even if it was someone he was arresting, he could make them see a bit of light at the end of the tunnel. Everyone who came across his path misses him. Hope you're hanging out with Adam West and the King right now.

This is also for my daughter, Anjel. You always know how to make others happy. Just don't forget to make yourself happy too.

Wednesday

Once upon a time, things seemed so much simpler. I'd get a call from someone, or stumble upon some creature with no right to be here, and I'd hit them back to the world where it belonged. A few times, here and there, it'd get hairy, sure, but all in all, things tended to flow better, to move like clockwork. I'd say close to ninety percent of the beings that find their way to Earth are trying to escape the worlds and realms they live in. They're refugees who hope to escape wars, death, or other forms of cruelty, so they're not always the rough types. A lot of them cry and beg to be left alone, but lately, things aren't as simple as they used to be.

Take these two for example. Five days ago, I dealt with a monster who'd taken over the corpse of a priest I considered a friend, and that was no fun at all. I figured on taking a bit of a break after the whole mess, but this morning I got a call from a family who told me they thought their laundry room was haunted. They explained about voices they'd heard, how clothing would go missing or would be found chewed up as though it had been put through a paper shredder, and asked for my help. I wasn't sure what it could be, and it might've been nothing at all, but since they put down a non-refundable deposit, I figured I'd make the trip.

They lived in the very west end of the city, almost into Mississauga, but traffic was light enough, so I made good time. On my way I sent Rouge a message to let her know where I was and I'd text her when I was done. She sent me a smiley face and a message about a gig offer she wasn't happy about. Apparently, the promotor of the show thought fifty dollars for a high-end act she was usually paid two hundred for was a great opportunity for her. I asked if bringing over some Swiss Chalet and my full attention would be of any help. She messaged back that I was her hero.

I do what I can.

When I got out to the house, a little bungalow with a tiny, cute flowerbed nestled up to the porch and a tire swing hanging from a monstrous oak, the family—mother, father, and two daughters— came out to meet me. I grabbed my bag from the passenger seat and was taken inside. The father smiled at me weakly, but the mother seemed so happy that I was there. I could tell she was freaked out about the whole thing, while her husband was no doubt trying to come up with a logical explanation for it all that wouldn't involve them having to pay for my services.

Some people might think saying this is sexist or wrong, but in my experience with the strange and unexplainable, that's just how it goes. Going only from the people I've interacted with, it's just how it works out more than seventy-five percent of the time. Women seem to accept what their eyes see, while men want to over analyze so much and try to make the impossible fit into the reality they know. If I had time, I'd love to study those that won't or can't accept the strange, but monsters and demons keep me too busy.

"We usually take turns doing the laundry, so we've both seen things we just can't figure out," the wife explained. "I've heard voices, I swear I have, but when I go into the laundry room, there's nobody there."

"I thought, and still think, it might be us picking up some sort of radio or cellphone signals," the husband cut in as we stood in the living room. "But, well, there are other things I just can't quite…"

"I think I get it," I said and smiled. I hoped it'd set their minds at ease. Letting people know they didn't sound crazy is a great first step to making them feel better. "I deal with things like this all the time."

"Do you think it'll be like one of the monsters you fought by those old buildings?" the youngest of the kids asked. I looked at her, confused, not sure what she meant, but she quickly went on and my stomach dropped a bit. "Those videos on YouTube are awesome. The monsters were so big and scary. That's why we told momma you'd be good at getting our monsters out of the laundry room."

"We haven't seen them yet," the other daughter said with a huge, mainly toothless smile. "But we know you're a superhero when it comes to monsters."

I said nothing. I'd known there had to be at least one video making the rounds from the fight in the Distillery District. When it all went down, I'd noticed a few people with cellphones out, pointed in my direction. It's the world we live in, but I really thought people would laugh them off. I'd hoped they'd think it was nothing more than movie magic or a viral video for a new creature feature.

Now, some might think it's weird for me to even care if a video of me fighting a monster gets out into the world. I mean, I have a website where people can come out and find me easy enough, though it's usually by stumbling on it while looking up porn sites involving large penises. A video on YouTube isn't the same thing. Especially if it's going viral, which I had no idea had happened, but if the kids had seen it, there was a chance.

"I don't know if 'superhero' is the right word," I said with a laugh, trying to brush it all off. "I'm more of a police officer or detective who's hunting down all the strange beasts that shouldn't be here." I looked from the girls to the parents and although the mother was still smiling, old doubting Thomas wasn't. In fact, his arms were crossed and he looked rather terse.

"So how much is this going to cost?" he asked, and I was prepared. I'm always ready for that question. I reached into my bag and pulled out a paper that contains all expenses. Normally, people are fine with it. I mean, if you really believe there is something supernatural in your house, what wouldn't you pay to get it out? There are always a few times where they look over the bill proposal and balk, but not often. The way he began to scowl going over it once, then twice, and then three more times, I was sure he was going to say no. "And how long will it take?"

"Depends on what's in there. I'm not sure what to think from the details you've given, but I think I can narrow it down to three or four possible species. Only one of them on the list is nasty. The others should be pretty fast and easy to tidy up for you folks."

"How long then?" he asked, sounding as thrilled as someone watching paint dry.

"Well, why don't the four of you go out for lunch while I go in and assess the situation? If it's one of the less threatening ones, it'll be done by the time you get back."

"And if not?" he asked, crossing his arms as if he would scold me if I gave him a longer time than he thought necessary.

"Well, if it is the other, more violent kind of creature, I'll have to go get something from my supplier to get rid of it. He's not far from here so I'd say regardless of what it is you'll be sleeping fine in your own beds tonight. Either way, I'll call one of you to let you know when it's done."

"We can't stay and watch?" the youngest girl cried out, and stomped her feet on the ground. "What's the point of having a monster fighter here if we can't see him fight monsters?"

I knelt down so I was eye to eye with both the girls, seeing as they were giving me equal amounts of stink eye. "So you saw that video of me with the big, ugly monster, right?"

"Yeah."

"Well, there are a lot of things like that. Some are big and gross, stinky things that could wilt a flower. Some of them smell so bad, they could turn milk sour. Worse than the worst fart." They smile at the thought of it, the youngest covering her mouth to hold in a chuckle. "But sometimes, it's not just the old stink faces you have to worry about. A few of them are real bad, and will attack anyone who gets near them. The last thing I'd want to see is any of you getting hurt. That would mean I'm not doing my job, and a bad *Yelp* rating these days is killer. So, you two should go with your mom and dad, go get some food, maybe even ice cream for dessert—mint chocolate chip is my personal favorite—and I'll make sure you guys can all sleep safe and sound tonight. Sound good?"

"I guess," the youngest said. "But I'd rather see you beat up a monster than eat ice cream. Dairy makes Daddy fart like a monster."

That was all that needed to be said, and they were off. Before they went though, Dad decided to give me a warning. He whispered that if he found out I was some kind of charlatan, he'd sue my ass back to last week. I just smiled and saw them off. It was the old *Leave it to Beaver* style where I stood on the steps of the house and waved to them as they drove off. Behind me, the house was silent. I took in a deep breath of the cool day outside before I turned to get to work.

My bag was on the floor, and I scooped it up and took a tour of the house, just to get a feel of it. The place was nice, tastefully if not plainly decorated with all the charm of Ikea and Wal Mart, but there was something cozy about it. It was a house that looked well lived in. Not messy and worn down, just homey.

It made me think of my own apartment. The sun doesn't always get in there, so there tends to be a dark, gloomy feeling at times. That's only made worse by the fact that I have so many oddities in there. Some of it is just specimen jars I've picked up at curio shops; others are things I've acquired on the job. I have bits of some of my stranger, more dangerous adventures. I have a piece of tentacle from the *Hellion* I fought, a claw and skull of one of many *Gloudians* I was attacked by, and even a tooth from one of the earthbound creatures I killed. My furniture is sparse and I could really use some time to give the place a good cleaning. Seeing this family's house made me feel as though my own apartment was more like Oscar the Grouch's place than a suitable place to live. It made me wonder what Rouge thought about it. She's never said anything overly negative in regards to it, not even something on the sly, which she's so good at. I could ask, but part of me is afraid of the answer she'd give.

It's strange to be worried about that. I mean the two of us sort of rushed head first into this relationship. Since I've never really dated anyone, at least on this planet, I'm not very good at knowing how fast or slow to take things, so I just let them happen. Rouge, on the other hand, is an intense person, someone who wears their feelings out in the open for people to see, for the most part, so she went with her feelings and we went from zero to sixty in no time. Since then we've slowed things up a bit. Not because we're afraid or getting bored, just because we want to keep it fun and light and allow the rest of it to take its course.

It was while I was thinking about all of that, lost in how happy I was with her and looking forward to seeing her, that I found the laundry room. I also found a surprise waiting for me.

The room was small, attached to the kitchen through a small doorway. The place was spotless and smelt of fabric softener and detergent. It was strong, but not unpleasant. I stood in the doorway, took it all in and waited to see if anything would happen. The way the mother described it, the washer and dryer would move on their own, jumping at times, even when they were off. She also said there were voices and the kids agreed: low, grumbling voices that sounded like monsters. There was nothing else to go on. No strange smells, no sightings of shadows, shapes or spirits. There was just a vague idea of what many would assume was a haunting. I sat my bag down, reached into my jacket and pulled out my *Tincher*, a dagger carved, blessed and branded with all possible curses, blessings and spells to defeat almost anything not of this world. Always assuming they're in range of the small blade. If they are, one swipe and it was lights out, dead or returned back to the place they came from, depending on the creature.

Nearly thirty minutes passed. I'm nothing if not patient. I stood there for half an hour, stared at the washer and dryer almost to the point of things becoming blurry, and waited for something to happen. A part of me wanted to sign into YouTube and see how many hits the video of me fighting those monsters had gotten, but I couldn't bring myself to do it. I tricked my own head into thinking I needed to be quiet to make these things show themselves, but the truth of the matter was that I wasn't ready to see it yet. There was a chance I was going to be in some sort of hot water with it, so I needed time to build the courage before checking.

I was pulled out of worry with a dull, metallic thud. I focused towards the source of the sound, the dryer, and waited for more. It came again, then a third time, and on the forth one, the sound was coming from the washer as well.

"Alright, who's in there?" I called out, still in the doorway. "Might as well show yourselves. It makes it so much easier on everyone."

The thuds increased, joined by a pair of low, deep, guttural growls. The doors for the machines began to open and slam shut over and over again. Clearly whatever was in these machines was trying to scare me. It was also clear, they had no idea I was a hunter.

"Get out!" the dryer bellowed and jumped a half inch or so towards me. I tried not to chuckle at the sight of the possibility of extremely slow pursuit. "Get out or die, human!"

"Who said I was human?" I said, juggling my Tincher. The machines stopped moving at that. I wondered if they were pondering the seriousness of my question, or if they were trying to come up with a plan.

"Of course you're human," the washer growled, and the thuds started anew. "We will eat you and taste your delicious human meat."

"You can try, but how do you plan on doing that? I don't see teeth in those machines, assuming that's what you took possession of when you crossed over. So, you can try to eat me with your dull metal doors, but in the end, you'll only piss me off and I'll make you suffer before I send you back to where you came from."

"What? Who are you?" the washer asked in a low whisper.

"He's a hunter," the dryer said, and even in the tinny, echoed voice I could hear panic.

"Impossible. He's no hunter. He's just a stupid Earther."

I walked over to the machines. The bangs and thrashing about continued. They growled words I couldn't understand, nor cared to. I wasn't going to play around with them. I just took my dagger and slammed it into the top of the washer. There was a scream of metal against metal as I thrust the blade in, and then dragged it out, but no cries from the monster who'd taken possession of the machine. The creatures continued to make the washer and dryer jump and thud as they growled at me.

That's never happened before.

I stabbed again, to no end. Like I said, things used to be so much easier.

"Get the human!" the dryer commanded and they both made a minuscule hop in my direction. They hopped again, and as I watched, looking down at them, I saw something. They'd given themselves away.

"Sneaky bastards," I whispered, and couldn't help but smile.

I grabbed hold of the washer and pushed it so it landed on its side, and then did the same to the dryer, shoving it the other direction. The creatures screamed out as the machines crashed to the floor and revealed them for what they were. Maybe wherever these monsters were from they had access to the Wizard of Oz because they'd tried to pull off a move the Great and Powerful Oz would've been proud of.

Under the dryer were two small beasts, no bigger than a medium sized cat. They stared up at me with dull, empty eye sockets. Their bodies were made up of dust and lint, and as soon as they saw me, their growls stopped. They ran to hug each another with false arms, and just stared up at me.

"Do you know who I am?" I asked.

"Some human," one of them said, sounding less ominous since it no longer had the machine echoing its voice.

"Not really," I told them. "Judging by your height, shape, and the elongated skulls, I'm guessing you're both Bronns?"

"Oh no," said the one who'd been under the dryer. "I told you he was a hunter!"

"You got me," I said, walking towards them. They quivered and held on to one another. There was nowhere to run. The fallen machines were on either side of them, and behind them was a wall. It was time to send them back, and they knew it. The Tincher would be enough.

"Please don't hurt us."

"You know I have a job to do. You shouldn't be here. You know the rules. Not to mention you're scaring the nice family of humans that live here. You're leaving this planet."

"No, but if you leave now and let us be, we won't let *Throg* hurt you," the one from the washer said through the sound of tearless crying. "We aren't hurting anyone. We don't want to hurt you."

"Who or what is a Throg?"

"Me is!"

The voice behind me was low and large. I turned to see what was there, but felt something grab hold of me and the next thing I knew, I was airborne. I didn't even have time to think before my body slammed into the wall next to a door that led outside. The drywall gave a bit, and I went crashing to the ground. Luckily, I still had my dagger in hand. I moved as fast as I could to get to my feet. I heard the thudding steps of something I guessed was Throg, and caught a glimpse of the monster before it hit me.

I had no idea where the goliath had been hiding. The creature was tall, a few inches above my six feet, and his body looked to be made up of things from a recycling bin. Newspapers, pop cans, dryer sheets, bottles of Tide, and other garbage took the shape of what was a lot like the smaller Bronns, only in a larger package. I'd heard how some of their species could be ten to twenty times the regular size of the average ones, but with that kind of height, smarts appeared to be sacrificed.

Strength was not.

"No hurt us," Throg grunted as he charged at me. "*You* hurt. *You* go away."

I *wanted* to get away, even more so when the big brute plowed into me and sent me back into the wall. At that point either the house shook or my whole body did, and my dagger slipped from my hand and clattered to the floor. I moved to pick it up, but Throg wrapped his garbage arms around me and began to squeeze. I gasped for air and struggled to get free.

"Kill him, Throg," one of the little bastards yelled out, cheering the brute on from the sidelines. "He wants to send us back home, so kill him."

He continued to try. His python grip around me was a killer, and I knew I had to do something fast. Without my knife there was no way to end it, but my gloves were tucked into my back pocket. I knew they were my only hope, if they worked on a Bronn at all, and I was about to put all my chips on that bet. The problem was the monster had my arms crushed to my sides and it was a struggle to reach them. My only hope was to let out all my breath fast, create just enough space between the two of us, and grab them. Problem with that was, if I missed getting hold of them, I'd be dead since his grip would be even tighter and pulling in breath would be next to impossible.

Since I've never been one to ponder things until it's too late, I did what I planned and grabbed them. One fell; the other was in my clenched fist. While I struggled to breath in his vice grip, I started to feel as though I was about to pass out at any second. I fought the calling darkness and slipped the glove on. After that, I touched it to him and hoped for success.

It wasn't easy, but it worked. Throg's arms loosened and released me. I stepped and swooped down to pick up my Tincher. Before he could regain his control, I plunged the dagger into his face and quickly swiped down. The garbage body went sprawling in every direction and a thin orange mist blinked out of this world.

After that, the two dust bunny Bronns could be dispatched and I would be done. As I walked over to them, though, they stood their ground. They looked at me with those dark, eyeless holes, and I realized they had stopped shaking.

"You have no idea what you're doing, hunter. Everything is changing. The worlds, realms and dimensions are falling apart. And you still stick to doing this. Why?"

"It's what I'm paid to do."

I didn't feel great sending them off back to their planet, but I did have a job to do. If I allowed these things to run wild, it wouldn't mean they'd be any safer here than there. What it would guarantee is I'd get pulled from Earth and another hunter would replace me. And since I had nowhere left to go, my own world and people nothing more than a memory, I had no plans to stop hunting. And sure, I've made exceptions before, but some things are easier to keep quiet than others.

Once upon a time, things used to be so much simpler.

I left the family's house and messaged Rouge to see if she'd be up for a visit. She was quick to get back, saying she'd love it more if I brought chips or chocolate. She also reminded me not to forget the Swiss Chalet. I ordered online, and then stopped by a convenience store on the way over. I parked beside a group of teens with skateboards who were listening to some of the most soul-shattering music I'd ever heard. Not loud or heavy, just auto-tuned and monotonous. It sounded like the kind of music you'd listen to if you wanted to kill yourself. I walked through a cloud of musty smoke and went through the automatic doors.

After I grabbed a few snacks, I headed out and noticed the group had their eyes glued on me. The music was thankfully shut off. They whispered to one another, and looked giddy and excited. Two of the group nudged the smallest over and over again until finally he stepped forward and opened his mouth.

"Hey, are you the monster guy?"

"The what?" I asked, barely hearing him.

"You know, the monster dude from that video on YouTube. That shit was sick, bro. I saw it, and was woke, knowing there's these dank monsters out there, man. Just like some crazy TV shit."

I groaned and continued to walk to my car. "I don't know what you're talking about. Pretty sure you got the wrong guy."

"No way, star, you're all over YouTube, like over a million hits. I saw you fight some sick monster. It was so fresh."

"I don't watch YouTube and there's no such thing as monsters."

"Sure, man, I get it, there's no real monsters," he chuckled like a brainless gnat. "We got your back, monster man. Keep on keeping on, dude."

I drove off and tried my best to ignore it. I knew one day I'd have an issue with people who posted everything to social media, expecting it to go viral. One day it might. There was only so long I was going to be able to keep doing what I do before it spread in a very public way. To some, that might be a good thing, a way for me to get more calls and more business; an easy way to clean up the mess these weak spots and portals cause. I have a website where I advertise what I do, but I don't go and spread it around the way this clearly would. See, I put up the website and let people find their own way to it. I don't put up fliers, or ads on TV. It's there, but not in your face because the last thing I want is to spread some sort of panic. You might think that the people who hire me could do that, start telling people about the monsters and demons in their homes, or places of business, but think about it. Would *you*? If someone had a roach or rat problem, would they want everyone on the world to know about it, would they video it and put in on some social media platform? Probably not. Most would be ashamed, thinking it would make them look disgusting, ward off friends and potential customers. So, they call an exterminator and keep the whole situation to themselves. Same thing goes with my clientele. None of them want people to know they were infested with some otherworldly creatures.

I don't blame them in that respect. Even though, like pests, it's not their fault. This kind of stuff just happens from time to time. I tend to tell a lot of them that to console them and make them know it's not their fault; it's just the nature of things. Then, when I leave and the problem has been resolved, they can pretend it never happened. And the rest of the world continues to sleep easy thinking nothing unnatural exists here.

Now there's this video. It might be nothing in the end. It could be that it had already gone viral. The stoner skater said it has over a million hits, but no doubt there's already an argument in the comment section about it being real or fake, monster or some government experiment. Some might even be calling it a distraction from some crooked politician, a little dog wagging to take your attention away from the latest scandal. If I've learned nothing else about social media and viral videos over the last few years, I've seen how nothing stays front and center for any great length of time. All I can do is hope something bigger and better comes up soon and people forget all about it, return to their regularly scheduled meme war or the everlasting battle between the far left and the far right.

I hoped it would happen fast. The last thing I need is for this to all get back to the higher- ups: the people I have to answer to would not be too stoked with that kind of publicity. I like being a hunter. I don't think I'd want to get in all sorts of trouble, be pulled from here and forced to do what Godfrey does.

Then again, I'm not the most likely to follow the rules. After all, I'm heading over to my human girlfriend's apartment to eat rotisserie chicken and treats, talk about my day, and do whatever comes unnatural. Most of those things are against every rule the *Collective* gave me when sending me here.

One of these days I may be the rule-follower, but I don't see it happening any time soon.

"We should have some pop and chips now. I think we earned it," Rouge said as she lay next to me. I was still struggling to catch my breath. I watched her as she got out of the bed. She was luminous, her pale skin reflecting the streetlight in the dark of the room. I was exhausted, satisfied as anyone could possibly be. Just the sight of her like that made me want a round two, though I knew she was right: we needed to treat ourselves, refuel before we went for another mattress ride.

After getting dressed and gathering our well-earned rewards, we sat down to watch some Netflix. Not too soon after did we get sidetracked with talking as we always do.

"Are you working tomorrow?" she asked, and sipped her pop.

"I have to pick up some supplies from Godfrey's, but as of now, I have no jobs scheduled. Why?"

"I have a show tomorrow and I was wondering if you wanted to come. It's one of Jason's and you know how I feel about him."

I did. In the time we'd know each other, I'd gotten to know a lot about the burlesque scene in Toronto. There were so many great people involved in it, amazing performers and producers, but there were a few real asshats as well. I'd listened to Rouge tell me all about the backstabbing, people refusing to pay performers, and others that were just smarmy in every sense and synonym of the word. Jason was one of those. He was a producer who liked to hang out in the change room while the performers were getting undressed and ready, pretending to need to talk about something important, but it never was. When it came to the end of the night and it was time to pay everyone who had given their all on stage, he would make excuses on how bad the door had been and even though he'd promised a certain amount of money, he could only offer a significantly less amount. He didn't always do it, but he did it enough times that Rouge had told him if she was to perform for him, she needed payment up front. He fought it at first, but since she had a big following in the city, he crumbled.

Still, there was a chance he'd be as lecherous as always, so when she worked with him, it was nice when I could be there to ward off the snake. I know Rouge is more than capable of doing it all on her own, but if she wanted my support, I'd give it to her any way I could.

"I'll be there in the front row."

"Yay! And who knows, it might be the last time you see me up there."

"What? Why?" I asked, and felt shocked to hear her say that. There had been times here and there where she would voice some sort of discontent, or explain how the polished sheen of the burlesque world was wearing off a bit, but I'd never heard her outright say she was considering quitting altogether.

"It's not as fun as it used to be," she explained. "I mean, I loved going out there, losing myself to the lights and the music, feeling beautiful and giving my all to everyone who watched. I still do, but the scene is changing so much. Everyone wants to be a political statement now, or some awkward, funny performer. I think the crowds are starting to like that more than people like me who do a more classic show."

"But you're so amazing at what you do. Won't you miss it?"

"Sure I will. I've been doing this for so long. It's a part of who I am, but I feel like the whole thing has turned down a road I don't really want to be on. I love the idea of being an escape for people, a bit of a fantasy. I get on stage and for that five or ten minutes I perform there's no worrying about your bills, how many likes your post has, who you're going to vote for, or anything else. But if I were to start making everything some political or social issue performance, that escape from reality is no more, you're being reminded of it. Maybe I'm just becoming an old biddy in this scene and it's time to take up knitting."

I laughed at that, and regretted it instantly.

"You think that's funny?" she said, crossing her arms, as she did her best to look indignant.

"No, but yes," I admitted. "I just pictured you in a rocking chair surrounded by cats, making piles of knitwear for your new feline companions."

She laughed to and gave my arm a little shot.

"First off, it would never be cats. They're the devil. Maybe a house full of puppies and I could make little gentleman sweaters and lady hats for them." That made me laugh even harder, and the dog shot us a look to let us know we were clearly being too loud while it attempted to sleep. "Or instead of that, maybe I could just work with you."

My laughter petered out at that, and I looked over at her, unsure if she was serious or not. The look on her face said she was dead serious.

"Work with me?"

"Yeah. Is that hard to believe?"

"Not hard to believe, but I'm not sure it's something that would ever really happen. It'd be kind of cool to go out to work with you every day, unless you'd get bored of me, but thinking about it realistically, it's dangerous and against every rule in the book."

"So is dating me."

"True, but what about the danger part? I'm not sure I'm cool with the idea of putting you in that sort of situation."

"Like when I saved you from being eaten in Innisfil?"

She had me there. If it wasn't for her, I'd be spending an

eternity being devoured by a demon. I couldn't really entertain the idea, though. It wasn't a good one. There's breaking the rules, and then there's shitting on them and throwing them into your boss' face.

"Well, saying you saved me is maybe an overstatement," I said, doing my best to try and downplay it. The fact was, when I was facing the Hellion, Rector, walking away from it in one piece seemed unlikely. If Rouge hadn't been there, I wasn't sure things would've turned out the way they had. Didn't mean I had to admit it though. Especially if she'd actually considered joining up with me full time. The kind of danger it would put her in didn't feel good in the slightest. "It's all how you look at it, I think."

"Oh, I saved you. Don't try and pee on my leg and tell me it's raining, hot shot. You owe me everything you got. But don't worry, I'm only partially serious. I would love to do what you do with you, but I don't think I want to go down that road just yet. But I'd need to cut my nails, and I just went and got these babies done," she said, smiling and shooting me a wink while flashing her manicure. "When they grow out, though, I may send you my resume."

"But if we're co-workers, do we have to stop dating? Not sure how the HR department feels about inter-office relationships."

"Well, what they don't know won't hurt them."

She had a point. I just hoped they didn't know, that nobody in the Collective was paying too much attention to what I was doing. My goal has always been to stay off their radar as much as possible, and then the rule-breaking doesn't really matter.

Thursday

After I left Rouge's, I went to my place to grab a few things, including a duffle bag to carry what I needed from Godfrey's. When I got there, I checked my cellphone for messages. I'd left it off overnight so I didn't get any calls while I was spending time with her. As soon as it powered up, I saw the light was flashing and when I checked I found it full. Sixty voicemail messages, but not one of them was worth the space they took up.

There were messages from people calling me a fraud, stoners telling me they think their mom is a monster, one from a woman who said she was a monster and needed the cute guy from the video to come over and slay her, and more of that. I listened to each and every one of them, and after they were all deleted I turned my phone off, not wanting any more of the same. After that I went to my computer and checked my email. Nearly two-hundred and fifty new emails in my inbox and just the previews of some of them made me not want to even open a single one of them.

This couldn't end fast enough.

Weaving through a sea of fake calls and messages, knowing that real clients who needed my help may not be able to get through to me, was something I should have dealt with yesterday. The way I find monsters, demons, and spirits in the section of the world I have to cover makes my life easier. I don't want to be like the others who actually have to go around and find signs or learn to sense weak spots in order to do the job. All of us hunters have a quota. I always exceed mine. I don't want to start failing because of all the prank calls.

I grabbed my bag, a few other things, and then got out of there. I needed to just go and stop thinking about all of it; I needed to allow everything to just get back to normal. I drove to Godfrey's and was thankful for it all being uneventful. I parked down the street from his shop, as I usually do, and then walked the two blocks there. As I was just about to the store, maybe three shops away, someone across the road yelled out "Holy shit! It's the monster killer!"

I refused to look over. I ignored it. Even when the guy started singing a version of the *Ghostbusters* theme, but changing the word to *Monster Killer*, I walked on and pretended I didn't hear him at all. I told myself it was fine, everything would pass as it always does. I opened the door and went into Godfrey's, but it was hard to ignore the chill in my stomach.

The little bell above his door jingled and my eyes took a second to adjust to the dim little store after being out in the bright day. Someone was already in there. Not unusual, but it was strange seeing Godfrey talking to someone in the shop in a quiet, calm voice. Normally, when anyone other than me is in there, he's a bit on the mean side. After all, the shop is a front. He's not really selling anything of interest to people, he's there to buy and provide weapons, relics, charms, and the likes to help me. I've never seen him buy from anyone, but I've seen plenty of people in the shop thinking they could pick up something weird and kitschy for a friend. Those encounters don't go over well. After all, running the shop wasn't really Godfrey's idea, it was his punishment.

On Godfrey's home planet, he did something wrong, something pretty bad: he's never gotten into what that was, but it couldn't have been good. It was bad enough that it got him sentenced to spend an uncertain amount of time on Earth, locked up in this store, until he was called back. In the store, he looks like a middle-aged Jamaican man, but if he steps outside, well, let's just say people would be freaked out to see an upright, fully dressed creature resembling a crocodile or dinosaur walking about town on two feet. I've seen it, and even I was a little freaked out.

Godfrey's a good person though. I didn't always feel that way, but things change. We've had our issues in the past, he nearly got me killed once or twice by selling me fake goods, but that's all in the past. Now I'm the one person he doesn't treat like a heel when they step into his store.

Except this guy.

When I shut the door to the shop, they both turned to look at me. The stranger smiled before he turned back to Godfrey. I saw something on Godfrey's face I'd never really seen before. The same look I've seen on the faces of creatures I'm about to dispatch.

Worry.

Fear.

It didn't look good on him.

I walked towards them, did my best to hear what the stranger was saying, but he spoke in a tone too low for me to catch any of it. Godfrey nodded over and over again, glancing from the stranger to me, and back again. The worry and fear never left his eyes.

Just as I got close enough to where I might be able to hear them, the stranger turned around and began to walk towards me. I stopped, my heart rate jumping. I thought he was about to come right at me. My hand went to the inner pocket of my jacket, my fingers wrapped around the handle of a small dagger I had there, and I readied for an attack.

"How's it going?" the stranger said as he brushed past me. He walked by and headed out the door, never looking back, and I was confused. He'd seemed like a threat as he came towards me. Godfrey had looked scared, and I'd felt something, but he barely paid me any mind. Then he was gone and I turned to Godfrey.

"Who was that?" I asked.

"Nobody. Just someone looking for something I don't have. No big deal."

"Really? So what was with the look?" I asked and Godfrey

stared at me as though he had no idea what I was talking about. As someone who deals with creatures that are frightened and willing to lie in hopes of getting what they want, there was no way I'd miss that fear in him. "I've known you for too long not to know something's up, Godfrey. You don't have anything close to a poker face, so you might as well just tell me who that was."

"I don't know what you mean," he replied, but his words couldn't hide the fear clearly written on his face.

"Your face tells me different. You might as well just tell me who it was and what they were doing here. I'll figure it out eventually."

"You mean you couldn't tell? I thought you were the best hunter around, but you couldn't tell what that was? I guess that explains why you didn't notice what was up with your priest friend."

That was a low blow, but I ignored it and turned towards the door. I replayed the whole encounter, from the moment I walked in to when the stranger brushed past me and left. There wasn't anything that popped for me. He was average height, brown hair, no marks or scars on his face, his eye colour unremarkable, weight average. Not one thing stood out in my memory-

I turned back to Godfrey. A thought popped into my head, but there was no way it could be true. I opened my mouth to say what I thought it was, but nothing came out. He nodded despite my loss for words.

"What's another hunter doing around here?" I asked when I realized everything about him was so similar to me. Nothing about us was out of the ordinary, not a single feature to make us stand out in a crowd. Average everything so it's easier to blend in, easier to be forgotten.

"He didn't say. He just said he was going to be around for the next little while and was introducing himself to me. Are you being replaced, Dillon?"

I had no idea. My stomach began to roll a little. Were the big bosses mad about the video, or me killing earthbound creatures, or maybe that I was dating a human? Was it one of those things, or all of them? I've broken the rules so many times over the years and never been called out them, so why now? What was the play here?

Those kinds of questions could eat a hole right through my tough stomach. I didn't need the stress, so I did my best to shake it off and talk to Godfrey about what I needed resupplies of. We talked for a bit, and I made a great effort to avoid thinking about all the possibilities. Yet try as I might, there was always a whisper of it in the back of my head, like an itch that wants, no, *demands* to be scratched. I didn't want to leave Earth, or my area for that matter. I had it so good here. Not just with the job and my life as a whole, but with Rouge too. We had a bit of a whirlwind relationship, things hit off fast between us, but there was a real connection there, real feelings I've never had before. I couldn't imagine leaving her.

"You okay?" Godfrey asked, and I snapped out of my downward spiral for a second to ask him what he'd said. "I said that I won't be able to get you any more silver water until I find a new supplier. The guy I used to get it off is in jail. Put some guy through a window at a bar. He thought it was no big deal. Cops said otherwise."

"No problem, but what about the other stuff on the list?"

"I got most of it in the back. Hold on a sec and I'll go get it. You sure you're okay? You look a little grey around the gills."

"I'm fine. I'm going to use your bathroom for a sec."

I went to the washroom and he went to the back to get my stuff. I felt a bit weak and dizzy out of nowhere, but I knew it wasn't out of nowhere really. It was stress. As someone who hunts down monsters for a living, it's something I'm on a first name basis with. Usually, I get adrenaline dumps to help me deal with stress so I avoid this feeling until much later, but I couldn't help playing out every possible situation that might occur if I was in trouble. And I had to be. There was no other way to explain it. Why would another hunter show up here, come see Godfrey, and say nothing to me when I showed up? In the past, if another hunter came here, or I ended up on some other hunter's turf, introductions were made and the reasons for the visit were explained. It's only happened a few times in my life, but that's what we do. It's kind of a protocol. This, it had to be something else, and that something was not good for me.

In the bathroom, as the scenarios rolled around in my overactive imagination, my knees felt so weak that I had to grab the sink to keep from falling. I looked at myself in the mirror. I did look like shit. Stir fried and served up cold. This was ridiculous. The same question rolled around in my head why now? Was this any worse than all the other things I'd done?

It couldn't be.

"You're blowing this out of proportion, dummy," I whispered to my refection. I tried to smile. It was as genuine as someone posing at Glamour Shots.

I drank some water and went back out to see Godfrey. I wanted to get out of there and call Rouge. I hoped she'd be home and not too busy. If anyone could talk me off the ledge, it was her.

"Feeling better?" Godfrey asked as I came out.

"As good as I can be."

"I'm sure it's nothing, but if it is, I'll help you any way I can. That guy seems like a real dick."

"We're all dicks, but thanks."

"You have a job tonight?" he asked, handing me the duffle bag and the list of items I'd given him. It was heavier than he made it look.

"No. With that video of me going around YouTube, all I seem to be getting are crank calls. So I turned my phone off. I'm going to see Rouge perform tonight."

"Good. That might be the best thing for you. I don't know what you're worried about with all this, but it can't be that bad. Just go out tonight and relax. Enjoy that woman of yours, because she could do so much better than you."

"Wow. You know just what to say to make a boy feel special."

Rouge was busy. She'd gone to a spa called Body Blitz with one of her performer friends. When I asked if I could swing by, thinking a spa treatment sounded like just what I needed, she told me it was a women-only place. She said after the spa she'd head to the venue so she could meet me there. That was still five hours away, so I decided to go to my place and kill some time. As soon as I'd turned my phone back on to call her, the little plastic nightmare went crazy beeping at me, letting me know more idiots had seen the damn video and wanted to call to curse, praise, or irritate me. I didn't bother to listen to them. I put the phone on silent, shoved it in my pocket and drove home.

When I got back to my apartment, I put my bag away, made some food and sat down to watch some mindless shows. I felt drained, so I set my alarm just in case Anthony Bourdain couldn't keep me entertain and distracted as he ate weird food in dangerous places. I didn't want to miss or be late to Rouge's show, no matter how shitty I felt.

I woke up to the overly loud alarm three hours later and nearly threw it across the room to shut it up. When I turned on the screen there was a call coming in from Godfrey. My mind immediately jumped to something bad, guessing the new hunter had come back and told Godfrey why he was there. I quickly answered it.

"What's going on?" I asked, and could hear the sleepiness in my voice.

"Did I wake you up?"

"Don't worry about it. What's wrong?"

"Wrong? Nothing's wrong, but I got a potential client for you. Interested?"

"Wait, someone called you to get me? How did that happen?"

"It was one of my sellers. They told me about this guy in Niagara Falls who's claiming he's haunted. The guy told someone about it, asked for a specialist in the occult. He says there's a demon or ghost following him around and *it* or *they* are going to kill him. Seller knows I deal with you so he told me about it. Since you're getting all those fake calls, thought this might help."

Maybe it would. Work had a way of making other things disappear. I took the number from Godfrey and thanked him. He told me he had my back and after everything he'd done for me recently, I believed him. It was nice to finally trust him. After all the years he came off as a sly, con-artist who couldn't be trusted to say an honest thing, it felt good to look at him as an ally.

After I hung up, I decided to Google the potential client, Chance Anderson. It didn't take long, as there weren't many people in Niagara Falls with that name. I opened up the first link and found out he was a real estate developer in the Niagara region. He owned some huge properties including many of the tourist attractions in Clifton Hills. He seemed pretty normal, nothing in any of the searches turned up potential that he'd be crazy or lying, so I dialed the number Godfrey had given me. The woman who answered the phone, Ms. Mittz, said Mr. Anderson was out of the office at the moment and wasn't expected back for the rest of the day.

"If you tell me what this is in regards to, I can get him to call you back at his earliest."

"Well, I'd like that, but to be honest, I'm not even sure what it's about. A friend of his contacted a friend of mine and said he had some sort of issue I might be able to help him with."

"You mean the ghosts?"

I was surprised by that. This guy clearly had no issue talking about his problems.

"That's what I've heard."

"Oh, thank goodness. He's been just a wreck over the last few weeks. Would you be able to come see him tomorrow? He's not really seeing any clients at the moment, so it's no problem fitting you in. The faster this gets handled, the quicker we'll have Chance back. He hasn't been the same since this all started."

"I can do tomorrow, but it'll have to be the afternoon."

"No problem. Whenever you can get here, that's just perfect. Like I said, things have been so bad lately; I'd just like to have my old boss back. Thank you so much, Mr. —"

"Just Dillon. And I'll see you then. Is the address the same as on the website?"

She said it was, and I jotted it down. And just like that, I'd forgotten everything else and was as calm as ever. Work has a way of doing that to me.

I left my car in a pay parking lot next door to the venue Rouge was performing at. The show was set to start in thirty-five minutes and I sent her a text as soon as I arrived. She asked if I could grab her something to eat since she'd been too busy with her tech setup to grab anything. There was a Tim Hortons in the plaza where the parking was so I went in, grabbed her some goodies and headed to the main doors.

As I passed the narrow alley, I saw there was already quite a lineup of people waiting to get in, but stopped in my tracks when I heard my name whispered from the shadows. I didn't know the voice. I turned and peered into the darkness. Something moved, shifted, and then stepped forward. My hand went towards my belt where the Tincher was, and I nearly dropped the food and drinks I was holding.

"I'm not here to fight," it whispered and finally the orange street lights found it and I saw what it was that had called me. "Come here."

Normally, I would have been a lot more cautious, especially when I saw it was a creature not of this world calling me into the dark, hidden space. Only I knew this one. The creature was a *Gargar*, one I'd actually let stay here on Earth when I'd first encountered it.

Years back, I was called by parents who believed their child was being hurt by a ghost or some other spirit haunting their home. When I got there, I found the Gargar in the room, but also realized he wasn't the one cutting the kid. He was trying to protect it. Another monster, a vicious little blood sucker called a *Daaf*, was the real issue. I let the Gargar stay there to protect the kid.

That's another rule broken.

"What are you doing here?" I asked as I stood at the mouth of the alley looking down at the short creature.

"I'm trying to hide. Something came through the breach in Sammy's room."

That's not good.

"What was it?" I asked, checking over my shoulder to make sure nobody was curious enough to come over and see what I was doing. Luckily, not a single one of them wanted to lose his or her place in line, so we were good.

He explained things to me as best he could. He described a fiery smell when the creature came through. He said it wasn't like a fireplace smell, but something more like what followed Sammy's only nightlight sparking and frying out. I imagined he meant it was an electrical fire smell, which helped to narrow down what it could be.

I asked him if he saw it when it came through, and the way he told it, the thing exploded into the room, more than just seeping in the way many will when they crossover. He told me it damaged the wall around it, used the fallen chucks to build up his very big body. It was an oddity, but not unheard of. Bigger and more vicious monsters could do that. So could demons. "What about Sammy?" I asked, trying to think what kind of creature might have crossed over into the kid's room.

"Sammy is off to college, and the parents are away, which is a good thing because I think this thing would've hurt someone."

"Maybe," I said, still not sure what it could be. "Where did it go?"

"No idea. I got scared and ran. That was three days ago. I was just sitting by the coffee shop drinking some puddles when I saw you. I wasn't even looking for you, but here you are. It must mean something."

Doesn't everything? Still, what could be big and mean and smell like an electric fire? There was something there, kind of familiar, but with all the species in this and surrounding universes, it was hard to come up with right away. Yet there was something about it, an idea right on the edge of coming to me, but I couldn't put my finger on it.

"You have anything else about it that might help me figure out what it was that crossed over?" I asked, hoping something might click.

"Big, mean, smelled like an electric fire, and it yelled out the word Zarn three or four times when it came through."

"Zarn?"

"Yeah. Does that help?"

I nodded. It did help. *Zarn* is a curse word, like saying *shit*. It's from a planet where creatures called *Volteer* live, and if that's what it is, everything else the Gargar says made sense. These things are big assholes. They feel as though they are the perfect being, that all others are bugs in comparison to them. They go across the universe enslaving any monsters or creatures they find or just trying to wipe them out completely. If that's what came into Sammy's room, I couldn't blame the Gargar for running.

"Are you going to go hunt it down?"

"I'll try and stop by the house when Sammy's parents get home, but if it's not there, I'm going to have to wait for it to pop up and show itself."

"Wait for it to pop up? But you're a hunter. Aren't you supposed to hunt things like this down?"

I shrug and was a little surprised by the tone he took with me. The last time I saw him, he was a small, timid thing. I guess that's what happens when you spend too much time in the company of a teenager. That kind of attitude is contagious. "That's not really how I do things. This city is too big for that. There are way too many hiding spots for me to just hunt down any and everything that might go bump in the night. But, you can go back to Sammy's to see if it's still there right now, and if it is, let me know and I'll go deal with it. If not, well, it's a waiting game."

"I don't want to go back there alone. Please, can you come with me?"

"Can't," I said plainly, and looked back at the venue doors. "I have something I need to do right now, but you go ahead and if there's any news, come back here and let me know. I'll be here for about four hours."

"You suck!" the Gargar cursed me and sank back into the shadows. There was that teen angst again. They grow up so fast.

Maybe he was right. Maybe I do suck. I know most other hunters hide in the shadows, stay out of the view of the public and hunt down monsters, demons, and spirits on a much stealthier level than I ever had. They actually track monsters down, and never make contact with people who are being affected by them. I, on the other hand, prefer people to find me. This way it's

27

easier and I get paid for my services. So even though I have a great monthly quota, I don't go out of my way to be some great creature tracker. I'd rather suck and do what I do than live in the sewers and creep in the shadows, although I'm sure those other hunters aren't being featured on YouTube the way I am.

Pros and cons, I guess.

At the thought of the video, my stomach started to do backflips. I did my best to shake it off, walked into the venue, and headed to the backstage area to drop Rouge off her bagel, tea, and Timbits. The people at the door knew who I was and let me in without a hassle. I sent Rouge a text to let her know her food had finally arrived and within a minute she came out, looking glorious with her Victory Rolls, her face in full performance make up. She was wrapped in an amazing deep green velvet robe. She smiled and kissed me on the cheek, and I wished I was the robe.

"Did you get lost on the way here?" she asked, taking the food.

"No. I, uh, got held up just a little."

"Coffee servers hitting on you, or was it the parking attendant?" she laughed.

"Neither. It was, well, work related I guess. No big deal, though. Nothing I have to worry about."

"Are you sure? I mean, if you have to go, I'd understand. Jason isn't even here for this show. He sent his boyfriend to do it, and Justin is as sweet as a mountain of Gummi Bears."

I shook my head. There was no way I was going. I'd missed her last two shows, and I had no plans to miss this one. It was a thrill to watch her perform, but I also loved being there as her personal cheerleader. Nobody could beat me at the hoots and whistles when she was up on that stage. And there was no certainty that the Volteer was still at Sammy's house. No point in wasting my time chasing my tail, or its. I'd wait and see if the Gargar came back with news.

"I have a job tomorrow, but for now, I'm all yours."

"For now? More like forever," she whispered as she leaned in and kissed my neck. Her touch sent a wave through me and I suddenly wished we were somewhere private. "Now, I'm going to go get ready. Your V.I.P. table is right over there. Hope you enjoy the show."

"As long as you're in it, it'd be impossible not to."

T he show was amazing and when we walked out, I was happy to see that the Gargar hadn't returned. I assumed it meant the Volteer was long gone. I wasn't jazzed with the idea of something that big and bad running wild in the city, but I knew I'd get a call about it one of these days. The mean ones never stay hidden for long. All good things come to those who wait, patience is a virtue, and so on. It was fine, and nice that we had the night to ourselves.

"Are we going back to my place?" Rouge asked as I put her bag in the trunk of my car.

"I think it's a better choice than my place," I laughed. My place was more of an idea of an apartment. It was a messy museum of the weird and unearthly, little more than trophies and oddities with a bed and a couch thrown in there amongst the bizarre. One of these days, I might have to just give it up and move in with Rouge, but I figured we'd get to talking about that eventually. "But I do have a job to go to tomorrow afternoon."

"Yeah, you were saying. Anything exciting?"

I pulled out of the parking lot and moved at a snail's pace in the late night club traffic towards her house.

"Not sure. Some real estate guy thinks he's haunted. So I'm heading to Niagara Falls to see what it's all about."

"Niagara Falls? Maybe I should come with you. Some people think it's kind of a romantic place. I bet now it's autumn, it'll be beautiful."

"What would you do while I'm at the meeting?"

"It's a tourist town, honey. I'm sure I can keep myself busy. Maybe we could even get a hotel room there. One with a rotating bed or a heart-shaped tub. It's the perfect place to curl up all cozy like and watch Superman 2."

"Sounds like a plan to me. I like your way of thinking. Nothing says romance like cheap gimmicks and '80s Superman movies."

"I'm all kinds of fucking fancy," she laughed, and went ahead and made us reservations at a hotel. I thought about how much fun it would be. I'd meet this guy and then have a great night with Rouge. And it'd all be a tax write-off.

Romance can be practical too.

Friday

The drive to the Falls was pretty uneventful. A little over an hour and a half of nothing to see but steel plants in Hamilton, plazas with the same six or seven stores in them, and little else. Rouge told me there was also an area called Niagara on the Lake where Ontario's wine region was.

"There's a cute little town there, one of those picturesque places with a Main Street straight out of a painting. They even have a big old clock tower right in the center of town, and horse drawn carriage rides."

"So why aren't we going there?" I asked.

"One thing at a time, Dillon. Since you have a job in the Falls anyway, we can stay there and tick that off our romantic-ass checklist. There's always another day for the other."

We drove the rest of the way and talked about other things we wanted to do. Rouge had a few ideas on the list she was really excited for and always wanted to go to. Disney World was on top of her list, but there were also chalets in Quebec, the mountains in Alberta, and glamping (glamorous camping) in Algonquin Park. She was so excited about some of those things she managed to get me equally as jazzed. Seeing as all this was so new to me, having never dated anyone before her, I had no real ideas of romantic places to go. Everything I know about romance I've learned from books and movies. Since I prefer horror movies and bad comedies, my ideas of romance are slightly warped.

My aim is to get better at that.

We arrived in the Falls with twenty minutes to spare before I planned to head to Chance's office. Rouge asked me to drop her off down by the hotel so she could check in and told me to text her when I was done. I watched her walk away and for a second had thoughts about just ditching the appointment and going up to the room with her. It would be way more fun than anything Chance Anderson, *Niagara Falls' number one choice for your future,* could provide me. There was a much more enticing adventure to be had in our cheesy room, which I'd been assured had a heart-shaped tub, than in the lame office of some suit and tie guy.

"Are you looking for valet parking, sir?"

The voice at my window pulled me from the picture perfect view I'd painted in my head, and I looked over at a kid who had more zits on his face than years on this planet. I shook my head and expected him to walk away. He didn't, though.

"Just dropping someone off," I told him, and yet he still lingered there.

"Oh shit! You're the monster guy from Toronto, aren't you?"

Oh no. Not here too. My heart started to race a bit at the recognition, and I felt like maybe staying here was going to be a mistake. I wondered how many people in the hotel had seen it. Was it getting shared all over Facebook and Twitter, so everyone and their grandmother watched as I battled that earthbound creature?

"Sorry, I think you got the wrong guy," I said as convincingly as I could manage.

"I've watched that video fifty times, bro. Ain't no way I'm wrong. This is so cool."

"No, it's not. And maybe you should spend a little less time on the internet and a little more on reading or figuring out a haircut that doesn't make you look like you use your hair as a paper towel when you eat your greasy-ass french fries."

It felt mean the second it left my lips, but I was seriously stressed out. When he'd brought up the video, the stress I'd been feeling was born anew, and my stomach rumbled uncomfortably. The worry washed over me, fear of being in more trouble than I ever had in my life. I drove away as fast as I legally could and tried to focus on getting to the meeting and potential work.

Traffic was almost non-existent. I turned on my radio, the car was instantly filled with the rough voice of James Hetfield, and I began to talk to myself. It was going to be okay. It had to be. I was a good, if not great, hunter. I'd managed to kill a Hellion not all that long ago, which is not an easy feat. Hellions are the worst kind of demon, vicious and bent on destruction. If it had managed to get completely through to this world, nothing would have been left untouched. That alone should allow me some leeway, in my opinion. I've never heard of a hunter or any other being come face to face with a Hellion and walk away unscathed, let alone the planet they showed up on being unharmed. It had to count for something. The Collective should turn a bit of a blind eye to some of the things I did, right?

So why was the hunter in Godfrey's? Why hadn't he introduced himself to me? Why, why, so many more whys. I was looking at questions and coming up with hypotheticals I had no real way of knowing, and it was eating me up. I needed to stop. Hopefully the meeting would help distract me. Work would have to be the great distracter once again.

I arrived at his office with nearly ten minutes to spare. It was one of the biggest storefronts on a street called Lundy's Lane. Along with it there were the usual small town shops: a Money Mart, a smattering of variety stores, a liquor store, more bars than anything else, a sketchy tattoo place with a poorly spray-painted sign over the door, and just around the corner from it was a not-so-classy-looking strip club called *Mints*. I thought I might have to swing by there with Rouge, just for the fun of it. Not so romantic, but one thing I knew about Rouge was her love of touring clubs she'd never been to. Sometimes, the grimier the dig, the better they were. And Mints certainly did have a certain air about it. And a strip club next to a funeral parlour: could you ask for something classier?

I think not.

I parked right in front of Chance's Realty and tried to walk in, but the door was locked. I peered inside, but saw no one. Most of the lights were off, too. I double-checked the time and saw I was a little early, but I figured someone would be there. I knocked on the plate glass, but nothing. I tried again, and when nobody appeared I pulled out my phone. I took a deep breath and ignored the forty missed calls from unknown numbers. Instead, I dialed the same one I had yesterday. From inside the office, I heard the phone ringing and figured I would wait there another ten minutes and if nobody showed up, I'd call it quits.

"Hello?" the woman I spoke to yesterday said, and I looked back into the dark store and saw nobody there.

"This is Dillon. I'm here for that meeting with Chance Anderson."

"Who is it?" a small, unfamiliar male voice said from the other end.

"It's him," she said, clearly not talking to me. "He's here, Chance."

"Thank god!"

"Sorry, we're in the back. I'll come out and let you in."

I said okay, and then hung up. The woman I'd spoken to came out a few seconds later and unlocked the door for me. She was a short, compact woman, with a tight perm and big glasses on her heavily made-up face. She wore a tweed jacket with a matching skirt and reminded me of some of the teachers I'd worked with over the years, ones that looked more like a movie producer's idea of how a teacher should look than how most did. The smile she gave me as she opened the door didn't seem quite genuine. She reminded me of a mother forcing a smile while she deals with a screaming three-year-old in full temper tantrum mode. Clearly, she had more of a sense of what she was about to let me walk into than I did.

"Something happened a little while ago, and Chance is a little freaked out. I'm so glad you're here. I really hope this is all going to be over soon."

"That bad?"

"I'm not sure how much more of this I can take." She shook her head and put her hand over her face after she relocked the door. "Oh that sounded so horrible. I'm not a mean person, it's just-"

"Don't worry about it. These kinds of things aren't easy for the best of us to deal with. Always assuming this is something at all."

"Oh, it is something. I've known Chance for fifteen years and I've never seen him like this. He's a mess. It's scary."

She led me to the back office. She knocked on the door three times and called out that it was just us. Inside, I could hear a whimper, like a dog whining for food or from fear. Slowly, she opened the door and peered in.

"It's just us," she said. "You can put that down now."

She opened the door fully and I followed her inside. First thing I noticed was a cot and blanket on the far side of the room, and a smell that was as stale as a college kid's room during midterms. It smelled hot, and sweaty. I didn't need to ask if he'd been sleeping there. If there had been windows in the back office, at least he would've been able to air the place out.

I moved towards the desk and knew there was going to be a gun on it before I saw it. I hate guns. And in my line of work, they're all but ineffective. Not unless you have bullets with the breath of a Shia'zz in them. If you have those, then I think your gun is just fine. Otherwise, they're just loud and useless.

The gun wasn't the only thing he had, though. In one hand he gripped a dark wood crucifix and he had a large black cross painted on his heavily creased forehead. His breathing seemed heavy too, and the hand holding the cross shook badly, despite the white-knuckled grip. I rarely if ever see anyone in that kind of state. Most people are a bit scared; more are just shook up, a little ruffling of the feathers. Chance, though, was in a state of absolute terror.

"Can I take your coat?" Ms Mittz asked me, and I passed it to her. She walked behind Chance's desk and hung it in a closet at the back of the office. I sat down and looked at a man trapped in a state I'd never really seen before. Whatever he'd been going through, it seemed terrible.

"Mr Anderson, I think you can put that cross down. In most cases they don't really do much to ward off the things that could be causing you to be afraid."

"Well, I feel better holding it. I'm not even Catholic, but, well, it makes me feel safe. So does this," he added, and caressed the symbol on his forehead. "They make me feel protected."

"Okay then, but can we get rid of the gun? I know for a fact that the only thing that's going to hurt is one of us."

He looked down at it, as though it was some foreign object he'd never seen before. He began to nod, and then asked Ms Mittz to put it somewhere safe. Once she left with the gun, holding it as though it was a dirty diaper, Chance took a deep breath and looked a little more relaxed.

"Thank you for coming, Mr—"

"Just Dillon. After all, if you're a paying customer, we should be on a first-name basis. Now, I need you to tell me everything."

"Where do I start?"

"When did all it begin?"

Chance took a deep breath and his eyes fluttered for a second. He looked haggard, and worn out. Even though I'd just met the guy, I could tell this was not his normal state. It helped that his office and the area surrounding it was plastered with pictures of him smiling with his perfectly white teeth, every hair in place, and a spray-on tan as perfect as a fake tan could be. The photos showed a man who clearly thought of himself as powerful and important, projected a sense of trust. The man who sat across from me was little more than an echo of those pictures. There was an idea of the same person, but he was worn around the edges: dishevelled, a faded portrait of who he once was.

"It started about two months ago," he began as Ms Mittz put down a glass of water in front of him. He thanked her and went on. "I was at a baseball game in Toronto with my friend Mike. We were having a great time in the box seats I have, and then it happened."

He scowled and drank a large gulp of water before continuing.

"I went to get a drink and something to eat. When I came back and sat next to Mike I saw it. He'd been laughing at a post on his phone, and when he turned to me, he wasn't Mike anymore. His face…it was wrong. It looked like, I don't even know, like he was crying and drooling black ink, or a bit like he was melting maybe. The skin around his mouth, eyes and nose had turned a greenish-black colour and ran down his face. I freaked out, dropped my drink. He leaned forward and opened his mouth. He might have been trying to say something, probably asking me what was wrong, but all that came out of his mouth was thick muddy stuff. It was real wet muck; looked like soil full of worms and maggots. I screamed and fell backwards. Mike came towards me, and that only freaked me out more. I had to get out of there, away from him, so I ran. I just got up and took off out of there in hysterics. I must've looked like an idiot."

"Did you talk to Mike after that?"

"He called me and I told him I was fine. I explained it to him—and maybe to myself too— that I was stressed out from overworking, and the heat of the day. I'd just settled deals on six properties in the last week, all multi-million dollar places, so it was no wonder. He told me he wanted to come by later in the week, make sure I was okay, but I told him I was totally booked up and couldn't. To be honest, I was just terrified. I'd never seen anything like that, and I was worried if I did meet with him, it would happen again. He told me to call him later and we'd hang out, that he was so concerned about me. He's always been like that."

"And what happened when he came?"

"He didn't. I put it off and off and then, maybe two weeks ago I found out he died. There was a work accident on one of the sites he supervises, a new condo being built in Toronto. He slipped and fell off an I-beam, fifty five floors. So no, I never got to talk to him again. But it wouldn't have mattered. I was too scared to call or see him anyway. Before I'd heard about his passing, I'd already started to see others changing the way he had, so I'm sure it's better that he never made it here. I would've just freaked out."

Chance began to tear up and his secretary handed him some tissues. He wiped the tears away, and as he did I tried to process everything he was telling me. Nothing he said sounded anything like a haunting, a monster, or something in the realm of what I do. I've been doing this for a while, and even though I haven't seen it all, I've seen a lot in my time. What this was sounding like was stress, some sort of nervous episode brought on by alcohol, overworking, too much on his plate at once, or all of it together. If anyone could relate to how stress can make you feel out of sorts, it's me. With everything going on in my life, I felt on the verge of cracking too. So I knew where he was coming from. The trick would be to tell him what I thought as gently as possible to avoid him losing his shit on me, or breaking down even more.

"So you've been under a lot of stress when this all started? Is that normal for you?"

"Oh, he's always stressed out," Ms Mittz said from behind Chance, her hand on his shoulder. "It's amazing his hair still looks so great with how much he's always letting everything get to him. He goes through more Tums than is medically recommended."

"It's not that bad," Chance said, trying to defend himself.

"Really? Remember when you were working on the Table Rock deal two years ago? You were barely sleeping it got so under your skin." She turned to me, smirking. "There's another agent in town who was trying to land the same deal. Gordon Symonds. He's like Chance. Not just a real estate agent, but also a developer."

"He's nothing like me, aside from the fact that he's always after the same places I am. It's like he has my office bugged."

That was a point I noted to look into if I decided to take on this case, which I was still uncertain about. It might not be monsters involved in any of this, it might be no more than stress and a guy who is out to get him, but that didn't mean I wouldn't do the job. There have been times in the past I took jobs I knew were bogus simply because I knew it would make the person trying to hire me feel better. They come to me with a report of monsters or ghosts, bizarre creatures made of shaped lights creeping around in their home, and when I get there, it's clearly nothing. I could turn them down and they'd go on feeling worse about it, maybe even have a breakdown. Or, I could pretend to help them, give them some sort of "talisman" to ward off a return, and they get better, they stop seeing things. That kind of thing won't work if someone has a deep-seated mental illness, but when it comes to people who have something going on in their lives, a fear, a stress, the loss of a loved one that sparks a slight break in their comprehension of reality, it can help. The trick is to know who you're dealing with, and how serious the cracks are. Is it a patch job, or do they need a full overhaul?

"I know this might sound insensitive, and you might be offended, but it's something I have to ask. Part of my standard questions before I take on a client," I lied. "Have you or anyone in your family been diagnosed with any sort of mental disease? Paranoia, schizophrenia, depression, or anything like that?"

"Well, my mom got pretty dark when my dad died, but she eventually got over it. He was only forty-one when he died in a car accident, so it was unexpected. Other than that, no; nothing I was ever told about."

"Do you take any drugs, illegal or prescribed?"

"No. Just Tums, but they're only antacids."

"Excessive drinking?"

"No more than four drinks a week. I don't really have time to drink or party."

Maybe you should start. Maybe your problem is never letting loose. Bottle things up enough and the pressure has a way of making you pop.

"You said you've seen others like Mike. Can you tell me about them?"

"Most of it was just random people. I'd be at the store and someone would pass me and their skin would darken, stuff pouring out of their eyes and mouth. I learned to sort of deal with it, to turn away and avoid it, but it's been getting harder and harder to do. I can smell some of them now. Before I even see one of these melted-face things, I can smell them. There's this strong reek of sulfur and something like my grandmother's basement after it flooded. I catch a whiff of that, and then I see them. It's starting to be like I can't go out without seeing one of them, and now my business is suffering. I can't deal with even the idea of having people come to the office. If they come here, I hide back here, let Ms Mittz start talking, and then I peek out. If they're not melting, I go out, but every now and then, one of them shows up and I have to stay in here, cover up my face so I can't smell them, and pray she can deal with it without my help. It's just too damn much to deal with."

He broke down then and Ms Mittz began to rub his back, clearly trying to calm him down. She whispered that everything would be alright, how I would find out what was haunting him and the world would go back to normal. I was glad she had the confidence in me that I didn't have in myself, but she was right: I was going to help him. I felt like I had to. I really didn't think any of this had to do with otherworldly beings, but that didn't mean I couldn't do my best to get him through this.

I asked him for a listing of all his holdings, most importantly the ones he had taken possession of and visited a month before the first incident with Mike at the baseball game. Ms Mittz said she would put a file together, and then left us alone. Chance took a deep breath. After a minute of saying nothing, he confessed something.

"It's worse than she knows," he told me. "I didn't want to tell her, she's so nice and sweet and innocent, but there's more to it than that. It's not just people I pass by and see like that. This morning, I woke up here. In case you couldn't tell, I've been living here. Well, when I woke up this morning I saw another one. I felt my whole world shake, and then spin. I nearly fainted when my own face turned into one of these melting, rotted things. I saw it first in the reflection of my computer, and then when I went in the bathroom. She came in when I started to scream, but I couldn't tell her what it was. She knows it's bad, but not how bad. Now, I've been spending the rest of the day avoiding any reflective surface. Do you have any idea how hard it is being afraid of seeing your own face?"

I shook my head, realizing that was why he'd looked so much more dishevelled than he did in his photos. Not being able to look at yourself in the mirror in the mornings, or after a shower, not being able to check your face or hair must be hard, especially for a guy like Chance who's clearly always had a love affair with what he sees in the mirror every day. Me, on the other hand, I could go either way. Some days I take on a more punk look and let my hair just live the life it wants to live. Why should I try and control something that clearly has other plans?

"I'm going to help you," I told him, and for the first time since I'd walked in he smiled and I saw something of what looked like a glimmer of hope in his eyes. He thanked me, and I told him to just stay strong and I would have everything sorted out as fast as I could. "You might just want to lay low for the next few days. Don't take any new clients right now or even see anyone if you can avoid it. Just take some time alone here or at home."

He agreed and then Ms Mittz came in with six pages of the most recent holdings, as well as those he'd visited just before the first occurrence. I told them both I would get started on looking into it as soon as I left the office, and then advised them on my rates. Chance said he didn't care, that if I fixed this for him he'd give me a million dollars. I wouldn't argue with that. It's well over my rate, but if he wanted to pay me that much, it'd be rude to say no.

"I'll show you out, Dillon," Ms Mittz said, and led me towards the front of the office. "I can't thank you enough for this. Chance has been such a wreck and I just want to see him better. Do you really think you can help him?"

"I do. I haven't really seen anything quite like this before, but if there's something to find, I'll find it."

"You think it might be nothing though? That it's all in his head, right? That's why you were asking him about mental illness and drugs?"

"No, that's just standard questions," I lied again. "I do this with all my cases, just to cover all my bases and make sure I don't waste my time and the client's money. This might be nothing more than a slight breakdown from being overly stressed, but if it's not, I'll find out. There'll be something at one of these properties that might give me some sort of clue. If there isn't, well, I'll find a way to get him back to where he was regardless."

"I really do hope so. I've known Chance since high school. He was always the life of the party and the guy who shined wherever he went. I used to have such a crush on him, but he was always too busy with debate team, or playing for the school football team, or hanging out at parties to notice me that way.

But we've been friends at least, and I miss him. I miss who he used to be," she said, and threw herself at me. She hugged me with all the ferocity of a grizzly bear and I was surprised by her sheer strength. She was only five feet four inches tall and I'd be shocked if she weighted more than a hundred pounds, but she managed to crush me with that hug. I hugged her back and she kissed me on the cheek before she let go. "Please do what you can. I'd love to have my boss and my friend back."

"I'll do my best," I told her, and went back to my car. I tossed the pages Ms Mittz had given me, and then used a tissue to wipe off the dark red lipstick she'd tattooed on my cheek. No need to let Rouge see it and get the wrong idea.

When I thought of Rouge, I took my phone out and dialed her number. I wanted to give her a heads-up on what I was doing. She picked up on the second ring.

'I hope you're not already done," she said with a chuckle.

"Actually, I'm not."

"Good. I'm just about to go and get a massage, and I mean to get it without being interrupted. Did you know they're free because of the room you picked?"

"Of course I did." I didn't. I just picked that particular room because it had a heart-shaped tub, and she'd wanted one. "I'm just going to go do a bit of work, check out some leads for this guy, and I'll be back in about four or five hours. Is that long enough for you to get your rub on?"

"There's always more rubbing that could be done, but maybe you can take care of that when you get back here."

"Challenge accepted. And I think I may extend our stay here a few more days. Did you want to stay with me, or do you have to get back to the city?"

"I think I can manage. I'll give Sue a call and see if she minds watching the pup a few extra days. But other than that, I'm good to stay."

"Perfect. I'll do that when I get back to the hotel."

"Can't wait to see you," she said, and then we said our good-byes before I drove off towards the first location.

There were so many places on the list. They ran the gamut of business types as well. Two were horror funhouses, one was a wax museum of sorts, and another three were variety stores. He owned a Tim Hortons, a Swiss Chalet, and an IHOP. He owned two hotels, five motels, and shares in a co-op. He'd even bought a church which, according to the papers, he planned on tearing down to build a condo, permits pending. There was no real indication of which ones he visited or when, so I figured I would start from page one and move along until I finished them all.

I hoped not to need to stop by each and every one of them, though. That would be a lot of stops to take on, so I hoped to find the source of his issue as fast as I could manage. I'd hate to check them all out and find nothing, leaving it all in the court of Chance's mental health. I knew how to beat monsters, not illnesses in perception. I kept my fingers crossed that things would stay in my wheelhouse.

The first place I stopped was Chance's residence. Ms Mittz had explained he owned another property further outside of the city, closer to the wineries, but apparently he hadn't been there since the spring, so that was unlikely. The house he lived in most days was close to the highway, well off the main strip. Huge houses lined the street. It took me over an hour to tour his nine bedrooms, four bathrooms, and a basement that looked almost like it could've been a BDSM dungeon if your idea of torture happened to be bad décor.

Aside from some strange, framed pictures of chairs and wagon wheels, the overwhelming smell of someone who suffers from athlete's foot, and Chance's apparent love of all things beige, there was nothing to note in the entire house. I left there, and headed to the first of his commercial holdings.

The first three places were all fast food chains restaurants. I went to each of them, ordered something small, and then sat there amongst the locals and the tourists for half an hour or so.

The idea was to quietly observe each place and look for any signs of something being off.

There were plenty of things off, things I will never be able to forget.

I watched a man shovel a dozen donuts into his mouth while drinking an unusually large cup of coffee. I saw a group of women eating inhuman stacks of pancakes, and then ordering more. I looked on as a couple ordered a full chicken each, with sides, and then devoured them in less than five minutes. It felt like everyone in each of the restaurants ate more food than I'd ever seen anyone consume in my life. I wasn't sure if it was a sign of something wrong here, or if Niagara Falls was just a city of gluttony. When I ended up going to the Chinese buffet Chance owned, I knew it must be the city, not some demon influence. I think even demons would be shocked by the sheer ravenousness lust directed towards food in these places.

By the end of it, four hours in all, I wasn't sure I could take any more for the day, so I called it quits. I knew I'd need to see these places after hours as well, but for the time being, I'd had all I could take. I didn't see or sense a single thing to hint at something unearthly or monstrous close by. No smells to let me know there was a monster or demon there. I saw no twitching shadows, felt no goosebumps as a demon crept around unnoticed. There was nothing aside from greasy chins and greedy mouths to make me want to run out of there.

I called Rouge to tell her I was on my way back to the hotel, but got her voicemail. I figured she must've been relaxing in the room or was touring the hotel even. When I got back to the room, I found a note on the table by the beds. I picked it up and read it. She wanted to let me know she'd headed to the casino to try her luck on games of fancy chance. I dropped off the files from Chance's office, and left my weapons in the room in case security at the casino were doing checks on people going in. I figured my Tincher, my gloves and the three vials of Hellion blood I brought with me might raise some eyebrows.

Even at the entrance, I felt my senses overloaded. The lights, the noise, and the din of people trying to talk over the bells and chimes, and over each other, was terrible. I'd never been to Vegas, but I imagined Niagara Casino was probably a slightly less flashy version—but only by a small margin.

At the main door leading from the hotel to the casino, there was a security guard conducting searches. In fact, there were five of them: huge men and women in black pants, black t-shirts, with more muscles than smiles. They ran metal detectors over people and checked all their I.D.s. I passed them by after a few minutes. The woman checking me grunted when she looked at my driver's licence before she flicked it back at me and called out for her next victim.

Once inside, I began to scan the crowd. I figured it would be easy to spot Rouge the way she looks, especially with her bright red hair. Turns out I was wrong. After fifteen minutes of moving through the village of the damned—people cursing at inanimate objects that refused to spill forth the fortune they held—I found her. I looked at her, did a double-take and had to wait until I was up close to make sure it was her.

She was sitting at a card table, playing a round of Texas Hold 'Em. She was wearing a dark green tracksuit with white stripes running down the arms and legs. There was a baseball cap on her head, the same colour as the tracksuit. She wore little to no makeup and was even wearing flip-flops. The look was something you'd expect to see at a retirement community as people sat outside and did chair aerobics. I could almost imagine her playing lawn bowls, or making small-talk about how humid it's been lately.

Who was this alien and what had she done with Rouge?

"What are you wearing?"

She spun in her chair and smiled brightly when she saw me. She jumped up and gave me a hug before she stepped back and turned around in a circle to give me the worst fashion show ever. She looked like a retired woman at a lawn bowling league game in Florida.

"You don't like it?" she asked, clearly seeing a look on my face that I had no control over.

"It's just so...uh...I don't even know what it is just so, but it is."

"It's so bad, right?" She laughed and sat back down to enjoy her game. "This was some of the free stuff in the room. They knew my colour and everything. It's so tacky, I thought where better to wear it than here? You should go change into yours. I want to see what you'd look like as my grampa."

"I'm not sure that stuff is actually free, but even if it is, I think I'll take a hard pass on it," I told her. There was no way I was stepping into anything that looked like that. I mean, what if it was so comfortable that I wanted to wear it all the time? That's what happened with me and hiking shoes. I used to think they looked ridiculous, but now it's all I buy. There was no way I was running the risk of looking like a member of a geriatric hip hop group.

"Your loss, sweet cheeks," she said, and folded her hand. "How are you doing? Winning us a fortune?"

"Not a fortune, but I started with two hundred bucks, and now I'm up to a thousand. So, not too shabby. How about you? Rid the world of any baddies today?"

Quietly, in case anyone was listening, I told her about my day with Chance, but left out my voyage to glutton town. There are some things that just need to be kept secret and hidden. Food mountain eater, bowel movements, and dreams involving Jell-O are just a few I can think of off the top of my head.

"That all sounds terrible," she said and took a sip of her drink—I guessed cola, since she's not much of a booze drinker lately. "You do know there are very few things in this world I hate more than maggots and worms, right?"

"How do you think I felt? Have you ever seen me around bugs? The idea of it was something I did my best not to picture. I'll take poop-eating monsters over a centipede any day."

"Want to head back to the room and we'll watch some Superman 2 and Canadian Bacon, which by the way, are my two favorite movies that feature one of the world's great wonders."

"Don't you want to finish your game?"

"I think I've won enough. Now we can go upstairs and I can

claim my prize." She reached over and grabbed my ass and I took that as a not so subtle hint as to the prize she was going to get.

Saturday

After breakfast, I drove Rouge to the Falls so she could go up to the tower, ride the giant Ferris wheel, and head over to the tourist centre where she said she wanted to peruse the never-ending aisles of stuffed beavers, items with Canadian flags stamped on them, and maple syrup. Apparently those are three of the main things people think of when they hear *Canada*.

"Do you know all the different ways maple syrup is sold in places like this? It boggles the mind," she told me as we pulled up. "You stay safe and call if you need me to swing in and save you like before. Just don't be afraid to admit you need me."

I laughed and she kissed me goodbye. I drove off and headed towards the next series of places I hoped would lead me to an answer of what was haunting Chance. I would prefer it not to be a mental thing after all. I have an easier time dealing with monsters and beasts than ruined psyches.

My first stop was a motel close to where I'd dropped Rouge off. I parked in the nearly- barren lot, and then moved along the outside of each unit on the first and second floor. I didn't linger too long in front of any of them, just to avoid looking like some weird creeper. My hope was to get some sort of sensation, catch a strange smell, or even hear something off in one of the units. After twenty minutes, the only thing I noticed was that it had gotten slightly cooler than when I first started. I went to the office near the parking entrance and spoke to a middle-aged woman named Marg, behind the counter. She had been working there for the last seven years, both behind the desk and as a cleaner.

If anyone knew of anything strange going on here, I figured it would be her.

"This place is full of weird shit," she told me as she looked out the window. "Over there in room nine there's a couple who I'm pretty sure never eat real food. They just smoke meth all day and scam tourists. I'd throw them out, but they always pay on time for the month, so, you know, the whole *money talks* thing."

"They live here?"

"Oh sure. Half the rooms are full of monthly renters. It's the only way we can manage to stay afloat ever since the bigger hotels closer to the Falls opened. You mind if I smoke?" she asked, and I told her I didn't, even though I kind of did. "We're not supposed to smoke in here, but as long as you won't tell, I won't either."

"You have my word."

She pulled out a battered steel cigarette tin, took a home-rolled cigarette out and lit it with a scented candle on the front desk. I doubted the Spiced Pumpkin Dream candle would cover the smell up for long. She took a long drag, coughed one of the worst-sounding coughs I'd ever heard, and then went on.

"There's another guy, over in room twenty-one, likes to dress up like Batman, but without the pants, and then flashes the curtains open now and then. Some of the non-regulars complain about him, but what can you do? In this day and age, if I throw him out for that people will lose their mind on social media, saying I'm discriminating against his sexual kink or whatnot. I called the cops on him, but they just laugh and say with a dick as small as he has, it's not indecent, it's a free comedy show."

Marg went on to tell me about a woman who eats her weight in bagel bites every day, a man who spends all day playing video games in the nude, a couple who cruise bars on weekends and bring people back for threesomes, and a single dad who stays there with his son, and makes some of the worst-smelling food on a hot plate.

"Sometimes I think I'm in India with the reek of onions and curry I smell coming out of there. Not that I'm judging or anything. Just saying it's no way for a kid to live."

She continued to "not judge" for another ten minutes before

I decided it was a dead end. I wished I had gotten out of there before she'd started smoking, because when I got back to the car, the smell had clung on to my clothes. I took out some cologne I had in the glove compartment and doused myself. I only managed to make myself smell like cigarettes and cologne, so despite the chilly air I drove with my windows down to avoid having to deal with the stench.

I hit eight places after that, and found nothing even slightly useful. One of them I was almost sure was the place. There was a smell like old, rancid meat and eggs, but as it turned out the store had a faulty septic system and for the last two weeks the smell of old bathroom fun times had been lingering there. The clerk working the front counter of the Money Mart looked embarrassed when I asked about it, as though it was all her former lunches and dinners responsible for the nearly eye-watering smell bleeding through the walls and floor. I told her that some of it was probably a year old and that only made her feel worse as she admitted to have been working there for over two years. As I left there, I reminded her we all shit, but like that comment, my day was a flush.

I sat in my car after, crossed off yet another property and thought of calling it quits. I checked my phone, saw fifty-two missed calls from unknown numbers—more cranks, no doubt—but nothing from Rouge. I guessed she was still busy, so I went through the remaining five properties on the page and tried to see if there was one close by. After a quick check with Google Maps, I saw there was one less than two minutes away. It was the church being converted into a condo. If any of the properties had potential to be the one place where I'd find something otherworldly, you'd think it was a church. It really should've been my first stop, but after what happened with Father Ted, I really didn't want to be visiting any church, not even one that was being changed into something hideous and over-priced.

I checked the list again, saw nothing else very close to where I was, so I decided to suck it up and head to the church, but I made myself a promise that it'd be the last stop of the day. By then it was already close to three in the afternoon. There's only so much work I can do in a day. Once I finished there, I'd check in with Chance or his secretary, let them know where things stood, and then get my romance on.

I already assumed it was going to be nothing before I got there.

I pulled up shortly after and checked the address again. At first glance, I was sure I'd gotten the street number or name wrong. The church looked strange. It was not really like any religious structure I'd ever seen before. There was no stained glass, no tall steeple or cross decked out on the front of it. I thought there was a possibility it wasn't a Catholic or Christian church, but since it said *former church* on the paper, not mosque, synagogue or other, I'd made an assumption. There'd been the chance it was already under construction, but to me, the church looked more like the burnt out husk of an industrial building. It was a flat-roofed, very boring rectangle made of off-white brick with the doors and windows boarded up, but there were signs of a fire. Black soot marks kissed the painted bricks at the top of each window and door frame until it simply faded back into the colour of the paint. I stood on the brown grass out front, looking at it, and wondered about the cause of the fire. Had Chance been inside here before or after it?

"Not much to look at, is it?" a female voice said from behind me. I turned around and saw her: a heavy-set woman in her late fifties, maybe. Huge sunglasses nearly swallowed her whole red, blotched face, and she coughed hoarsely as she pushed her wheeled walker toward me. "Can you believe they're going to tear this place down and build a condo here? Who the hell is going to buy a condo in Niagara Falls, especially here? There's something not right with that place."

Bingo. I guessed I should've started there after all, and wanted to kick myself in the ass for bothering with all the other places. What a waste of time.

"I'm kind of new here. Someone told me they were building apartments here and I should check it out," I lied, and hoped to get something informative out of her. "A real estate guy named Chance Anderson said it would be a prime place to move, so close to Lundy's Lane and the Falls. I take it it's not?"

"Are you kidding me? You'd be better off moving in to some sleazy motel close to the bus terminal than whatever they build here. This wasn't a real church, it was evil." My interest was sparked. Churches are notorious with weak spots to other planes and dimensions. Creatures, especially demons, are drawn to them. It's as though a strong belief and faith in something somehow draws these monsters forth. One day I will really need to look into it. I keep saying that every time I have an incident at a church, but I really should.

Add that to my to-do list, I guess.

"So if it wasn't a real church, what was it? Satanists? Molesters?"

"Not even. This preacher, a shady-looking guy who called himself Pastor Herb, bought the building off Mary and Bob Grieves. When they owned it, it was a pottery store, and then Pastor Herb comes along and makes it a so-called church. Only the whole thing is a front for damn potheads. Instead of preaching the word of God, they talked all kinds of nature and Mother Earth bullshit. Instead of hymns, they sang songs by Bob Marley and Peter Tosh. And, instead of consuming the holy sacrament, they smoked that awful-smelling devil's grass. You could smell it all up and down the street. Pastor Herb would lurk in there, corrupting the youth all day long, while good Christians wanted to save them. We all started a petition to get it shut down, complaining to the police, but nothing came of it. They just stayed in there, a false house of God, and smoked and sinned. That is, until someone with some good sense and high morals burnt the place out. During the night, a Good Samaritan, a warrior of the Lord, threw a Molotov cocktail right through one of those windows and we rid our city of his pestilence."

"He died?" I asked. I was shocked by the cavalier way she talked about it. But if he did die, it would explain a lot. A place where someone passes in such a horrible way might not even mean a demon or an otherworldly creature had passed through the barrier into this world. Humans can become earthbound, menacing spirits if they die in the right conditions.

Being murdered, burnt to death, would be just the right set of them.

"Oh no, he didn't die. He was barely even burned. Just a spot on his arm from what I heard people say. But when the fire department and the police came out, they found he had one of those grow-ops in the basement. The whole city would've been higher than Denver if the fire department hadn't shown up so quick and put the fire out before it torched it all. Guess Pastor Herb was worried about getting charged so he ran and nobody has seen him since. Still can't believe anyone wants to build something on such a disgusting hole. A false house of worship is a cursed place. I wouldn't suggest moving in there if I were you."

I nodded and realized this was all another bust. Maybe I had it all wrong. There was a chance none of this had to do with any of these properties on the list. Most of them, aside from this and a few others, were open to the public, but nobody else seemed to be affected the way Chance was. I could go back to his house and try there again, but there was a part of me starting to lean heavily towards this being some sort of mental strain. At this point, it seemed more likely than not. I planned to meet with him tomorrow if I could, and would find a way to try and set his mind at ease. My idea was to hold some sort of made-up ritual, an act that would give Chance the idea I was warding off the ghosts causing him to see the nightmare visions. It was the best thing I could come up with. I'd give him a good deal so I would feel better about it. I had to charge him something for all this, but maybe just enough to cover expenses.

I thanked the woman for her information, telling her she just saved me a bad investment, and went back to my car. She smiled and slowly walked away. I felt frustrated at the case and was about to leave, but I looked back at the church and decided to go peek in anyway. I'd come all that way, I figured I might as well look inside, just in case Chance had been in there, and something had found a weak spot in. Just because nobody had died inside didn't mean I could just cross it off my list.

I walked around the building to the back. There were boarded windows and a door there too, and when I checked how secure they were, I found they weren't at all. No wonder. It's the reason

I went back there too: it was out of the view of anyone passing by.

I struggled to get in, but once I managed to shimmy my body through space between the plywood and a door barely hanging on its hinges, I was greeted with the terrible, lingering smells, most of it probably from the plastics and other synthetics that burn in a fire.

I covered my mouth and nose with my shirt and pulled my cellphone out to give me some light. I checked each of the rooms on the first floor. There was some graffiti here and there, symbols carved and sprayed on the walls, but nothing I recognized as anything important or meaningful. They looked more like things a teen would do, thinking they were being edgy and Satanic. When I found nothing else of note, I walked down into the basement.

The stairs felt weak from water damage, so I walked down cautiously. Right away I could tell the basement had been the source of the fire. On the far side of the single room there was a small, broken window. This one was smashed inward, instead of being blown out by the flames. My guess was that was where the Molotov cocktail had come through. More symbols were down there too, many like the ones upstairs. Nothing that struck a chord with me, and again I started to feel that old familiar feeling that I was wasting my time.

The room wasn't overly big, and there was little to note. The remains of carpeting, a couch, cots, books, and a few small end tables were all there was to see. There were areas of the wall where fresh, unburnt plywood had been nailed, but it was attached pretty secure and I didn't have anything I could use to pull it off. I knocked on the boards, hoping for an echo that would indicate there might be a room, a chamber, something hidden and suspicious on the other side, but there was only a dull noise and it sounded as though there was just wall behind.

Not my lucky day.

It was another swing and a miss in my opinion, but at least I could cross Pastor Herb's house of ill repute off my list of possibilities.

The night was fun. Rouge had made reservations for us at a local restaurant she'd googled she thought might be nice, and she was right. We sat in a dimly lit room, dressed in our best—no green track suit today—and ate food that was better than I'd ever had before. There was even a violinist playing by a huge window with a view of the Falls behind him.

"This is so nice," I told her, and took a bite of my dessert, which was a Maple Crème Brule. She was right, they really did do it all with maple syrup here. "We should do nights out like this more often."

"I don't know. It's nice, but there's nothing wrong with snuggling on the couch with some Swiss Chalet, watching Grace and Frankie, and trying to ignore the pupper as she begs for a little more chicken."

"You're right there," I laughed, and thought of the little dances her dog likes to do to get our attention. "I think we'll be back there tomorrow night, or Monday morning at the latest. This all seems to be a bust."

"No monsters?"

"Not that I've found. I mean, you should've seen the guy who hired me. He was a wreck. Looked like a mess. I should've just admitted right off the bat there was nothing to this, that it was all in his head, but I had to try."

"So what are you going to do now? Are we just going to go? What about this guy?"

"I'm going to see him in the morning. I'm going to try and help him." I then explained my idea of a fake ritual to make him think I'd fixed it all. It wasn't guaranteed to work, but I was also planning on taking Ms Mittz aside and telling her the truth: I could only do so much. I was a monster hunter, not a therapist.

Sunday

We had a quick breakfast in our room before I got in my car and headed over to Chance's office. I tried to call before I left, but there was no answer. I was going to leave a message, but the machine was full. I thought it was possible he wasn't there, it being Sunday and all, but judging by how there'd been a cot in his office and his house had that smell they get when people aren't living in them, I was positive he'd be right where I'd last seen him. I didn't think he was in the right state to risk going outside and seeing more of those faces he'd described.

Without getting in touch with him, I made the decision to just head over to the office regardless. If nobody answered, I'd leave a note for him to call me ASAP. I wanted to be back in Toronto no later than nightfall. Realistically, there was little I could do to help Chance other than to offer him the idea of being safe. I've dealt with mental health cases in the past, and they're never fun. It's a delicate thing, and making sure I don't make things worse is the most difficult part about it. You never want to treat someone with a mental illness lightly, just brush them off as some "nutjob" who isn't worth your time. I'm not a doctor, but a sense of closure and relief can be a first step to them getting better. All I had to offer was a placebo, but if he swallowed it, there was a chance it would work for him.

The city was quiet on a late Sunday morning. Not unlike Toronto that way. In Toronto, people spend all night partying right until the very crack of dawn, so by the time Sunday morning unfurls, there's little life left on the streets. Aside from the ever-decreasing number of churchgoers, and the unlucky few who have to work on the day traditionally set aside for rest, Sunday mornings usually give people a glimpse of what they expect a post-apocalyptic world might look like. I've seen what apocalypse can really look like, though, and quiet, empty streets is so far from reality.

When I pulled onto the street where Chance's office was, I saw something was wrong. It was busier there, especially further up the road, right near where I wanted to go. There were lights flashing and cars blocking the way, and they were mainly emergency vehicles. That couldn't be good.

A part of me considered turning around and getting out of there. Police cars had a way of doing that to me. After all, I was a stranger here, someone who'd just met Chance two days before, and if it was bad, if anything had happened to the office, or worse, to Chance himself, I would be suspect number one. It would be easy to pull a U-turn on the all-but-empty road, but I knew if I did, there was a chance someone would see it and I'd look just as suspicious. It was best to just drive up, get told to turn around, ask what happened as people often do, and then drive away and just forget about this whole case. That was, assuming this had anything to do with Chance Anderson or his office. As I got closer to the emergency vehicles, I could tell it did.

There were seven police cruisers, a fire truck and an ambulance there. I didn't know what that meant, aside from the fact that when you dial 911 and ask for police, fire, or paramedics, you usually get them all showing up. I was able to see police tape surrounding the front of Chance's office, so I knew it was serious. I slowed down and a cop stepped out into the street and held up his hands to tell me to stop. I did, and he walked over to my window.

"Sorry, road's closed here. You're going to spin around and use another one," the woman told me, with more authority in her voice than was necessary. Cops have a way of doing that.

"Sure, no problem," I told her, but had to add the usual line on the end, to keep up appearances: "What happened there? Was it a fire or something?"

"I can't go into that, sir," she told me with a huff, and crossed her arms. "Just turn around and —"

"Dillon? Is that you?"

The cop looked as surprised by that as I was. We both looked over to the sidewalk, and there was Ms Mittz, a wool coat wrapped around her, mascara dribbling swathes black down her face from the tears she no doubt had been shedding for whatever happened. If I wasn't sure how bad things could've been there before, the condition of Ms Mittz gave me some confirmation to that end. I waved to her, and as I did the cop looked back at me.

"You're Dillon?" she asked and I nodded, even though I didn't really want to. "Park right over there, and come with me," she said. "The detectives need to ask you a few things."

Great! There were detectives involved. The number of vehicles, the condition of Ms Mittz, and the involvement of detectives together equalled the one thing I'd been dreading since turning onto the street. Chance was dead, or badly injured. I doubted there'd be all these people for narcotics, fraud, or some sort of white-collar crime. This was going to be a long day. I was instantly full of regrets.

I did as I was instructed. I was slightly worried because I had my Tincher and my gloves on me, and if for whatever reason they wanted to take me to the station, they might be discovered and would be hard to explain. I thought about taking the blade off my belt, but the cop was watching me closely as I parked, so shifting to remove and hide it would arouse too much suspicion. I would just wear it, ensure my coat kept it covered, and hope for the best.

As I got out of my car, Ms Mittz was there and she threw her arms around me the way she had the day before: vice-grip tight. She was still sobbing, so I hugged her back and hoped she'd tell me something to offer enlightenment on the situation before the cops started in on me.

"What happened?" I whispered to her, still held tightly in her arms.

"It's Chance. He's...oh God, he's dead."

I'd figured as much. "How? What happened?"

"I came in this morning to make coffee and see how he was.

He'd been sleeping in his office lately and…" she tried to say it all, but was wracked with a bout of heavy sobbing, and before she could continue, the female officer was right beside us.

"Come on. You two can talk later. The detectives want a word with you."

"I'll be right back," I told Ms Mittz and pulled away from her, but she was reluctant to let go. I assured her I wouldn't be gone long, and when I did, the cop chuffed and muttered something along the lines of *yeah right*, but I ignored that. This wasn't the first time someone I worked for had died and I was questioned by the police. I would have to play things smart and safe, but seeing as there was no way I'd done anything wrong, I really had nothing to worry about. It also helped being in a hotel with cameras which would give me a good alibi, assuming this happened overnight.

The cop led the way towards Chance's office and the police tape. Once there, we ducked under it and went inside. There was a weak smell of death, the early signs of which were mild decay and the expelled body fluids. There was also a strong smell of blood: a thick, coppery smell, so I knew whatever had gone down, it had to have been pretty bad and messy.

We started to walk to the back room where I'd met with Chance two days before, and for a second I braced myself, sure she was going to bring me in to the room where Chance had died. I've seen plenty of death over the years, enough so that I wasn't likely to puke or have nightmares, but enough to know that if there was a way to avoid seeing it, I would. There's a part of me that is fascinated by death, but for my own sense of well-being, I avoid my exposure when I can. I found it interesting to see a body, especially if there was trauma to it, but looking at a lifeless shell was something I preferred to avoid: it was the reason I never went to funerals and tried to steer clear of crime scenes. Luckily we stopped just before the doorway, and she cleared her throat before calling out to the detective.

"What is it?" a hoarse, male voice asked from inside the room.

"I have that Dillon guy here. The monster guy the secretary told you about."

"Really?"

From the open door two people came out. One was a needle-thin man in a wrinkled suit, and the other was a sharp-faced woman in a suit that fit as well as anything I'd ever seen and looked expensive. The two of them seemed completely opposite in so many ways, but the way that each looked me up and down was a mirror of the other. The woman walked over to me first and held out a hand.

"Thank you for coming out. I'm Detective Winger and this is Detective Korkis. We just have a few questions for you."

She said it as though someone had come and collected me instead of the fact that I had driven over to the office with no idea of what was going on.

"I'll do whatever I can to help out, but there's not much I can tell you. I only met him on Friday, and haven't seen him since."

"Anything you can do to help would be great. This isn't a run of the mill homicide here. It's, well, a new one for us. Now, first thing we need is your full name, date of birth, and where you live."

I gave them the regular lie. I passed over my driver's license to Korkis to jot down all the information and waited. I didn't look around the room. I tried my best not to notice if there was anything out of place, or pick up on any details at all. Winger watched me like a hawk, so I just stared at Korkis as he wrote. I know from my own experience that looking around too much while under the lamp, so to speak, was a sign of nervousness, and that could be the type of thing they'd misread as guilt. Unlike the way it's perceived on TV, police usually form an opinion of guilt within the first twenty-four to forty-eight hours, and then spend their time finding ways to make the evidence stick to their theory. The idea that most crimes are solved thanks to DNA and forensics, well, it's not true, but it is a great scare tactic for the general public.

"Thanks," Korkis said and handed my I.D. back. "So what is it you do for a living?"

"I'm a private investigator," I told them. Cops in Canada tended to hate the term private detective, as though I was trying to put us on the same level. It's the same reason they hate when security tries to use the term officer, instead of guard. They enjoy their elite status.

"And you were hired by Mr Anderson?" Winger asked with a quick look over at the room he was no doubt still in.

"I was. He contacted me in regards to an issue he had and hoped I would be able to help him in some way."

"And what was the issue? Ex-wife, former employee, something to do with the bikers in town?" Korkis asked, and I took in a slow deep breath. This was going to have to come out, so best to play it all straight. I had no idea what Ms Mittz had already told them.

"Mr Anderson said he was being haunted by something. He contacted me because my specialty is finding things not of this world: ghosts, demons and monsters. He thought I might be able to find the source of his problem because he said it was ruining his life."

Nothing from them. They just stared at me with deadpan expressions, and seemed to be waiting for a punchline. It's to be expected. I think if I said that to anyone, but especially to people who are more straight-laced and who believe only what they see, they'd give me the same look. We've all seen it. It's the same one a mom or dad have when their kid tries to pass off some tall tale as the truth; or when a cheating spouse gets caught red-handed in something, and they tries to spin it. They all get *the look*. It's the one where nothing is said, but everything is being said.

"I'm sorry if I misheard you," Winger started, and there was a snarky smile playing at the corners of her mouth. "Did you say you're a supernatural private eye? Is that what you mean?"

"Yeah, I am. And I know you're not going to believe anything in that regard, but that's why I was hired by Mr Anderson. He thought I could help him."

"And I guess, judging by the state he's in right now, you didn't," Korkis said. He actually sounded mad. I wasn't sure why, but even his face had grown harder as my words sank in. "So, are you going to tell us some ghost or demon did that to him? Because if he hired you to help him before anything bad could happen, you did a piss poor job of it."

"Actually, I was coming here to tell Mr Anderson that I'd hit a dead end. The way I figured it, there was no real sign of anything actually after him, nor was there any sign of what might've caused him to see the things he was seeing. It looked like it might be in his head, a stress break down."

"Really? Well, someone, or according to you some*thing*, came in here last night and killed him. He fired his gun five times. Hit nothing but the wall," Korkis told me. "There's no sign of forced entry, so it would appear whoever did this was known to the victim. Where were you last night?"

"I was at my hotel room with my girlfriend."

"We're going to need to speak to her too, then."

"Or you can call the hotel, check security cameras and see I never left my room after we got back."

"And what time did you get back to the hotel?" Winger asked me.

"Around ten-thirty, eleven at the latest. There should also be a record of when I used my room key at the hotel."

"You seem pretty familiar with police procedures. Maybe you're familiar enough to even set up an alibi for yourself."

Unbelievable. Even though I was doing my best to show I was on the up and up, give them no reason to distrust me, I was already suspect number one. This was the first time I'd ever dealt with Niagara Police, so I had no idea what to expect, but after all my years of dealing with police as a whole, it wasn't this. There have been a time or twenty where I've been a suspect in someone's death or injury, but in those situations, suspicion was warranted. Once it was because I was in an elevator stuck between floors of a building, and when they finally got the door open, the guy who I was in there with was dead. It took some time and a lot of talking before they'd listen to my explanation that the guy had been dead for two weeks before he'd ever gotten into the elevator with me. Luckily, the coroner in Toronto is someone who knows me well enough that she actually listened to my story, checked the body for decay and found I was telling the truth. It's not always so easy to convince people who only see things in black and white and ignore the spectrum of colours when in comes to the truth and reality. I knew, with these two, it wasn't going to be an easy road.

"The reason I'm familiar with it, detectives, is because I'm not new to how things work. I've been doing this a long time and seen more than you'll ever be able to accept. If you want to speak to detectives in Toronto, Port Hope, St. Catharines, or Hamilton who I've worked with over the last couple of years, I can give you their names and personal cell numbers. I can also give you the number of the coroner's office in Toronto, and the head M.E. will vouch for me and what I do as well. But, if you want to ignore all that and try to peg this on me, make me your focus so you miss actually catching whoever or whatever is behind this, then I think I'll just shut up and lawyer up. You want to waste my time, well then... I guess all our time can be wasted."

When I stopped talking, the mirror faces shattered and each had a different look on it: from Korkis, more anger brewed forth, but Winger actually looked as if I'd wounded her, as though I had misunderstood what they were trying to get at with their line of questioning. I didn't misread a thing. It was as obvious as the nose on Korkis' face.

"Maybe we should just take a step back," Winger said, and motioned for her partner to turn away from me so they could have an aside. He reluctantly did and they whispered hastily. I took that time to finally give the room a once-over. I wanted to see if there were any signs of the unnatural in the front part of the office. It was possible that whatever killed Chance had come through there, and if it was a demon or certain types of spirits, there was a chance they'd left a trail or trace, or some other bit of themselves that would cause a eureka moment.

When they turned back to me, I saw nothing of the sort, but I could see Korkis wasn't pleased at all with whatever it was his partner had told him. He said he was going to step out and ask the secretary a few follow-up questions, and left me alone with Winger and whoever was in the inner office with Chance's body.

"I think we should start this again," she said, trying to offer a smile. "It's all just a bit strange, you know. The body in there, and then you come here and say you're a private eye who investigates X-File type stuff."

"Not really. I'm more of a monster hunter than an actual investigator."

"That's even weirder. Good thing Esho didn't hear that. His head might've popped."

"You didn't look too convinced either," I said, and preferred the way this was going. She seemed more at ease. It could be she was playing good cop, but if I could just give her a chance, she might actually listen.

"Oh, I wasn't, and I'm not saying I am, but you're not really acting like a guilty person. Esho knows it too; I think that's why he's so mad. We already had two other cases in the last month go unsolved, plus there was the three from earlier in the year that died at the church."

"Wait, what?"

"There was a church fire—"

"I think I know the one you're talking about. The weed preacher."

"Yeah, that's the one. There was a bunch of arsons around the same time—stores, houses, parking garages—but this was the only one where people died. At first we thought it was related to the other arsons, but the evidence at the scene made us re-evaluate that conclusion. Different gas used at the church, while all the others matched; not to mention the bottle used was different as well."

"I spoke to someone and they said nobody was hurt, aside from the preacher who had his arm burnt a bit."

"He's actually one of the ones who died. We kept it quiet, and people just talk and come up with their versions of what happened. He died, as well as two teens living there with him. Someone smashed the basement window in and tossed at least two bottles full of gas down there, then tossed a lighter in. They wanted to make it look like a Molotov cocktail, but it wasn't. The place went up fast, and the three who died had been sleeping down there. I doubt they even woke up. Doctors said they were dead before the flames found them."

"Did you know Chance owned that property? It's one of the

places I investigated for him," I told her, and began to wonder if I was all wrong about this whole case. It really didn't seem like the church was anything at all, but maybe I should've listened to my own gut right away. If there's a church somewhere in the picture, that's usually the door to the story.

"We did, but we really don't think the two are connected. Although it might explain the torch marks in the victim's office," she said more to herself than to me. She drifted off mentally, looking at nothing in particular, and I knew she was trying to put pieces together in a puzzle that made no sense. After a few seconds, she came back to the moment and looked at me. "You want to see what I mean? It might be easier than explaining it."

"I'm sure it would, but I'm not one for crime scenes." She gave me a look then, one that told me *"You have to see it to believe it,"*, so I nodded and we did what I didn't want to do.

I followed her to the office I'd been sitting in only two days before. There were four forensic people already inside. They were taking pictures, bagging random items, and putting markers in areas where items had been removed. None of them were near Chance, so I was able to see him right away. At least, I saw what was left of him.

Chance was against the wall in a seated position, dressed in plaid pajamas. His hands lay open on either side of him, and he wore slippers. I was surprised by the lack of blood, though, as my eyes found where his head had once been. As I was led in closer, it made sense.

"In my nine years in this job, I've never seen anything quite like that," Winger said with a hint of sadness in her voice, or just tiredness, and a bit of an *I give up* attitude.

To be honest though, I had. Well, it wasn't exact, but I'd seen something close to it once. There were too many parts of this that didn't match the previous case, though. In the other one, there'd been a strong odour of brimstone, and the path the demon had taken was marked by scorches along the floor, but in Chance's office there was none of that. The room smelt the same as it had a few days ago, and the only scorch marks were on the skin of Chance's neck, where his head had been removed. That part was the same. Not just severed, but from the way the skin looked, there was little doubt it had been twisted off. In the previous case, because the culprit was a Gortho, a species of demon bounty hunters I've crossed paths with only once. They come here, looking for criminal demons who've escaped whatever Hell they're from, and send them back by twisting their heads off. Chance looked like a victim of the same bounty hunters, but there were too many things not right about the whole scene. In short, it looked staged.

"Have you ever seen anything like this?" she asked me, and I told her about the demon hunter. She listened, and even though she seemed a bit amused by the whole story, she let me finish without laughing at me or calling bullshit. "So, you think this is a demon bounty hunter?"

"Not really. I mean, I've heard of things like this, but not quite the same. There're too many things missing here; details are just not right. There are signs of demon hunters, but even more signs *missing*, so I think whoever or whatever did this, it's trying to cover its tracks by redirecting our attention."

"Well, at least I don't have to put that in my report. I can just see my boss' face if I did, though. I'd be locked in a looney bin."

"Where is the head?" I asked as I looked around the room for it. When the bounty hunters removed the heads in the last case, they were placed on a pile of salt with the eyes removed and an Azerviel symbol (the Lord of Defeat) carved into the center of each forehead.

"No idea. It's not here. We figured whoever did this took it, like a trophy. You said you're staying at a hotel? Mind if we check there? Just to cover all our bases."

"Really? You still think I did this?"

"I don't know what to believe, to be honest. I'd be more satisfied if you were just some nut who thought monsters and demons were real and killed this guy, than to think anything you're saying might be true. Given the options, crazy person is easier to swallow that crazy reality."

I only nodded. I understood what she meant, but that didn't mean I had to be happy about it. I agreed to let her check my car and my hotel room if it'd make her feel better. She said it would, and then asked me what my plan was now that Chance was dead. She asked if I was going to stay in town and try to find what did this or not.

"I think you guys can handle this. If you're asking me if I could say a demon or human did that to Chance, I don't know. I wouldn't swear to anything under oath. In a different world, I might try and look into it more, but since my client is gone and I'm not getting paid to be here, there's nothing left for me to do here."

Though there was a curious part in me that really did want to know what happened to Chance. I'd blown off any possibility that a monster, demon or ghost had been haunting him. After checking out all his holdings, including the church, I'd found nothing out of the ordinary, yet there he was, dead, and there were signs of it being by an otherworldly agent. I did have to assume there was something unnatural at work as most humans would have a very hard time twisting another's head off. Yet, my client was gone so I wasn't going to be paid to look into it any more. Of course, as a hunter, I'm not really supposed to get paid at all for chasing things down, but Toronto is an expensive place to live, and unless I was getting something for my work, my time there was done. "But, hey, if you guys find a lead you can't explain, something that seems a little out of the ordinary, give me a call." I handed her my business card. She took it, read it over and her eyebrow immediately rose.

"'Dillon the Monster Dick'?" she laughed. "Really? That's what you went for?"

"It seemed like a good marketing idea at the time. I've been reconsidering it more and more lately."

After that, Winger followed me out to my car, and I let her check it. She found a bag of my tools in the truck, and I explained what they were. As most of them didn't resemble any real weapons, she moved on and found nothing else worth noting in there. She spoke to her partner and told him she was going to go to my hotel room to see if there was anything there to link me to the murder. He was still talking to Ms Mittz, his hands in hers as she cried while he clearly did his best to console her. He nodded to his partner, and we went back to the hotel. I asked if I could text my girlfriend, but she said no.

"I'm not saying you're guilty of anything, so don't get me wrong, but I have to cover my own ass here. You said you've worked with cops before so you get it, right? What if I let you call and you give her a signal to hide the head you have there? Not that I really think you do, but, well, better safe than sorry. No hard feelings."

Oh sure, no hard feelings at all; of course. Why wouldn't I have a code word for Rouge to let her know to put the severed head somewhere safe? It only makes sense that I twisted a man's head off, snuck it back to my hotel room so we could sit around and admire it. And there'd of course be a code word I could use in case I brought company or the cops over. I didn't say any of that to her, I just nodded as though it made sense to me and there were no hard feelings at the suggestion.

We pulled into the casino, and one of the concierges started to smile brightly as we walked over towards him and the elevators.

"Oh my God! You're the monster guy! Bobo told me you were staying here. Dude, this is so fresh. My bro is never going to believe the monster man is staying here and I met you. Can I get a selfie with you?"

"Maybe later. Can't you see I have someone with me?" I said doing my best to sound annoyed with him.

"No worries, dude. Monster man has a lady to slay. Sweet!"

"I'm a cop," Winger said, and I didn't think she had to try to sound as annoyed as she was by the guy's comment.

"Yeah, right. Never seen a cop in the Falls as hot as you. But if that's your bag, cool with me. Role playing is freaky, but you do you."

Without another word we got into the elevator and I could see the frustration on her face. "At least he thinks you're hot. I never get that. People just keep call me monster dude, or monster guy. Some even called me liar and asshole. They never see my cute side."

That at least made her laugh for a second before she asked

how the kid knew who I was. I explained about the viral video on YouTube, and how, on the last check, over five million people had watched me fighting a creature in the distillery district in Toronto.

"So there's an actual video of you and some monster online?"

"Yeah. I'd hoped people would think it was a fake. Not everyone does."

"Must be giving you a ton of business."

"More like a ton of bullshit calls, and an ulcer. Ever since that started, I've been getting terrible headaches and stomach aches. To be honest, this thing I was doing for Chance was a little vacation away from all of that. Aside from a few younger people in Niagara Falls, I could almost forget the video was even out there." I had also forgotten about the other hunter in Toronto, or the potential trouble I might be in. Then, just as I thought of it all again for that brief moment, the pains and nervousness were queued again and I felt shaky. I took a deep breath and tried to move on. I had enough to focus on at the moment than to worry about what might happen on our return to Toronto.

When we got to the room, Rouge was sitting on the couch in a robe, watching a Disney movie and eating some chips. She looked over with a smile, but when she saw I wasn't alone, it faded and she looked confused. Before she could say much, Winger introduced herself and gave her a very brief version of what happened at Chance's office.

"You're client is dead? That can't be good," she said, stating the obvious. "So why are you here?" she asked the detective.

"Well, there is something missing from the crime scene, and because Dillon here had contact with the victim in the last forty-eight hours, we need to see if that item is here. You can stay there. I'm just going to have a look around."

Winger started her search of our room and Rouge looked at me and mouthed *missing*. I gave her a look, one of those that would tell her she wouldn't want to know, but when she persisted, I mouthed *his head* to her and made a gesture to give her the sense of what had happened to Chance. She looked appalled.

"You think there's a dead guy's head here?" Rouge blurted

out to Winger, not even bothering to try and keep it in. "Are you nuts? That's so disgusting."

Winger looked over at her from across the room where she'd been checking the mini fridge. "I don't really think so, but I have to check. I can't write my report and say I didn't cross everyone off my list. I'll be out of your amazing hair in no time," the detective said with a wink.

"No time" turned out to be another ten minutes. I walked Winger to the door and told her again to call if anything popped up that made no sense. She said she hoped she'd never see me again, and I didn't blame her. After that, I told Rouge we should pack our stuff and get ready to blow that popsicle stand.

"We're leaving? What about the case?"

"What about it? The client's dead. And the cops are on it. I don't think they want my help."

"But they can't handle this kind of thing, can they?"

"Since I don't even know what this thing is, they're just as likely to solve it as I am. Plus, I gave the cops my card and told them to call me if they find anything too weird or need me."

"Did you give it to them, or to her?" she asked, and there was something in her tone and look I'd never really seen before. It almost came off as jealousy.

"Like you have anything to worry about, gorgeous. I know what side of my bread is buttered. Don't fret. Now, let's pack up and get the hell out of here."

Monday

The next day I tried to turn my cellphone back on to regular service. As soon as I looked at it, getting food and coffee in me while it powered up, I saw over a hundred missed calls, thirty-two text messages, and fifty voicemails—which is the max I can get. I scrolled through and deleted every message first. They were all garbage. Each of them either called me awesome or a liar. It was more of the same with the voicemails. I found I could skip and delete each of those within the first sentence. There was one inquiry that sounded as though it could be legit, so I wrote down the info and thought I'd call back after I messaged Rouge to see if we were hanging out later.

A few minutes after I sent her one, she messaged back saying maybe later tonight. She needed to go pick up the pup, do some shopping, and run a few other errands. That would give me time to call back the potential client and see if it was something worth my time or not.

I dialed the number while I made a second coffee. On the third ring, a man picked up.

"Hi, I'm looking for Don Parks," I said.

"Speaking."

"My name's Dillon. I'm returning your call."

"Oh, thanks for getting back so quick. I saw your video on YouTube the other day and really hoped you could help me." I instantly worried it'd be more of the same. Another crank, a waste of my time, and I readied myself to hang up. Still, there was a chance it could be real. Fingers crossed.

"Your message said something about a weird shape in your basement, and a certain smell, too. Can you explain it a bit more?" If he was lying, he would probably mess up recalling what he'd left on the message.

"Yeah, sure. So, I don't normally use my basement, it's kind of a dark and creepy place I just keep my Halloween and Christmas decorations. I went down to grab my Halloween stuff about five days ago, and when I did, there was something down there. I didn't get a real good look at it. It was just out of the corner of my eye, but it wasn't a rat or a raccoon. It was way too big for that. It was about the size of a small kid."

"And the smell?"

"Well, you might think it's weird, but it smelled like someone was burning rubber down there. I nearly choked it was so bad."

I mentally added it all up: small body, burning rubber smell, and hiding in a dark basement. My guess right off the top of my head was a *Bakoo*. They're not too dangerous, but they hate the light and come from a planet that reeks of something close to burning rubber. They even have an ocean there, dark as coal, that burns all the time and yet, things live in it. The universe is a strange place. This didn't sound like a prank, so my day was off to a good start.

"Okay, I think I may be able to help you. My suggestion is, don't go back down there unless you have to, and if you do take a high-powered flashlight with you. Should be fine, Mr Parks. When would be a good time and day to come over?"

"The sooner the better. My wife gets back from her sister's in two days, so I'd rather her not come home to any of this."

"Would an hour be fine?"

"Perfect."

We spent the rest of the call talking about rates and passing on directions. I got off the phone with him, messaged Rouge to let her know what I was going to be up to, and then checked my supplies. I had a huge, powerful flashlight ready to go, my gloves, my Tincher, and just in case this Bakoo was a dick, I grabbed a *Refulgent*. It was something that goes beyond light. This was kept in a metal bottle and had been taken from the heart of a fire demon. Once unleashed and aimed at your target, they'd be blinded before the light devoured them. I'd prefer not to use it on something as simple as a Bakoo, but if it turned out to be a nasty one, I'd have to prove a little nastier than normal.

I packed up, had a third coffee—though drinking it caused me too feel more nervous and jittery than I had as of late—and then I got changed into something somewhat presentable. Before I left, my phone started to ring and out of habit I picked it up without even checking who it was.

"This is Dillon," I said, and was bombarded with curses and accusations of being a fraud.

"You should rot in Hell. God would never make a world with monsters, you blasphemer. I hope you die from cancer."

There was more of that, but I hung up without a word and put all unknown numbers back on silent. Only people in my phone book would be able to get through. I hated to do it, but I was busy enough now, thanks to the job at Don Parks' place.

My head started to pound and my heart was beating a little too heavy in my chest. I knew it would eventually go away, but it was really shitty for the meantime. I decided to down a few Advil before I headed out and drove over to Mr Parks' house in the East End.

The house was just off of Woodbine, near Kingston Road. In that area, all the houses had a certain look to them, a similar style. They were also very close and cramped together, as though at some point the spaces between houses had been sold off and new houses had been squished into the resulting slots. Nobody had driveways there, or even alleys between them. I'd have a hard time fitting my arm between one property and the next. It was too close for comfort, as far as I was concerned.

Halfway down the street, I found his number and pulled up close to the curb. I didn't see any signs saying I couldn't park there, so I risked it. These side streets can be tricky, though. Sometimes it's just certain hours you can park, other times you have to be parked on a specific side of the street to avoid the dreaded parking enforcement officer.

I walked up the steps to the porch of the house and tried to see if I could smell the burning rubber from out front. There was nothing, so it was unlikely the smell Mr Parks had described was coming from an outside source. I rang the bell and waited. If this was just a Bakoo, I knew it should be no more than an hour until I was on my way again. The work was nice. It gave me time to step away from all the dumb stress I'd been overwhelmed by. I didn't really want to think about anything that had been going on lately. Not the video, not the whole mess with Chance Anderson, and not—

"Ah, Dillon! Thanks for being so quick. Come on in."

I couldn't believe it. My heart sank, my stomach turned into a sea during high winds, and my anger nearly got the better of me. I hate being lied to. When I get tricked, my first thought is throwing a fist at the very least, but I knew whatever the reason for the charade, letting my baser instincts take over would be even worse than anything that might come out of all of it.

"You look surprised to see me," the hunter who'd been in Godfrey's the other day said, a smirk on his face. "I figured this would be a good way to meet you on your own ground, in a way. Having you show up in work mode, it's better than me just showing up at your place, or at your girlfriend's house."

"What the hell is this about?" I asked, and bit back all the rage boiling in me. The day had already started to feel like a bit of a rollercoaster. That was the story of my recent life.

"Why don't you come in so we can talk? I think we have a lot of ground to cover, so we might as well get comfortable."

"What do I possibly have to say to you? I don't even know you."

"We can start with why I'm here. You've been fucking up a lot, Dillon. And I mean so much more than ever before. The Collective is not happy. I've been sent here to evaluate you and see if we need to take you off this planet, as you are clearly not willing to follow the rules. Now, would you like to come in so we can talk about this, or would you rather everyone on this ugly street know our business?"

I felt trapped, and more than a little afraid. All my fears were coming true in one brief statement. *They* knew. The beings in charge of all the hunters on Earth were watching us and knew what'd been going on. A few isolated breaks in the rules was one thing, but add them all up and I might be on a one way ticket to some horrible corner of an unknown universe.

"Come on, Dillon. Let's go inside and we'll talk about this. I have a friend inside as well, someone who would love to see you."

My mind went right to Rouge. Had this piece of shit grabbed her and brought her here to punish me; threaten me? I needed to get in there and see. I all but pushed past him aside, and walked quickly into the house, and he grabbed hold of my wrist.

"You need to relax, Dillon. You'll see them soon enough." He shut the door and I tried to pull my hand from his, but his grip was surprisingly strong. "I'm a *Thrak*. We're a lot stronger than your species. You're a *Treemor*, right?"

"Where is she?" I asked, ignoring his remark and question. I knew what a Thrak was, and yes, they were much stronger than my species. In fact, I always found it strange that a being so large could fit itself into one of the human hosts we use when on Earth.

"What do you mean, *she*? I don't think it's a girl, but hey, what do I know?"

I relaxed a bit at that and Parks let go of my arm.

"Oh! Did you think I had your little girlfriend? No, that's not allowed. She's an Earthbound being. You, of all people, should know we're not allowed to harm something from here. Or maybe you don't. That might be the problem. Can I get you something to drink?"

Since it wasn't Rouge in there, I thought for a second of just leaving altogether. What would any of this accomplish? I stopped in the hall and turned back towards the door, ready to go, when Parks put a hand on my shoulder.

"I know you want to leave, but I think it's time you stop to see how serious things have become, Dillon. I'm going to put all the cards on the table, and then you'll see where things stand. The Collective isn't very happy, so maybe, just maybe if I tell you what you're doing wrong, you can stop it and secure your place here. They don't want to pull you from here and stick you in some terrible sector of the universe, but with the path you've been on as of late, it's exactly what they'll do. Now, like I asked a second ago, can I get you something to drink? You look like you could use something."

"I'm fine," I said with reluctance, and followed Parks down the hallway to the living room area. It was dark there, but I could tell something was in the room. I could hear movement, and a slight, almost whimpering sound.

Parks turned the lights on and in the middle of the floor, surrounded by a bright blue couch and a rocking chair, was a Gargar. Not just any Gargar, but the one who had been left to protect Sammy. The very one I sent off to see if the Volteer was still at the house he was living in. It was a bad thing he was here. It was yet another rule I'd broken that Parks and the Collective clearly knew about.

The hits just keep coming.

"I think you know this little guy here. He says he knows you," Parks said, and leaned down so he was closer to the Gargar. The creature lay on its back, a small black stone sitting on his chest. It looked like it could be a *Swart Stone*, a crystal from Aaxees region. It has the ability to paralyze certain types of creatures, but can also be used to turn types of liquid solid. The Gargar's gaze was on me. He looked pathetic as he struggled under the crystal, but it was no use. He wasn't going to be able to move while it was there.

"Why are you doing this?" I asked Parks in a low voice, already feeling very defeated.

"I'm doing this to show you the errors of your way, Dillon. You let this thing stay here, a creature with no allowable reason to be on this planet. You were sent here by the Collective to ensure order is kept and rules are followed, so tell me, why is this Gargar still here?"

"I left him to protect—"

"No, that's your job. You're here to protect this world from things like this ugly little worm. So, try again. Why didn't you send him back? Why didn't you dispatch him?"

"You don't know the whole story. You weren't there. There was a Daaf and—"

"Did you let it go, too?"

"No! I took care of that, but there was a baby in the room. The Daaf had been attacking it, and it wasn't the first one to show up there. The Gargar was protecting the child. I made a choice to leave it there to keep the kid safe."

"You know I have a name," the Gargar whispered, still wiggling under the crystal.

"Nobody's talking to you, slug," Parks said, and gave the Gargar a light kick to the head. That shut him up. "Fine, there was a Daaf there, but you could've sealed the breach and made sure none of them came through. Right?"

"Not at the time. I was all out of *Firma Pitch*. Godfrey said it would be a while before he could get his hands on any, so I made a call and let the Gargar stay."

"Okay. And when you got some, did you go back?"

I shook my head. "The Gargar was never a real issue, so in the weeks after when my supply had been refilled, I never thought to go back and seal the breach and send the Gargar back to his world. It was an oversight on my part, but nothing bad happened."

"Until the Volteer came through the breech you failed to seal. Just a little oversight, right, Dillon?"

Oh, shit.

"I can see by your wide-eyed expression that you knew about that too, but did you go and check it out?"

"I never had a chance," I lied, but it wasn't very convincing.

"You had time," the Gargar moaned. "I came to you and asked for help and you told me to go deal with it so you could watch your girlfriend peel her skins off."

I shot the little bastard a look and wished I had dispatched him all those years ago. It's the kind of thanks you get. You help someone out, and they find a way to fuck you hard the first chance they get. Sure, I could have dropped what I was doing and gone to deal with it, but there was no sure bet I'd find the Volteer right then and there. I had made a promise to Rouge to help her with a smarmy producer, but as it turned out, he hadn't even been there. Hindsight is 20/20, I guess.

"So, you thought seeing your girlfriend strip—and we'll get to that soon enough—was more important than going to stop a Volteer? You do know how dangerous they can be?"

"I do. That's why I sent this little shit to go see if it was still at the house. But he never came back to me."

"But *you're* the hunter. You should have gone and if it wasn't there, you could've tried—oh I don't know—hunting it down. Luckily, I ran into this thing and he told me the whole story. I went to the house and took care of the Volteer and then brought the Gargar back here to tell me everything. Apparently, he's not the only one you've let stay here. Is that true?"

I said nothing. I wasn't going to admit to it, nor was I going to deny it and have him pull some other monster I'd given a break to out of the wood work to throw in my face. I was starting to feel too overwhelmed, and thought again about leaving. I felt choked by the stale air in the house. I shifted the collar of my shirt as though it would help, but the feeling was not physical, I knew that. I was stressed in a way I rarely am, and needed fresh air.

"You okay, Dillon? You sure you don't want, or need, a drink? You're looking a tad pale."

"I don't want your fucking drink! Got it?"

"You need to calm down. Snapping at me—a guy who's here to see if you even deserve to be on this planet—is not a good thing. Maybe you should take a deep breath and relax a bit."

"Just get on with it. I need to get out of here."

"We'll see about that," Parks said, pulling out a silver knife from inside his coat. In the dim, light I could see symbols swirling like smoke on the blade and knew what it was. Similar to my Tincher, it was a spellbound blade, blessed and cursed, used for one thing: to dispatch creatures not meant to be on Earth. With lightning speed, the blade zipped through the air, seeming to cut through the light and leave a trail of shadows behind it. I tensed up, ready for an impact I had no time to stop. There was so much I had wanted to do before leaving here, but he wasn't going to give me the chance. I closed my eyes, brought Rouge's face up in my memory, and heard the knife hit home.

I was still there.

The Gargar was not. Only the crystal and a pile of what had made up the creature's body lay where he had been just moments before.

"Now that that's done, let's go sit on the couch like civilized adults and try and sort this out. I have a report to submit."

We sat there for over thirty minutes and Parks went through all my wrongdoings. He had it all down on paper. He had the Gargar, the Volteer, the fact that I'd allowed seven other beings stay on Earth aside from that, and that I had killed earthbound creatures. He also had the website, the YouTube video, the fact that I had allowed Godfrey to leave his store, and of course the icing on the cake for him was my relationship with Rouge. I listened to it all and was glad he only knew a fraction of the things I'd done wrong. I was actually surprised no mention was made of the fact that I worked with humans at all. The Collective really wants us to roam the shadows, to keep it all quiet, but there's no real point. It's easier to work with the people affected by the experiences and with law enforcement to get things resolved faster. In the end though, it seemed as if most of his focus ended up coming down to Rouge, which didn't surprise me that much. It was pretty much the number one rule one not to break.

And I'd shattered the hell out of it.

"What were you thinking? Having relations with a human is, first off, disgusting, but you know how the Collective sees that. It's not just the law they set that you've been breaking; it's the laws of the natural order. What if you got her pregnant?"

"I would deal with that when it came," I said.

"See, there, that's part of the problem with you, Dillon. You're way too cavalier about all of it. It's like you don't take it seriously at all."

"I take it more seriously than you can know. You have no idea what this is like, the stress I'm under right now. You've been on Earth—what? A week, two tops? The Collective sends you to fuck with me, stress me out, to what end? I do my job. I've been doing it a long time."

"Since 1884 it says," Parks reads off a paper, and I nodded. Sounds about right. "That's a long time to be here. That could be part of the problem. You think you're untouchable, you became complacent and that led you to making mistakes."

"Mistakes?" I laughed for a moment, though I wanted to yell it at him. "My track record is pretty damn good. And I stopped a Hellion not that long ago."

"Which the Collective appreciates, but it doesn't mean you can abuse the rules."

"Maybe they should appreciate more, instead of sending you here to make my life harder. Aren't there bigger fish than me to fry in the whole universe? Maybe they could try focusing on the little uprising going on instead of my stupid mistakes and judgement calls."

Parks looked confused.

"Are you telling me you don't know anything about the uprising? For the last two years I've been dealing with more and more creatures coming through. Most of them are running for their lives because whatever is going on out there is threatening them. But they're not the only ones getting through. The Hellion used a Porter to get here. I've put this stuff in my reports. More than half the creatures I deal with are talking about an uprising, a whole underground fighting against the Collective and what they stand for. You can't not know about it."

"Of course I know, and so does the Collective," Parks said, doing his very best to lie to me, but his eyes gave him away. He had no idea what I was talking about, but that didn't mean the higher-ups were as blind to the turnings of the universes. "We're getting sidetracked here, Dillon. All that talk about uprisings is just fluff right now. You are the subject. So, what are we going to do about all this?"

"Clearly, you're going to write your report and they'll do what they'll do. Either way, I'll be allowed to stay and deal with these monster and demons, or I won't."

"You don't even sound like you want to stay."

"Of course I do. Earth has become more of a home to me than my birth planet ever was. I was barely thirty when I left there, when everyone I knew and loved was killed. This is my real home, and I'm surrounded by people who actually care about me. I do something I enjoy, and I do it well. But sure, take it all away. Or even threaten to. It'll ruin my life, but it will also open the floodgates to this planet, and you know it. Whoever this underground uprising is, they'll see you removing me as weakness, so do whatever you're going to do. Write your report; go tattle on me. Let the Collective know I'm such a turd and in need of a time out. Then we can watch this world go down the crapper."

"You really do have an ego, don't you?" Parks said, looking disgusted with me, but I was already done with all of it. I was stressed out, worn out, and willing to punch him out. "I will write my report, but I have an easy way to redeem yourself so the Collective will see you want to change."

"And what's that?"

"You end it with the human, the one you're in a relationship with. You cut off all ties to her and I can guarantee you that the Collective will let everything else slide. It's the major issue they have right now."

I sat there in stunned silence. I couldn't think about not spending time with her any more. Trying to imagine her face as we sat somewhere and I told her we had to end things, it made me feel queasy. The two of us met because of this work I do. We got involved pretty fast, and fell for one another even faster. Some of her friends thought it'd been way too quick, as though the concept of love at first sight is new. They told her she tended to rush into relationships far too often, and despite her explanation of how different it was between us, they stuck to their guns on their opinions and suggestions she should step back and slow things down. Sure, we might've moved quickly, going from a date to saying we loved each other in record time, but there are no rules when it comes to the heart. There was no rule book, especially when it comes to interplanetary dating.

"How am I supposed to do that? I love her," I said, my voice softer than I meant it to come out. Even to my own ears I sounded quiet and defeated. That was probably because I was replaying different breakup scenarios in my head and seeing her heart break over and over again.

"That's the way it has to be if you want to stay on Earth, Dillon. You can think on it for a few days, but if it's not done by the week's end, I can't guarantee you'll be allowed to stay. You end it with her, and that'll at least show your willingness to move forward and follow the rules. Again, think on it, but not for too long."

I wanted to jump at him and punch him in his stupid, smug face over and over again while screaming *Fuck you and your fucking rules*, but I didn't. I sat there on his couch, breathing in his stale air, looking over at the remains of the Gargar, and tried to figure out my next move. Could I break her heart and my own? Could I follow these rules I didn't really care about? It seemed like either choice I made, losing Rouge was the end result.

Heads you win, tails I lose.

Without another word to him, I got up and left the house. He said something to me as I was going, but I didn't hear a word of it. It was just sound: a muffled, muted voice like an adult in a Peanuts cartoon. He was nothing but background noise as I walked to my car, got in and started it. I didn't drive off right away. I just sat there for a while, seething, and staring at the steering wheel. At some point I began to scream over and over again, long and loud until my ears hurt and lights burst in my vision. I felt dizzy and sick. I leaned back in my seat, closed my eyes and tried to wish it all away.

Nothing changed.

Once my head seemed as clear as it was going to get, I drove away from Parks' house. I tried to call Rouge, but she didn't answer. I sent her a text and told her I needed her to get back to me as soon as she could, but as soon as I hit *send*, I wanted to retract it. What was I going to tell her? I needed to vent, but didn't want to drop this kind of bomb on her, not yet, not until I had a chance to figure out exactly what I planned to say and do. I drove with no ideas finding their way into my confused brain. I was positive I didn't want to leave her, but it seemed as though any way I sliced it the results were going to be the same. Stay with her and I'm sent off the planet; leave her and I could still never be close to the one person I wanted to be with. Either way, we couldn't be together.

I'd been painted into a corner.

I drove around aimless. I talked to myself as I turned from one street to the next. At some point I stopped off at a drug store and bought a bottle of Pepto-Bismol. I barely remembered doing it, but there it sat in my cup holder, half gone and my mouth tasting vaguely of peppermint, cherry chalk. My stomach rolled acidic waves and turned somersaults, so I drank more of the unpleasant, vile liquid.

I thought about calling Godfrey. At least he was someone I could lay it all out before and he might have some understanding. In the end I didn't think it was right to unload on him, especially since it was clear they were watching him, too. And if I ended up taking option number three, the one Parks never mentioned, I didn't want him knowing anything about it. The less Godfrey knew, the better off he was. After all, choice number three was going rogue with Rouge and running. Not the best option, seeing as it'd make me one of the hunted, but there were places to go on this planet where they'd never be able to find us. I knew about small towns and villages that hunters would rarely, if ever, venture to, and looking human meant I could at least blend in. It might be the only choice, though if I was caught it would mean a lot more than losing Rouge. It would mean losing my life. A rogue hunter was a risk, and wouldn't just be sent off the planet. They'd be sent to whatever was beyond the mortal world.

At some point I drove all the way to the west end of the city, to Etobicoke, and noticed Sherway Gardens was just up ahead. I pulled into a shopping mall parking lot. I shut off the engine and sat there, turning it all over in my head. Time slipped from me and I started to feel dizzy and tired. I felt like a hamster on one of those wheels, going nowhere fast. Sitting there and thinking about it all wasn't helping anything, so I decided to go walk through the mall and just blend in. I thought about grabbing some junk food from the food court and eating away the stress, even if the idea of eating made me feel a bit queasy. Maybe some salt, oil and sugar would chase the blues away, even momentarily.

For a Monday afternoon, the mall was busy. I hadn't been to the place in years, and had never seen it full of so many people who clearly didn't have day jobs. People with arms full of bags, or kids; packs of people talking so loud my head started to hurt even more than it already had been. I wondered if I was coming down with the flu, or if was only stress-related. If it was stress, I figured there'd be a nervous breakdown in my future if I didn't find a way to wrangle it in. I felt like utter crap.

I made my way to the food court, and that turned out to be a mistake. Apparently, part of the reason the mall was so busy was a meet and greet right in the hub, next to the stairs which led up to the second level food court. Some teen idol who sang about his little bits needing to be with someone's lady bits had been set to perform, sign posters, and whatnot. It appeared the whole shindig was free, so cue the slew of rabid fans.

The problem was, foam-drooling fans were young and had made the singer popular by watching all his videos on YouTube. Guess what else was on the same digital platform?

That's right.

"OMG! It's the monster man!"

"Monster guy! Over here!"

"He's so cute."

"He's shorter than I thought."

"You're a fraud."

"Loser."

"I love you."

"Sign my poster, monster dude."

"Die, you turd!"

"What a dick! Get it? He's a dick!"

The whole area exploded with calls and screams towards me. I backed up as the crowd surged in my direction. Young girls and boys charged at me as though I was a member of some currently popular auto-tuned pop band. A sea of braces, pimples, greasy fingers came at me like a tsunami, and I felt near-panic grip me, and the urge to get out of there was overwhelming. I think I may have screamed as I turned to run, only to come face to face with a nightmare.

Across from the surging sea of teens, a woman I didn't know stood looking in my direction. She filled me with dread. I had no idea how old she was, but as my eyes fell on her, something changed in her face. The space around her nose and mouth became shadowy, and her eyes darkened. Her features liquefied and swirled, as though the blackness was made up of something alive. The darkness began to bleed down her face, looked as though it was melting her flesh as it went, and when she opened her mouth, globs of black, tar-like mud fell from it. I screamed as the wads of blackness fell to the ground. I looked down and saw it moving. The sludge inched towards me, alive. It looked like soil mixed with old motor oil, and was full of all sorts of tiny, disgusting bugs.

I hate bugs, but I hated whatever she was even more.

I started to back away from her, but only ended up crashing into the crowd of kids behind me. Their shouts and my screams at the melting monster before me blended to become a cacophony. I had to get away from it all.

Panic took over and I shoved and pushed everyone out of my way. Young hands tried to grab my arms and I ripped myself free from them. I'm sure I knocked a few of them flying, but that woman was still there, still spewing clumps and blobs of nightmare from her face onto the floor. Someone told me to watch out, another to relax. I told them all to fuck off and let me go.

Once I was free, I ran from them and then from the mall.

The cold air hit me hard, but it was so welcome. I bent over, trying to catch my breath and fighting back a need—a real need—to bawl my eyes out. I felt so overwhelmed, and once out and away from all of that, the panic hit me like a truck. I began to breathe in slow, deep breaths, trying to calm my speeding heart. I turned and shot a quick look over at the mall doors I'd just run from, expecting the kids, or the melting woman, to be coming after me, but was relieved to see nobody there.

"What the *fuck* was that?" I asked myself as a group of people passed me to go into the mall. One of them—a dad with a child of maybe four years—shot me a look and told me to watch my mouth or I wouldn't have a mouth to ever watch again. "Yeah, sure. Sorry about that. Not sure what you mean, but sorry."

They went in and I continued to watch. I expected others to run out of there screaming at any second. As soon as they all saw the melting woman, they'd see why I was freaking out, and they'd run for the hills. I'd made a spectacle of myself and most of them were focused on my hysterics, but after a few seconds I expected someone else would've notice the melting woman and join me in my exodus. There's no way one melting woman could attack them all at once, but someone *had* to have the good sense to make like a library and book.

Nobody did.

I inched my way back to the doors and before going in, I put my hoodie up, hoping it was enough to disguise me for a bit as I surveyed what was going on. I wasn't planning on going all the way in, just enough to see if I could hear screams and see people running away. I knew there was more than one entrance/exit in Sherway, so maybe everyone else had gone one of the other ways.

Inside, though, I heard nothing. Not a scream of terror, or the slap of feet as they dashed through the tiled mall. There were a lot of voices, and some yelling, but it was all in the realm of normality.

What the hell was going on?

I inched back towards the food court, and stopped in the area where everything had happened, keeping my head down so nobody would see me. There was nothing out of the ordinary. Even the spot where the melting woman had spewed her mouthy goo on the floor looked as clean as a mall could look. I was at a loss.

I turned away from the food court, my back against the Tory Burch store, and tried to get my head around what had just happened. Music started to thump off in the center and I could hear a chorus of screams from the kids as their pop sensation began to do what is these days called *singing*. The background noise sounded more like the electronic chirps of Star Wars' R2D2 than anything you'd call music.

"Everything alright, chief?" a woman asked to my right, and when I turned to look at her, I almost expected it to be the melting lady. I jumped a little and nearly ran, but saw it was a security guard and her partner.

"Yeah. Sure. Everything's fine," I said, as convincingly as I could muster.

"Well, you're going to have to take down your hoodie. We don't allow that or any other gang stuff here, boss." The two of them stood in front of me, hands on their duty belts as though they were just waiting for a reason to grab the baton, cuffs, or whatever else they thought would be fun to use on someone. The guy had a hand on his radio, holding it as though there was a gun in the holster instead of an ancient Motorola walkie-talkie.

"Seriously? I can't wear my hoodie up because you think it's a gang thing?"

"You heard my partner," said the other guard. He was tall, and had no neck I could see. His hands were the size of my head and his fingers looked more like pale sausages than actual digits. "I think you're going to just need to leave."

Whew! That went from zero to sixty in no time.

"Okay. Sounds good to me. And if I come back, is there anything else I shouldn't do or wear?" I asked as I pulled my hoodie down.

"Oh, you're not coming back here, buddy," the female told me, taking my arm. "You clearly have some attitude, and around here, we don't put up with that kind of shit."

I was taken a bit aback, but just went with it. They each had an arm, and began to escort me out of the mall. This wasn't the first time I'd been physically removed from anywhere, and I doubted it would be the last, but there was something that felt a little excessive about it. From the way she kept referring to me as boss, chief and buddy, as though she knew me, to the way she was still trying to talk down to me while they escorted me out for wearing a hood up, was ridiculous.

"You know, you may want to put a sign up somewhere, letting people know these rules of yours."

"Yeah, we'll get on that, pal," she said, as we approached the exit.

Before we got there, a group of about seven walked in through the doors, and my feet nearly stopped working, my legs almost gave out. A man and a woman, holding hands, walked in, and at first they were smiling. But a second later, their faces were doing the same thing as the woman's by the food court. My stomach turned cold, and as I began to back away, the guards squeezed my arm and yanked me towards the melting monsters.

"What the fuck do you think you're doing, shithead?" the female security guard barked at me. "You're going out that door, or we're putting you in cuffs and calling the cops."

I looked at her, and then back at the couple with the dissolving faces. They were coming right at us, but the guards didn't seem to care. The big guy was looking right at them, yet they were more focused on tossing me out than they were at the bug-filled sludge splattering on the mall floor.

I almost screamed, but the couple veered away when they saw us coming, as though I was the one with the face looking like the German guy from Raiders of the Lost Ark. We continued forward, but I was staring wide-eyed over my shoulder at the couple, even though they never bothered to look back at me.

"Did you two see that, or am I losing my marbles?" I asked. But already knew the answer.

"You'll lose a lot more than your marbles if you come back here, fucktard," she growled, and then I was back outside. "I mean it. You come back here and you'll find out what it feels like to get hit with Matt's canned hams." She motioned to her partner, who slammed one massive hand into his equally massive palm. I got the point.

"No worries. I won't be back. Your mall's overrated, anyway. Stop acting like this is somewhere special. It's Etobicoke, Toronto's butt crack. This place nearly makes Scarborough Town Centre look upscale."

I walked away from them and headed back to my car. They called out some insults, no doubt trying to egg me back inside so they'd have a reason to arrest me, but I had more important things to worry about than two overpaid rent-a-cops. Mainly, I needed to wrap my head around what was going on, about what I'd just seen. It was obvious I was the only one seeing the melting faces. None of the people around, or the guards, had reacted, so there was no doubting it. Why I was seeing it was what I couldn't wrap my head around. It was clear the melted-faced monsters were the same thing Chance had been seeing, and I knew why he was so freaked out. The sight of them had turned my blood cold.

The real question was: what caused it? Why had I start seeing the same thing Chance had? What had been the cause of the visions for him? Was it stress? It could've been. I was stressed out quite a lot. Or maybe I brought something back with me from Niagara Falls. This could be some demon or monster, or even some alien virus I'd never heard about.

I needed to get home and try to work it all out. I had to try to figure out why I was having the same visions as my client. I wanted to know if I was going to end up with the same head-twisted-off fate he had.

Things only seemed to be getting more stressful these days.

When I got back to my apartment, I locked the door and checked my phone. Still nothing from Rouge, but maybe that was for the best. There was too much to try to work out, and I wouldn't be very good company. Nor did I like the idea of her seeing me in that condition. With what happened at Sherway Gardens, and the bomb dropped on me by Parks, I felt as though I was coming apart at the seams, and then being pulled in four different directions at the same time. My stuffing had started to fall out; my mind was little more than mush. I felt restless, unable to stay on one train of thought for longer than a moment or two. If I sat down and tried to focus, to close my eyes and work through any of it, the images of those melted-face people crept into my mind. This led to Chance sans head, and the idea I would end up the same way. I mean, it was logical thinking that whatever made Chance see what he did, could very well be the same thing that caused him to have his head twisted off like a pop lid. If I followed that track of thinking, I could surmise the same thing was likely to happen to me.

The questions were: why, and what was causing it?

I decided it would be better to focus on that. Never mind what Parks had said for the moment. There was something way bigger at play than him and his threats. I needed to put him on the back burner and turn all my attention towards work. If I was lucky, it would all turn out to be something huge, maybe even bigger than a Hellion. If it was, and I was the one who figured it out and ended it, the rest would work itself out.

One could only hope.

I went to my books. I had several on demons and demonology. Since I knew bounty hunters from certain demon realms had a knack for turning head hunter, I looked them up first. I needed to find a link between what I'd seen at the mall and how Chance had ended up.

I turned page after page of ancient—and in some cases alien—text. I took notes, found interesting items here and there. I found points very close to the details involving Chance's case, but none of them were close enough. There'd been nothing at the realtor's office to point to any demon or creature I could find in the books. Normally, when that kind of violence was brought, there'd be a certain amount of energy used, and that would leave some sort of trace. Often there'd be a smell, markings, items floating freely in the air, or even the swarming of bugs or rodents. None of that had present in Chance's office. There'd been nothing in the room which hadn't been there the day before, headless client aside, of course.

I threw one of the books across the room in frustration.

After two and a half hours I was no closer to an answer than when I started. Aside from eliminating every possible species of bounty hunter or collector in the world of demons, I was empty-handed and even more frustrated than when I'd started.

I thought about checking Google. I knew it was bad when I was so desperate for answers that I'd been ready to deep dive into the hopeless world of human opinion. Luckily, my phone rang and saved me from certain disaster.

I dreaded the thought of looking at it, but did anyway. Of course it was Rouge calling me. I wasn't sure I was going to answer it. I knew I'd sent her a message a while back asking her to call me, but I wasn't ready for it. I needed to get my head on straight. I was a mess, and I wasn't sure unloading any of this on her would make me feel any better. I had a good idea this would only take a turn for the worse and my pot of stress would overflow.

When my phone stopped ringing I felt a bit of relief. I'd text her back as soon as I could, and let her know I was alright; just working. That wouldn't really be a lie. It was just a different way of looking at the truth. I'm not sure if that's as bad, but it would have to do. I could feel guilty when this was all over.

I turned back to the computer, still thinking about searching it through the dreaded message boards, when I heard a muffled voice calling my name. It was soft and close, but surveying the room, there was nothing and nobody there. I closed my eyes, focused on it as it continued and could still hear it: small and female.

Oh no.

I looked down at my hand, at my cellphone. I'd been wrong. Rouge hadn't hung up after all. I'd answered it without even trying. This day was like bad breath. It wasn't going away until I did something about it.

"Rouge?" I said as I lifted the phone. "Sorry about that, I was just in the middle of something and didn't even realize I answered."

"No worries, Dill. You okay? You sound weird."

"I'm fine, sort of. It's been a day."

"Sorry about that. It's been one here too. Internet problems, had to run the pup to the vet, and then this weird guy came to the door asking a shit-ton of questions. I wasn't even going to answer, but he wouldn't go away."

I had a bad feeling.

"What was it about?" I asked, but I was pretty sure I knew where this was going.

"Actually, it was about you more than anything. He said he was a friend of Godfrey's and yours; that he was part of some group of super friends you're part of and wanted to know how we met and a few other things. He said his name is Don Parks."

I guess asking if the day could get any worse was an invite for something like that. "When was this?"

"Less than ten minutes ago. He seemed fine, but I didn't tell him anything. I told him he could talk to you, if you guys are actually friends. He said you are, but I know you're very private about us, and I have never heard you mention him, so I told him again to talk to you. I just didn't feel right about telling him anything about us. So he left. Sort of."

"Sort of? Is he still there?"

"He's sitting in a car out on the road, typing away on a laptop. Do you actually know this guy, or should I go get my baseball bat and give him my two cents?"

As much as I would've paid to see her tune this asshole with a baseball bat, I didn't want her to get hurt. I didn't have any idea what he'd do in that situation, but I couldn't let her find out for herself. I told her to just lock the doors and wait for me, to stay away from the windows.

"Should I be worried?" she asked, and I could tell it was already too late for that question. She *was* worried.

"I'll handle him, Rouge. Just sit tight and I'll be over soon."

"You know, I wouldn't have to sit tight if you moved in. Maybe think about it." She hung up before I could say anything. Not that I had much to say about it. With everything else, moving in was the last thing on my mind.

I didn't pull up in front of Rouge's house. Instead, I parked at the end of the street and walked to where Parks was sitting in his car. I could see him, his face stuck in his laptop, but even though his attention was diverted, I decided to keep low so he couldn't see me. I had my Tincher with me, tucked up in the left sleeve of my hoodie in case I needed it.

I hoped I wouldn't. I was already in enough trouble, and it would be worse if I attacked and stabbed another hunter. Especially one sent to investigate me.

Still, I needed to put a scare in him, let him know he had to leave Rouge out of this.

I opened the passenger door the second I was beside it and got into the car with liquid ease. I slammed the door behind me. Parks jumped, which was good. I wanted to catch him off guard.

"I'm sorry, did I scare you?" I said with a smile, loving the look of fear on his face.

"What the hell are you doing, Dillon? Holy fuck, man. I almost gutted you."

I looked and saw he had the blade he'd killed the Gargar with in his hand, ready to strike. I didn't care. He wouldn't have had a chance to use it before I got him.

"Maybe I wanted to make you feel the same way you made her feel," I told him, and he turned towards the house. I wondered if Rouge was watching us. She wouldn't have listened to me when I told her to stay away from the windows. She would've been peeking out waiting for me to show up. So she was probably seeing it all. "Why'd you come here?"

"It's my job, Dillon. That's what—"

"No. Your job is to deal with me, not her. That's not how it works. So, again, what are you doing here?"

He said nothing. I reached over to pull the laptop from him, see what it was he was writing, but he stopped me, slamming it closed and putting it beside him.

"Maybe I wanted to see what the big deal was, Dillon. I came here to look at her face to face and see why you'd be willing to throw away everything you have. And you know what I saw?"

"No. Do tell."

"Nothing. Just a human. She's nothing but a weak, inferior species with nothing special about her worth noting. She's just like the rest of them. There's a reason we have to be here on Earth. They couldn't handle being part of the Collective. Humans are small, dumb, and closed-minded. Your Rouge is no different. She's just a little thing that needs to be protected from everything else in all the universes."

The words left his lips, and just as they did, the driver's side window exploded inward, raining safety glass all over us. Parks screamed, but I'd seen it coming, so I just covered my face. I'd been listening to Parks ramble on and saw Rouge walk out of the house with her Louisville slugger in hand and a look on her face that showed what kind of business she meant.

"You want to tell me why you're still here, motherfucker?" she yelled, pushing the bat through the broken window and poking it repeatedly into Parks' throat. "I don't think you told me everything, did you, you weasel?"

"Get away from me!" Parks tried to yell, but he sounded afraid, and raised his hands in surrender. His blade dropped from his open grip and hit the floor of the car. "Please, you don't know what you're doing."

"Why don't you tell me what I'm doing then? The way I see it, I'm protecting my property, my person, and my boyfriend. So why don't you tell me what I don't get about all this?"

"He can tell you. After all, the reason I'm here is because of him. Go ahead. Ask him."

"Dillon? What's this dickbag on about?"

I got out of the car and went to her. "Come on, let's go inside and talk. This guy isn't worth it," I told her and reluctantly, she let up on Parks, removing the bat from his car. As she went to walk away, though, she spun away from me and brought the bat down hard on the hood of his car.

"You come back here again, and it won't be your car I hit. Got it?"

Parks nodded and Rouge seemed satisfied with that. She headed back towards her house. I went to follow, but turned back towards the hunter.

"You're an idiot, you know that?"

"I told you that you need to get rid of her. Break it off, or you're leaving this planet. Time's ticking away," he said, clearly trying to sound unruffled, but as he swept the glass off his shoulder he turned to look at Rouge and there was fear in his eyes. "But for now, I'll stay away from her. As long as you know, you have to make this quick. I'm sending my report in by the end of the week. Don't make me say that you're still with her, Dillon. It won't go well for you."

I said nothing else to him. I left him to clean up the broken glass and followed Rouge to the house. I wasn't ready to talk about this, but I had no choice. It was on the table.

Time to face the music.

When I walked into her house, she was already sitting in the kitchen, her fingers tapping on the scarred wood of the small table. She had a look on her face I'd never seen aimed at me, and I knew it wasn't good. This was the face she saved for line jumpers, people on the street who'd call out lude suggestions, and other acts that would get equally under her skin. She was pissed, and rightly so.

"You want to tell me what that was all about?" she asked as I sat down across from her. I felt as though all of this would go better over some mulled wine or whiskey, but as Rouge wasn't much of a drinker, she never had that kind of stuff in the house. "Clearly you and ass-face out there are friends like he claimed."

"No. We're not friends," I said, and had no idea what else to say. I didn't want to get into it all right then and there. I was still feeling stressed by everything else in the day, and didn't want to pile on an emotional meltdown.

"So, who is he? Is his name really Don Parks?"

"It is, and he's a hunter."

"There's another hunter in the city? I thought you said you were the only one in the area, in this part of the province for that matter."

"I am, or I was, but now he's here."

"I know there's more to it than that, Dill. Don't keep things from me. Your face gives it all away. What's he doing here?"

I took a deep breath and tried to find the words. It was harder than I'd imagined. This would have been better if I'd had time to roll it around in my head for a while. I would've preferred playing out all kinds of different scenarios so I could have a better idea of what to say, and more importantly, what *not* to say. Instead, I'd barely spent a second figuring the right words, so I just came out and told her, hoping for the best.

"He's here to investigate me. Apparently, I've broken a lot of rules, and he's here to see if I need to be taken off the planet or not."

"What rules did you break?"

I raised my eyebrow and gave her a look. I'd only told her a hundred times, after all. "Well, the gist of the more recent ones is killing Earthbound creatures, letting other creatures stay on Earth that should have been sent back, having a website, the YouTube video going public, and..." I trailed off and sighed. I didn't think I could say it.

"And what? And me?" I nodded. "You're saying that us dating is *that* bad?"

"For them it is."

"So, they're going to send you somewhere else because of our relationship?"

"That and the other things I said. Yeah."

"Can you fight it? I mean there's got to be some kind of way out of this. You do so much for them." I didn't respond to that, because if I did, I'd have to tell her the rest of it, and I could see where it would go from there. Instead, I reached out across the table and took her hands and tried to smile. "Oh, my God! There's something more, isn't there?"

"What?"

"You are easier to read than the funny pages, Dill. Your palms are sweaty, your left eye is twitching, and the smile you just gave me looks like an overcooked noodle. Please tell me what it is."

"It's nothing because there's no way I'm willing to do it."

"Just spit it out."

There was going to be no dancing around it. "He told me I'd be allowed to stay, if I stopped dating you. He said otherwise, I'd be shipped off somewhere and the Collective would choose my punishment."

"So it's break up with me or get removed from Earth. Not much of a choice."

Rouge let go of my hand and deflated in her chair. I could see the realization on her face and it hit me so hard. I watched as her bottom lip started to quiver and she casually caught it with her teeth in hopes of keeping it all in. She thought I was easy to read, but this was the same way she got when Mufasa died in the Lion King; a part we now skip over when we watch it.

"Darling," I began, but as soon as I spoke, a tear came from her eye and she covered her face. Clearly she didn't want me to see her cry, but hearing it tore me apart. "I don't know what to do. I don't want to leave here, but I don't want to leave you either. I've never felt like this with someone before; I never loved anyone. It's been eating at me since he dropped this bomb on me this morning. I really have no idea what to do."

"You don't?" she sobbed, and moved her hands from her face. I nearly screamed.

For a second, no more than the blink of an eye, she looked like one of them. Her eyes had turned black and that blackness ran down her face, her mouth twitched and swirled living darkness. And then, it was gone; Rouge looked as she always had. My heart pounded in my chest and the scream that had died in my throat felt like a stone. She didn't seem aware of my strange reaction, something I felt lucky about. I wasn't sure she'd want to hear about any of that.

"How do you think I feel? I don't want you out of my life, but it looks like no matter what we do, you will be. I can't deal with this right now."

"What do you want to do? We can just set it aside and—"

"I can't set this aside, Dillon! Are you kidding me? This isn't something you just put aside while you watch movies or play cards, then take it out after and see if anything's changed. I need to just think about all of this. I need some time alone, I think."

"Alone?" I asked, and nearly expected to see the melting face thing start again, but it never did. Small favours there.

"Yeah. I think I do. I need to think and cry and throw things. It's not going to help with you here." She stood up and held her hand out to me. "Come on."

I got up and she walked me to the front door. I wasn't so sure leaving was the best idea, but it was hers, so I went along with it. I'd come to accept that Rouge usually knew best.

When we got to the door, she wrapped her arms around me and pressed herself tight against me. I returned the hug and whispered that I loved her.

"I love you too, but this isn't going to be fixed with words or feelings, Dill. I need some time to think and deal with it. I know this can't be easy for you either, but please give me some space to work through this."

"Of course. Anything you need."

She kissed me on the cheek and let me out. She closed the door without another word.

None of it felt good, especially how broken-hearted I felt.

Tuesday

I woke up late on Tuesday, after spending a night in bed tossing and turning. Nothing that happened the day before felt great or right, and my whole body ached when I finally slid out from my sheets to face the day. Beyond the window rain fell, matching my mood. Wind smashed hard against the glass, making it shake in its frame, and I thought about crawling back into bed and just staying home all day. I thought I might find some solace in my oversized comforter, wrapped up in my sheeted cocoon. I still had a lot to try and figure out, and I wanted to avoid it. Between Rouge, Parks, the melted-face people and Chance, my life felt full to the brim with stress, and sleep seemed a better choice. I stared at my bed longingly for a moment, but knew hiding away would be pointless.

I went to the bathroom, and then headed to the kitchen to put on some coffee. As it brewed, I checked my phone. I was surprised to see nothing from Rouge at all. I thought at least a text message, but not that or a missed call. I sent her a quick one, just to say hi and that I hoped we could talk later.

By the time my coffee was done and I had finished two cups, she'd sent no response so I was pretty sure she was avoiding it all too. As hard as it all was for me, there was little doubt it was equally as bad for her. We had such a great relationship. We laughed, got out and saw all kinds of amazing things, had some incredible sex, and talked about our future together. It was perfect in my opinion, and then, it was all coming apart. I felt sick to my stomach from it. Every time I tried to think about something else, her face popped back into my head. I figured the best thing to do was get to work on solving the Chance case. I hoped if I buried myself in research it would be enough of a distraction from the things that made me long to sleep my day away. I put on some music, needing something dark and hard to wake me out of the funk I was in. A playlist of Bad Brains, Killswitch Engage, Wu Tang, and Propaghandi was just what the doctor ordered.

Three hours melted by before my head started to pound from all the time I'd spent poring over books and staring at page after page on my computer. I spent all that time reading and it turned out to be all for nothing. Not one thing I read brought me any closer to answering the mystery of what had killed Chance, or what would cause me to see those people drooling from every facial orifice. I leaned back in my chair, frustrated, and felt as though I needed to step away from the research, too. Work didn't seem to be working the way it normally did.

I stood up and checked my phone. There was still nothing from Rouge, so I sent her another message asking if she wanted to see me later. I didn't know what else to say.

When I got nothing back from her after thirty minutes, I knew I had to do something else. I couldn't go back to reading, as important as it was. I needed to move, to get out; I figured fresh air would do me some good, even if it was raining out. I was worried about going out, though. If it was somewhere public, there was no saying I wouldn't see another of those melty-faced people, and I was sure I'd freak out again if I did. Skipping the mall was easy enough.

I saw it was still pouring outside, but even if all I did was go for a drive, I was sure it would help. I could pick up something from Tim Hortons and drive out to the Bluffs and watch the storm. It'd be better than sitting around the house moping and feeling useless. I've never been in this way before, feeling as though everything around me was a fragile house of cards, with a hurricane on the horizon. It wasn't something I felt suited me too well, either.

I left the house five minutes later.

The storm wasn't as bad as it had seemed from my apartment,

but the wind made it harder to see. That was good, because not many people were out and about, and the ones that were had their faces cover up. If they had their faces covered, I was less likely to see one of them melting away.

I picked up some coffee, Timbits, and a bagel, and changed my mind about driving all the way to the Bluffs. The rain had picked up, which meant a higher possibility of bad drivers. The Timmies I went to was pretty close to the lake though, just down the street from the old Sunnyside pool, so I decided to go out there instead and look out over the lake as the winds made actual waves.

I parked in a deserted lot very close to the water, and just let the serenity of the scene relax me. I turned my phone to silent. I wanted to talk to Rouge still, but if I was going to have any success at using the time to relax and try to work through everything, I didn't need to keep worrying about whether or not she was going to call. I did send her a quick text though, let her know I was going to be offline for a little while, but really wanted to talk to her. I asked her to message me when she could to let me know when we might talk later. I then tossed my phone into the back seat and forgot about it.

I wasn't even sure where to start with everything, but I knew I needed to pick a jump-off point or my mind would just wander and eventually take me down a path that would only make me freak out even more. I'd had enough of freaking out to last me a life time.

I went back to everything that had happened in Niagara Falls. I replayed the moment I met Chance Anderson, right up until I left the city and headed home. I retraced my steps through each holding he was owner or part owner of, pulling up every little detail I could, and in the end, it brought me right back to where I thought it would. Through all the details, small and major, there was only one real place my focus fell on that felt right. The church: it was the only thing that added up.

I used a pen and paper to write down the name of the pastor, Herb Dank, an obvious alias, and drew the symbols I'd seen spray painted on the walls, and those that were carved into the walls and into the wood beams and pews. Most of the vandalism was just a blur, but some of it had really stuck out and I picked it out of my memory easily.

I delved deeper, remembered burn patterns there, recalled the area that was the start point of the blaze, and what the property had been before it'd become a church. The woman I'd talked to said it used to be a pottery store, but I wondered about its history beyond that, or if the people who owned the old store had had any incidents before they left. I would look that up when I got a chance to, but it was a good starting point. I'd been so ready to brush off the church after the woman had told me all she had, but when the cops explained that Pastor Herb and two others had died in the blaze, and that the fire was deliberate, well, it meant it was top of my suspect list of the source of all the madness.

That act of murder, especially in a place that might even be only perceived as holy, would be just the type of thing to call a demon. It was especially so if the building already had a weak spot in it. If I could find signs of previous activity there, then there'd be no doubt. Some of this seemed like it could be a stretch, but it was more than I'd had a day ago. I'd look into it, the symbols, the history of the building, and Pastor Herb. I just hoped it would turn out to be a demon, and not some other Earthbound spirit, like the vengeful souls of Herb and the others looking to curse anyone who stepped in there. If that's what it was, it would mean having to break the rules once again to save myself. Better to break the rules and keep my head than to be a good boy and end up looking like a ruined action figure.

With everything lined up there and ready to go, I turned my attention to Don Parks and Rouge. That was more stress than I really wanted, but there was no way to not deal with it. He wasn't just going to go away, as much as I would like that, and my feelings for Rouge weren't simply going to be squashed because he ordered me to. The two of us had started our relationship in a whirlwind of monsters and potential death, which is probably why it happened so fast. Some people might think it's not the best way to start a relationship, but it seemed to be working out just fine for us. I wasn't going to let this asshole come out of nowhere and try to squash it, just because it was against someone's rules. I've been on Earth for so long, I've come to realize that many of the rules the Collective try to put on us is based on outdated and unchecked facts. It's not like we were planning on having a pack of little monster hunter babies. We just dig each other.

But he'd shown up at her house, and that made me think he might do something to her, as well as to me. I have no idea what the Collective might've okayed him to do if I refused to leave here, or her, but I had a hard time believing they would harm her. It sort of went against their laws and rules.

Yet, I remember a few decades back, when another hunter had gone off reservation with a human companion. The two of them had decided to stop hunting monsters, and instead began robbing banks and killed a few people. All the active hunters on Earth were told to keep an eye out for them and kill them on sight: both of them, not just the hunter. So there was a history to consider.

The waves began to slam into the rocks along the shore with a thunderous bang as the wind picked up and I continued to ponder the conundrum before me. There was no good way to deal with this, but it would have to be dealt with. I still held hope that if I solved the Chance issue, found out what had killed him and was causing me to see all the melty-faced people, I'd have something to hold over their heads and it would allow some leeway.

I didn't know for sure though. A boy can hope, though.

I spent another forty minutes parked there, staring off at the ebbs of the stormy water and feeling a connection to it. The waves rose from a dark colour to a foamy white rage, crashing against the still waters, or against the rocks that lined this area of the shore. Further down the way, it washed against the sand where, in the summer, kids would be playing. In October, though, people rarely came down, especially in weather as foul as this day had served up. When I figured I had settled my mind as best I could, made firm plans as far as Chance's case went, I reached back and grabbed my cellphone.

Still nothing from Rouge, but I had two missed calls from

numbers I knew, forty from unknown ones. The two I knew were Don Parks and Godfrey. I ignored the call from the asshole hunter and called Godfrey back. He picked up after the second ring.

"Screening calls?" he asked me, without saying hello.

"I had my phone off; needed some thinking time. What's up?"

"You hear from that other hunter yet?"

"Unfortunately. Why?"

"He was here today asking a lot of questions. Some of them were about you, some about your girl. He even asked me about leaving the shop. How'd he know about that?"

"I have no idea, but he mentioned it to me, too."

"Are we fucked, Dillon?" he asked, and I didn't want to lie to him. I told him I wasn't sure, but things weren't looking too good for me. "Well, if they get you, they're going to get me, too. The best I guess I can hope for is extra years in this shop, but there's worse ways they can get me, right?"

"Aren't there always? Want me to swing by?"

"Only if you want. Maybe you can grab some whiskey or rum for me if you do. Might as well drown these thoughts in my head, or at least settle them down with some hard drinking."

"I could join you there. I'll swing by with a bottle or six. I also have some drawings of some symbols I'm hoping you'll recognize."

"You still want to work with all this going on?" he laughed.

"It might be something good enough to take the heat off. You never know, but it won't hurt to try."

"You've said that before. You're not always right in those cases."

How true that was.

On the way to Godfrey's, I stopped by the plaza at Bloor and Dundas Street West where there's an LCBO (liquor store for those who have no clue how different it is to buy alcohol in Canada; look it up). The plan was to grab some JB and a bottle of spiced rum I knew he liked. The store wasn't as busy as usual, but there were still a fair amount of people in there since it was just after most people were off work.

I was in my own world going in, still thinking about Rouge and wondering why she wasn't calling. I felt so terrible, and I could only imagine where her head was at. I hoped she'd call before too much more time passed, but I didn't want to come off like a clingy boyfriend. I had to accept she'd call me when she was ready to, no matter how much I didn't like it.

I grabbed the bottle of whiskey first, and headed over to get the rum. I saw a shelve with a bunch of Autumn-inspired drinks, and shook my head. Most of them were fine, ciders and dark ales, but the ones that made me want to hurl were the rows of pumpkin-spiced beers. I'd fallen for them once upon a time, when I actually had drinks on the weekend, but they never tasted the way you wanted them to. You hear chocolate beer, or one that's pumpkin-spiced, and you get this warm, delicious image in your head that makes your taste buds start to dance with excitement. Then, you open it, try it, and your taste buds become taste foes. They want to pack up and leave your mouth from the pure disappointment of what you just forced them to savour. You taste the false pretenses and say you'll never do it again, but you do. Usually it takes three or four failed attempts to make you steer clear of the bottles of regret. For me it was four, and from there on in I swore to my mouth I would never show it disrespect again.

So, I shook my head, avoided the bad decisions, and grabbed a bottle of spiced rum. As my hand wrapped around the neck of the bottle, I heard someone say something behind me, and it made me not want to even turn around.

"This is so cool. Davey, do you know who that is? It's the fucking monster killer from YouTube, bro!"

I closed my eyes and wished them away. I didn't want to turn and see two or three barely-legal bros grabbing some brews for the rest of their frat brothers. I just wanted to get what I'd come for and get out of there without another word. They continued to talk, though. The one guy who'd called to Davey began to call out to me, asking me if he could get an autograph, or take a selfie with me. I bit back the urge to spin around and swing the bottles in each hand at him and whoever he was with. That wouldn't do me any good. There were other people in the store, cameras everywhere, and I was already in enough trouble. The only thing I could do was turn around, tell him he had the wrong guy and be on my way. It was doubtful they'd believe me, but I'd just have to ignore their disappointment.

Trying to relax a little, feeling my shoulders already tight from the first words, I turned around to tell them I had no idea what they were on about. My mouth opened, but the words died on my lips as the three people standing there in matching Blue Jays jerseys drooled oily blackness from every orifice on their faces. I saw their oozing, melting faces, the globs of muck falling from their mouths, and took a step back, hitting the wall of bottles behind me, nearly bringing them all down.

The tallest and broadest of the group took a step towards me, and a sound came from the sludge-packed mouth. It sounded like something that wanted to be words, but they were like nothing I'd ever heard. It was as though his speech was playing in reverse, but was also muffled. The sound came out it bubbling hisses like the sound mud makes near a hot spring. He raised a hand towards me, and a logical part of my brain told me not to be afraid. I tried to remind myself how nobody else could see what I was seeing, that it might not be real. I even told myself that I was just breaking mentally, or infected with something I'd gotten from Chance's case. I knew there was a rational explanation to it all, and freaking out wouldn't solve anything.

Yet, despite that, as soon as his hand touched me, another part of me—my survival instinct, maybe—just snapped. I reacted without any real thought. His hand was like fire on my skin, even though he was touching me through my coat and hoodie. I dropped the bottles of booze I'd been holding and without fully realizing what I was doing, I reached back and pulled out my Tincher. A howl came from the closest of the melted-face jocks, and his equally liquefying friends joined in. That was probably because I threw myself at the one who'd touched me, knocked him to the ground and put the cursed, spellbound blade to his throat. Some of the goop touched me, and I felt darkness swirl all around me. The LCBO started to smell of wet dirt and rot. I could taste earth and mould. I shrieked and tried to get it off me as the melty one under me began to buck, trying to get me off him.

I nearly dropped my blade as I fell sideways, landing in a pool of whiskey, rum, and the remains of the bottles. Glass cut into me, but all my attention was on the alien substance from the melted thing's mouth. It was on my left forearm and moving in every direction. It reminded me of a scene from the blob, only this was blacker than the midnight sky out in the country. It felt like cold death as it spread over my arm. The more of me it covered, the more the room stank of decay, and the darker the lighting in the store seemed to get. I was about to try to get it off with my other hand, but a sudden terror of it infecting that as well stopped me. What if it covered my whole body, ate me in its muddy darkness, the squirming things under the mainly-liquid surface finding their way into my mouth, nose, or ears and suffocating me?

I took my Tincher to it instead. I used the blade to try and scrape it off my arm, careful not to cut my coat or my skin. The blade disappeared into the mess, and there was a hissing sound that rose and became more intense the longer I held it there. The blackness boiled on my sleeve. Alien insects with bleach-white legs and millions of eyes rose to the surface and then fell to the floor, where they thrashed around until they appeared to dry up and turn to dust.

The black goop also fell off and evaporated before it ever hit the ground, and my heart rate finally slowed down a bit. I went to get up, forgetting for a moment where I was, but then heard the commotion around me and knew as bad as that had been, things were about to get worse.

"**D**rop the knife and get on the floor!"
There was a huge crowd there watching everything as it went down. Mixed in with the onlooker were the three melting-faced jocks that nobody seemed to be reacting to. Masses of blackness continued to glob out of their mouths, but that wasn't

my biggest concern. My full attention was on the cop working a Pay Duty gig. His gun was out and aimed at me as I knelt on the floor, still with a sizable knife in my hand. I wasn't sure if he'd seen everything that had taken place, but as nobody was reacting to the three melters in amongst them, it wasn't likely he would have any idea what was actually going on.

I wasn't even sure I did. Not fully, at least.

"I said drop it, or else!"

I let the knife fall from my hand, and it clattered to the ground in front of me. I kept my eyes fixed on the cop, not wanting to look away or act shifty at all. Cops had a way of shooting people lately, even when they were doing as they were told, so I wanted to avoid giving him any reasons to use me to scratch his itchy trigger finger.

"Now get on the ground, face down, hands behind your head."

I did as I was told. I tried to avoid the glass as best I could, but some of it poked into me regardless. As soon as I was on the ground, the cop was on my back. He dug a knee into the back of my neck, and placing me in cuffs. I was limp, not going to struggle, in hopes of avoiding some extra attention from his fists or boots. Seeing as I was in a very public place and no doubt people had already started to pull out their cellphones in hopes of recording some tragedy they could post online, it was doubtful the cop would try anything until we got somewhere much more private.

Once I was secured, he called in to his dispatcher and told them he had someone under arrest and needed additional units. He asked someone close by if they needed medical attention. I heard an unearthly sound that could have been a voice, and knew it was the melted-faced guy who'd touched me.

"You're sure you're okay?" Another strange, gurgling noise. "Okay, but I'm going to need statements from the three of you. So stay put."

I was then pulled to my feet. My wrists strained against the cuffs and I winced at the pain, but it was short-lived, at least. Before taking me to the back office—as he was Pay Duty, he didn't have a cruiser—he grabbed my Tincher off the floor. He told the store manager to stay with the victims and we were off.

The room he took me to was small, with a scarred desk and a few chairs. Not much else. I wasn't sure if this was supposed to be a lunchroom or where they just brought people who might get arrested for shoplifting. Whatever it was, it was nothing to write home about.

The officer pushed me down into a cheap, weak chair and tossed my knife down on the other end of the table. He pulled out his notebook, scribbled down a few things, and then began to read me my rights.

It's weird. If you watch a lot of TV or movies from America, you get used to the Miranda warning there. The whole *right to remain silent* speech appears in almost any movie or TV show with a cop as a main character. Well, in Canada, it's nothing like that at all. You pretty much have one right here, and that's to telephone a lawyer.

"Alright, sir, I'm letting you know you're under arrest for assault, and possession of a weapon. It's my duty to inform you that you have the right to retain and instruct counsel without delay. You have the right to telephone any lawyer you wish. You also have the right to advice from a legal aid lawyer. You may apply to the Ontario Legal Aid Plan for assistance..."

He went on, providing me a phone number from the back of his memo book, and asked if I wanted to call a lawyer and if I understood my rights. I told him I did understand and no, I didn't want to call a lawyer. I didn't know any lawyers, really, so what use would that be? I could try calling some legal aid lawyer, an underpaid newbie that might be good one day, but what where they now? Nobody. They'd be someone more willing to try to deal my life away than listen to the truth.

There was one choice though, something that might help.

"I don't want to call a lawyer, but I would like to call one of your detectives. Jonathan Garcia? He knows me, and he'll believe what I'm going to have to tell him."

"Why don't you tell me instead? If a simpleton like me can't wrap my head around the story of how you smoked some meth or crack and attacked three people with a huge-ass knife, I'll call the detective for you. How's that sound?"

Not good. There was no way I was going to be able to tell him or anyone else they might send about what had happened or what I do. It had to be Garcia or someone else I knew. I accepted that this was not going to end any time soon, so I just lowered my head and let him rattle off about how I was an asshole, a psycho, and he'd make sure he showed up at court to throw the book at me.

"Guys like you, I'm sure you have a record as long as Yonge Street. You think you can just wig out and get away with it, and you usually manage to wriggle out of any real charges, right? That's why you're still out here walking around with normal people. You probably gave up your dealer or some other skid, and you're back out to get your fix and fuck with people. Well, not this time. My brother's a crown attorney, and I'll be the star witness against you."

Maybe I did want a lawyer after all. I sat back in the chair and stared at him for a second, trying to think of something to say; clever or helpful, I didn't care. He was looking at me like someone he'd just caught having sex with his daughter, and every time I had an idea, I bit it back, not wanting to make it worse.

He pulled his memo book back out and started writing again. "So, what's your name?"

"Dillon," I told him, knowing I was defeated for the meantime.

"Last name?" I told him my wallet with my driver's license was in my back pocket. I didn't really want to talk. I wanted to think, and it looked like I was about to have quite a bit of time to do that. It was still early enough that if they took me down to the station, processed me, saw I had no previous charges, and maybe contacted Garcia, I'd get out of all this and still make it home before midnight.

He told me to lean forward, pulled my wallet out, and then ordered me to stand up. I did as I was told and he asked if I had any weapons, needles, or drugs on me. I told him that aside from a pair of gloves, a set of keys, and a cellphone, I had nothing else on me. He relieved me of all of that, and when he threw my cellphone down on the table, I saw the screen was shattered beyond anything salvageable. Great! Another notch added to the amazing day and week I was having.

He continued to roughly search me for anything I might have missed. Sure, maybe I had a rocket launcher, or a dildo hidden somewhere. He found nothing, and pushed me back down onto the chair. Then he went back to writing, and I went back to thinking.

What was going on? Things were starting to make less and less sense. It would be one thing if I was just stressed out and my mind had snapped, but could I be so far gone that I was seeing the crazy shit I'd just seen, hearing those weird sounds, and feeling that darkness spreading over me? That was something, it had to be. There was no way that could all be in my head. I was starting to feel like someone on a bad trip, as though I'd had a drink spiked with LSD and the world had gone batshit bananas. I was off the wall like Lucille Ball.

The memory of the melted-face guy touching my arm and the black stuff on me made me want to suddenly puke. I could still feel the cold darkness all over, surrounding me, trying to pull me down to some hellish death place. There was nothing to compare the feeling to. It was like a physical form of depression, or what a slow death must feel like. If this was what Chance had been going through, maybe having his head ripped off was the best thing: a relief. And there was still the chance I would be joining my deceased client in the world of twist-off tops. If this wasn't just some sort of madness I was sharing with the man, something I was seeing because of his case and my own personal break down, then there could be something out to get me, something from the church. I needed to get back to Niagara Falls, or at least give Winger a call and see if she'd pieced anything together.

There was a knock at the door and the officer turned to me.

"Don't move a muscle, fuckhead!" he barked, and I obeyed. I watched as he opened it. "Oh, I wasn't expecting them to send a sergeant. How are you, ma'am?"

"Fine. What've you got?" a woman asked, and then the cop who'd arrested me moved out of the way and she walked in.

I was fine for five seconds.

She was normal-looking, dark hair pulled back in a bun, dark eyes, and a face as stern as one could be. She walked right over to me, hands on her hip, shaking her head as she came, and then it all went to hell.

I couldn't help the sound that came out of me as she came apart. It was my new living nightmare. I opened my mouth and made the most unflattering sounds as I pushed away from her, toppling over in my chair, doing everything I could to avoid her drooling all over me. I was in mid-fall and she reached out, the arresting officer running across the room yelling at me to calm down. I hit the ground hard, my cuffed hands behind my back crushed under my weight and for a second I was sure my wrists were broken.

I lay there, looking up at the stained ceiling, but the lady's melting-chocolate-bar face came back into view, trying to coat me in her mud-slick mouth drippings. I tried to kick her, yelled for her to get the fuck away from me, not to get that shit on me. I may have even called her a monster, or a demon, or both. I'm not sure. As soon as I swung my leg at her head, I saw something in her hand and felt my world light up in a way I've never felt before.

It was the first time I'd been tasered.

But not the first time I pissed myself and passed out.

The darkness of unconsciousness was kind of nice.

And Then the Days All Become One

The next time I opened my eyes, I had no idea where I was. I was groggy, and found I could barely focus my eyes. My mouth felt as though it was full of paste and I was filled with a terrible need for water. I tried to call out for someone to help me, to give me something to drink, but when I couldn't find the words, so I quickly gave up on that. I figured it might be better to figure out where I was and how I'd gotten there.

One thing I could tell: I was strapped down on a very hard bed. My arms, legs and head felt as though they were glued down. It was so bright in the room; the hum of the florescent lights sang out like cicadas on a hot summer day. I did manage to call out then, but nobody answered, so I guessed I was alone. I tried to sit up, but the straps held me down firmly. There was no way this was a jail. I've never heard of getting this kind of treatment at a police station, so that could only mean one thing, and it wasn't good.

Towards my feet, I heard a door being opened and I started to call out.

"Hey, who's there? Where am I?" I was surprised anything came out of my mouth this time, though the sound of my own voice seemed alien to me.

"Oh, I see you're finally awake," said a man with a soft and gentle voice "Good. I guess the sedatives we gave you when you arrived have worn off a bit."

"Why was I given sedatives? Was I in an accident?" My mind was still a shadowed hallway, too foggy to remember anything beyond waking up in the morning. "How bad is it?"

From my peripherals, I could see a man pull up a chair and sit down beside me. I assumed he was doctor, though he wasn't dressed in a lab coat. Instead, he wore a light blue sweater over a plaid shirt, no tie, and looked down at me through thick, horn rimmed glasses. He smiled and sat down so he was just out of sight. I stared up at the ceiling while he flipped through some pages and cleared his throat.

"I'm Doctor Marshall. Can you tell me your name?"

"It's Dillon, I think," I said, confused, hoping he was going to untie me and tell me what was going on. "Can you let me out of these restraints?"

"Not right now. They're on for a reason. Can you tell me where you live and the current date?" I had to think about it for a second, and then I gave him the best answer I could. I hoped it was right. "Very good. Now, I know you must be a bit confused, out of sorts, but I want to ask you a few questions and help you. What's the last thing you remember, Dillon, before you woke up here?"

I tried to recall, but everything seemed so foggy still. My head hurt, my body ached, and my mouth was so dry. Still, I ran through my memory as best I could and tried to bring anything up—just catch a whiff of a small memory, a piece of something I could grab hold of and ride towards something bigger. I looked for a ripple, a trickle of my past, and there was something there. Water. The lake. I was sitting in my car, drinking coffee, and looking out over the water during a storm. But why was I there? Did something happen there? Did I fall in the water?

"Anything coming to you, Dillon?" he asked, and I told him about the lake. "And why were you there?"

"I wanted to think about something. I was stressed out, I know that, but I'm not sure what it was."

"That's just the sedatives. It's good you're getting pieces. It'll all come back soon. Now, do you remember what you did after leaving the lake?"

"No. Not really. I guessing I fell in the lake or there was some sort of accident. I figure whatever happened next was bad, and that's why I'm here."

"I don't want to give it to you, Dillon. I need you to think and let it come to you. Think back to the lake, you're in your car. Where did you go after you left there?"

I closed my eyes and used my memory like an old VCR; let's hit instant replay. There wasn't much to see there. Everything was grey. It was like I was sitting in my car, looking out at the water again, only a fog had started to roll in and was burying the world, my memory, in a blanket of haze. I went to the lake to think, to sort things out. Then I left. I drove my car away from the lake, headed down the road to...

"I was going to Godfrey's," I said, as something crept back into my head. It was a small, but certain memory.

"Who's Godfrey? A friend?"

"Sort of. He's more of a business acquaintance," I told him. At least that was still there and easy to remember, so I at least knew it wasn't amnesia. I knew him, my name, Rouge...oh no...I knew why I was at the lake! I was messed up about her, and having to break it off with her, but I didn't really want to. So why was I? Why did I think I needed end my relationship if I didn't want to? I didn't share that with the doctor, though.

"Alright, Dillon. Let's follow that road and see where it leads us. You left the lake and started to head over to Godfrey's. Do you remember why?"

"I needed to talk to him about something."

"Was it personal or work-related?"

"I'm not sure," I told him, unable to remember where he even lived at the moment. I knew I was going there, but every time I tried to put it together, I just kept coming back to thinking about Rouge, her face dancing around in my head.

"Okay. I'm going to show you some pictures, and I want you to tell me if they mean anything to you."

"What kind of pictures?"

"Sketches for the most part. We found them in your car."

I told him it was okay, and then from his direction came a note pad. My eyes had a bit of trouble focusing as he opened it to a page that had been marked with a small red flag sticker. I blinked a few times to clear my vision and saw a few strange, hand-drawn symbols. I knew them, but how? They seemed familiar, but it was more like déjà vu than an actual, solid memory. I couldn't remember the context of any of them, though I knew I was the one who'd drawn them. How I knew that detail is anyone's guess.

"I'm not sure. I think I remember them, but I can't put my finger on what they are. Did I draw them?" I asked, wanting some sort of confirmation to my suspicion.

"I was hoping you could tell me, Dillon. There's a lot I hope you can tell me, but maybe you should rest a little more and we can take this up later."

"Can you tell me what's going on? Please. Am I hurt? Is Rouge okay?"

"Who's Rouge?" Good! If they didn't know, that meant she wasn't with me when whatever happened, happened.

"My girlfriend."

"You have a girlfriend named Rouge, as in the French word for red?"

"Her name is Rouge Hills. Well, her stage name is, but I just call her that all the time."

"Stage name?"

"She's a burlesque performer," I explained, and gave her real name and tried to give her phone number, but it wasn't all there. Not a surprise. With smartphones, who remembers anyone's phone numbers these days? "Her number is in my phone. You can get it there. Can someone call her and tell her I'm okay?"

"Your phone was broken when they brought you in. Guess it happened during the incident."

"What incident? What happened?"

"I need you to let it come back to you. The sedatives and the medication may be making things a little difficult right now, but it'll come back to you, Dillon. It's better the memories come back naturally so we can know what happened wasn't a psychotic episode. So, do your best to work things out, and when I see you next, you should be able to tell me what happened and then we can go from there."

Psychotic episode? What the hell happened? Suddenly I wasn't so sure I wanted to know.

"Can you at least take these straps off me?"

"I'm afraid not. I will remove the one for your head if you promise not to try anything improper. Deal?"

"Sure," I said, a little indignant maybe. What was he expecting me to do, bite him or something?

He reached over me and undid something and the pressure on my head was relieved and it felt so good. It felt as though a weird tension was suddenly gone from my neck and shoulders. He pulled the straps away from me, and I turned to look at him, and almost laughed when I saw he looked almost exactly like Mr Dressup, the guy from the kids show in the 70's and 80's. I didn't though, because I got a flash of his clipboard and there was something on there that told me I really had no idea what had happened.

"Where am I?" I asked, even though I'd started to have a pretty good idea where we were.

"All in good time, Dillon. Try to get some rest and I'll be back soon. When I do come back, maybe we'll both have a few more answers for each other."

He stood up and walked across the room. I watched him go, and a nurse met him there. He told her to ease up on the sedative, but to continue with the Clozapine. I knew what that was, and it made sense seeing as the clipboard in his hands had the *CAMH* logo on it. CAMH was the new way to be politically correct about it. Calling it the *Center for Addiction and Mental Health* sounded so much better than the *Queen Street Mental Hospital*.

What the fuck happened? What did I do?

The nurse came in and gingerly gave me two injections through an IV, and before I could come up with an answer, I was off to a dreamless land that only made my memories more dampened. How was I supposed to remember anything when I was falling down a dark rabbit hole?

There was a nurse standing over me the next time I opened my eyes.

"I think I need to piss," I whispered, my mouth still cotton-ball dry.

"You can go ahead," he told me with a smirk. "You have a catheter in. Whizz away, wacko."

I had no idea what a catheter was, but I wasn't going to piss my pants. That was rude. And gross. But where was I? Why was this guy in white standing over me humming *Seasons in the Sun* and injecting things into a tube.

I slept on it, not caring anymore the second he pulled the needle free. I didn't give a shit who he was, what he was doing, nor the propriety of peeing myself. I let my bladder go as I fell back into my dark state of nothingness.

"Are you there, Dillon?"

Slowly, I opened my eyes. I felt the voice call me out of the void I'd buried myself in. The room was too bright and I wanted to find my way back to the places where light couldn't find me. The emptiness was nice, forgiving, and asked nothing of me. It was a place I could let go of every worry and fear, and accept contentment. How dare this person call me away from that to a place where the lights vibrated and tried to burrow their way into my head.

"Dillon," he said again, and I knew the voice. It sounded like Dr Dressup. I squinted against the intrusive light, and found him sitting beside me again with his CAMH clipboard in hand, ready to take notes. "How are we doing today?"

"Tired," I said with little emotion. "Can I go back to sleep, please?"

"I've been told you've been sleeping quite a bit, Dillon. Why don't you stay with me for a while? We can talk and maybe we can get you up and about. I'd like to see you walking around. I want to help you."

"Then let me sleep. It's nice there. Quiet. Dark. Perfect. Just give me more of whatever you're giving me and let me sleep."

"I'd prefer to talk, Dillon. I think drugs can help, but right now we still don't know what's going on with you. We're only giving you a common-enough mixture to help settle you down after what happened."

"What happened?" I said. My words sounded lazy and slurred in my ears. "Was it the monsters again?"

"Monsters? What monsters, Dillon?"

"Monsters, demons, spirits…all of those damn things on this planet, the things that aren't supposed to be here. The ones I'm here to hunt."

The drugs were affecting me. I was spilling too much, telling this man of medicine and science things I normally wouldn't, but I was barely there. I was still one foot in the subconscious, the land of slumber. If I'd had control, I would've kept my mouth shut and just let things get back to normal, pretended I was fine and mentally healthy. The drugs though, they weren't reacting well with me. Not being completely human might've had something to do with it.

"You're here to hunt monsters? In the hospital?"

"Not in the hospital, but everywhere else. They come through weak spots. They find their way here any way they can, and I have to find them and send them back to their worlds."

"Is that what the knife is for?"

"My Tincher? Yeah. It works on almost all of them, but sometimes I have to go see Godfrey to get something better, more affective. Sometimes, these things are tricky little bastards."

I looked over at the doctor and he was busy scribbling down words on his pad. At the time, I thought nothing of it. I wasn't fully aware of what was coming out of my mouth. Apparently the mix of Clozapine and sedatives were acting like a Dillon the Monster Dick truth serum. I was on a roll and had no plans or sense to stop.

"Can other people see these monsters, Dillon, or do you have something that helps you see them?"

"People can see them, usually. They call me up and have me come to their homes or businesses to get rid of them. Sometimes, though, I have to let them stay. Sometimes, I feel so bad for them, the more helpless ones that only come here to get away from their terrible lives."

"Okay, this is new, but it's also progress, Dillon. Was it monsters you saw the day you left the lake and ended up here?"

"I don't know, was it?" I asked, and rolled back through time. I still just wanted to sleep, but thought if I told Dr Dressup everything I could about whatever he wanted to know, I'd be able to close my eyes again. "I was at the lake, hoping Rouge was okay. I have to break up with her, or they're going to take me away."

"Who is?"

"Parks. The Collective sent him here because I broke the rules and started to date Rouge."

"Why can't you date her? Is this Collective like a religious group?"

"No. They're more like universal police. They send us here to protect the Earth from beings that aren't supposed to be here. And that's what I was doing, but then I met Rouge and we started dating, and that's a no-no. We're not allowed to date humans."

He went silent, scribbled some more and just sat there. I can only imagine how crazy I must've sounded to him.

"So, you're not human?" he finally asked, after nearly five minutes of saying nothing. I'd started to drift off by then, but was jolted back into the overly-bright world.

"No, yes, and maybe. It's hard to explain. This body is human. I'm not. I'm a Treemor. But you can't tell anyone, okay? Ssshhhhh! It's a secret. We've got that whole doctor and patient thing going on here, right?"

"Of course, but I would like to know more about what a Treemor is."

"I am. The last of my kind, and that really sucks. And if I don't break it off with Rouge and they send me away from here, I don't really have anywhere to go. I have no home planet any more, no family, and no friends. Do you have any idea of how much that sucks? Makes me just want to jump ship and go underground."

"Okay. I think I get that." He scribbled more stuff down on the pad before he turned back to me and smiled warmly. He seemed like such a nice guy. "Now, can we go back to the day you were at the lake and drove away, the day you came here? You said you were on your way to Godfrey's. Did you ever make it there?"

Did I? I didn't think I did. I went back through the waves of time. I could see myself sitting in the car again, watching as the wind drove the surf into the rocks and into the sand further along the shoreline. I'd been thinking about my life and how it all seemed to be going off the rails. There was Rouge, Parks, the earthbound monsters, the video up on YouTube, and the case in Niagara Falls. I couldn't forget that, especially after what had happened in the LCBO. Those three with the melted faces, how they came at me; and there was the one who tried to touch me: there was no wiping that away from the old memory banks.

I put myself back there, in the middle of the store with them, their faces drooling black flesh that began to lose all solidity. I could hear the mucus-filled voices bubbling out incoherent words. And then the one closest touched me and got some of that muddy substance on me.

In the room with the doctor, I wasn't only remembering it, I began to relive it. I could feel it all over again. The coldness of the shadow muck as it spread over my arm, trying to pull me down into the darkness where it had come from. I could feel the small, unseen legs of the bugs living in the black sludge and I had to look down at my arm to make sure it wasn't actually there, that it was just a memory. Even though I couldn't see it, and there was a part of me that knew it was only a memory I was experiencing, I began to scream and cry out for help. I sounded insane as I begged the doctor for my Tincher so I could cut it away from me.

The doctor stood up and backed away as the cold, deathly slime spread its invisible self up my arm towards my chest and face. He was no doubt glad I was still strapped down as he called out for a nurse to hurry over. I could only catch a bit of his voice over the terrible sounds coming from me. My voice didn't even really sound like me, but I was the only one in the room other than the medical staff, so it had to be me, right? The doctor wasn't screaming. I looked from my arm to him, the din deafening by that point, and he was talking to a male and female nurse, so it wasn't them. It had to be me, but I wasn't fully aware of trying to scream out. That was, until I looked down at my arm and once again felt the cold shadow on me. The feeling made me start to scream even louder until I heard my own cries, which led me to try and figure out who was making that terrible sound. I was in a loop of screaming, confusion, realization, and then right back to screaming. I thought it was never going to end. There was a calm voice in my head, which appeared out of nowhere, telling me that the feeling wasn't real, to relax and take a deep breath before my howls ripped my throat apart and I drowned in my own blood. I was okay with that thought too, because then I wouldn't feel the stuff that had fallen on me from the kid's mouth. The rational part tried to explain that the muck was gone, the cold death feeling was all in my head, but its voice and my nerves were on two separate planets, speaking languages neither understood.

The screaming didn't stop.

Well, not until the doctor was back beside me and one of the nurses had jammed a syringe into my IV. The doctor told me to calm down, relax, it would be fine. I wanted to, I really did. I even tried to tell him it was okay, I knew what was going on, but those words were lost in a mass exodus of *AAAAAHHHHHHHHHH!*

I thought it would be the last scream before I either fainted or choked on my own blood, but then, there was the void of sleep. It whispered in my ear like a lover come back after a month-long trip. All I wanted to do was embrace it. The world around me had the volume turned down, and the director called for a fade to black. Who was I to argue?

One day turned into the next. Hours and minutes came and went and I had no idea if it was night, day, summer, fall, winter, or the end of times. Nor did I care. The doctor would stop by and sit with me, and I tried my best to talk to him, to work out things with my memory so that I wasn't reduced to making the constant sound of a cat getting its tail stepped on. We'd start with my full name, what I did for a living, and then get to the

LCBO; cue madness. It wasn't that I was in terror of the moment; it was more having no control over my own thoughts and sanity because of the damn drugs. I'd never felt so out of control of my own emotions, and the drugs were my way to explain the abandonment of command I had over my own will.

I tried to explain it to him, begged him some days, or all in the same day to take me off them, but he said he was worried I would become violent and hurt someone. I guess the fact that I attacked three boys barely out of high school with a knife had them guessing I was a madman. The waking night terrors and screams probably hadn't helped my case either.

Hours passed and days did as well. Or at least, I think they did. For all I knew, being locked in a room with no windows and only one solid door, it could've been all the same day. The only thing that ever changed during that time was the doctor's shirt and the nurses who came to pump drugs into my IV. I assumed the doctor wasn't changing his shirt over and over again just to make it appear as though time had passed.

Soon, my voice didn't sound like my own. My throat became raw and sore from screaming in endless loops before I was drugged back down into my living coma. I was strapped down the entire time, and I'd given up asking to be freed long ago. They came and changed my piss bag, moved the pads they placed under me to catch my shit like I was a dog being housebroken. They gave me several sponge baths. I wasn't even conscious during some, but woke up smelling of the weird soap they used. This had become my life. I had no strength to fight back, so I went along with it all; objections, and even the thought of complaining, melted from my mind.

Then, one day I woke up and I was sitting in wheelchair by a window. I was wearing a Disney nightgown, and had knitted slippers on my feet. I lifted my hands up and looked at them and they didn't seem real, as though I'd never seen them before. I blinked, wondered if it was all a dream, or maybe they'd changed my medication and I was finally being pushed out of the warm blanket of dreamless darkness I'd used as a security blanket for so long.

I looked up again, out the window, and saw the sun high in the sky. Trees rained leaves, and a strong wind blew. Normally, the leaves in the fall are vibrant reds, yellows, and oranges, but these seemed dull, as though the saturation on them had been turned down. They were still those colours, only less intense. I wondered if it was the drugs causing that, too. If so, I needed to get them to stop giving them to me, but I wasn't sure they'd listen any more than they already had.

"How's it going, buddy?" someone asked to my right. I turned my head as fast as I could to see who it was, but it felt like everything moved in slow motion. The sensation was similar to trying to run underwater.

When I finally managed to turn and look at him, I saw it was a guy with crazy hair and a shaggy beard sitting on a chair in a robe just like mine. Mickey and Donald danced around on the cartoon print with Minnie and Daisy, stars and rainbows taking up the empty space. They seemed just perfect for the setting.

"You okay, buddy?" the patient asked, and started to chew on the sides of his fingers. I tried to say yes, but my mouth was still very dry and my throat hurt, so I nodded slowly instead. "They got you pretty loaded up. You the guy who's been screaming over in Isolation?" Again I nodded, guessing it had to be me. "You sound nuts, you know that? It's hard to sleep here as it is, without you howling like a wolf."

He threw his head back and made a wolf howl, but it was short-lived, as one of the nurses came over.

"That's enough of that, Harrison. You start anything and you'll be back in your room before lunchtime."

"But it's pudding day," he said, looking terrified.

"Then you better behave. Don't be giving Dillon here a hard time."

And with that, the nurse left us alone again.

"He's mean, that one. We have to be good and quiet all the time or he gets all bossy and takes away our pudding or TV privileges. He's not as bad as that woman in the *Cuckoo Nest* movie, but he's still mean. You ever see that movie?"

I shrugged. I wasn't sure at the moment, and I didn't want to think about it.

"Well, they play it once a week in the TV room. Weird movie to show us, but it's the only one they put on. So, your name's Dillon? Mine's Harrison." He held out his hand and I looked at it as though it was a foreign object. I knew what he wanted to do, but there was no way I could figure out how to get my hand from my lap to his outstretched one. He laughed, nodded and pulled his hand back. "By the way, you're drooling all over yourself."

So I was.

I ate.

I slept.

I sat in the recreation room.

I sat in the TV room.

I met with Dr Marshall, Dr Dressup's real name.

I listened to Harrison talk.

I used the bathroom.

And between it all I took the pills they dished out to me. Swallowed them dry and then had my mouth inspected to ensure they were gone. My dignity became a thing of the past, but the field where I grow the fucks I give had stopped growing the day I came here, so I couldn't have cared less. My life was a haze and a daze, and I didn't think of anything other than what was right in front of me. Even Dr Marshall had started to get frustrated, as he wanted me to delve into my past, my delusions of being a monster hunter, and the attack at the LCBO. But I didn't want to talk about any of that. I just stared at him blankly, hoped he'd take the hint that my brain wasn't working right with the drugs he was giving me. And it wasn't. I try to recall Rouge's face, bits and pieces of my life, but like the colours in the leaves, and the Jell-O they loved to feed us, it all appeared desaturated of life and vibrancy. I didn't know what to tell him, because I just didn't know much of anything anymore.

Most of my time was spent in the recreation area where other patients coloured in giant colouring books. Others played checkers, while some put together puzzles. It smelled of old feet and medical rubs, with a hint of piss everywhere. Whenever I was there, Harrison was close by talking to me, telling me stories and asking me questions I couldn't answer.

"You ever play World of Warcraft? I love it. But there are people out there, real sickos who use the game to hurt people. One time, I had fallen asleep eating Beefaroni—you like those, they're the best thing in the world—and this guy found my game on from inside the game, and he came through it, into my house. He must've been a level fifty-one wizard at least. It takes someone that good to make a portal. Well, he comes in, steals my bones right out of my body and puts them up for auction on eBay. Can you believe that?"

No, I didn't believe that, but shrugged to avoid him trying to convince me of his story.

"Yeah, well, I had to buy them back, but I couldn't get them in my body right, so I had to change bodies again. I do that every so often, you know. I've been alive for three hundred years, and every now and then I have to upgrade my form to stay alive. If not, I die in this body and that would suck, I mean, look at me. I have the body of a God, sure, but that God is Buddha."

In my normal life, I might've laughed at that, but my normality had been upended and I'd turned into a walking vegetable. I opened my mouth to try and say something to Harrison as he began to dig up his nose in search of some lost treasure, but when I blinked, he was gone and I was sitting in a room with Dr Marshall. He wore another of his sweater-and-plaid-shirt combos, but I could barely tell what the colours were they were so muted. The doctor leaned back in his chair, looking at me with concern as he chewed his pen.

"Dillon, you really need to snap out of this. Lately, you hardly take note of our meetings. Are you hearing me?"

I tried to nod, but wasn't sure anything happened. I coughed hoarsely and felt spittle pooling in my lap. This was getting old.

"You need to start working through things. This idea that you're a monster hunter, that you attacked those boys because they were melting, and getting something on you that would kill you; it's just not what's real." I told him about the melting faces? I didn't remember that, but I wasn't remembering much any more. I knew I had a girlfriend, but what was her name? How old was she? What did she look like? Or was she just in my head? "This desk, this chair; these things are real, Dillon. Monsters and ghosts are—"

"—and then I found a cat and it was actually a friend I'd gone to school with reborn inside the little fella," Harrison told me, and I realized I was back in the rec room. Dr Marshall had just disappeared, and I was in another room. "I took him home, tried to feed him Beefaroni, but then he got lost in my place and I was so sad. I thought he ran away because I got athlete's foot real bad and it was smelly. Then I found him under my bed and he was smelly because he died a while ago. I hope he's going to find another body to live it, because I still..."

The words stopped and I was back in my bed staring at the ceiling. I felt sore and stiff. I looked down at myself and saw my knees were red and scraped. I had no idea what had happened, but it felt terrible to move my legs. I reached down to touch them while my roommate, Dougie, snored up a storm. My fingers found the cuts already scabbing and I—

"—and three today," one of the nurses said. I was sitting in a room with most of the other patients. I had no idea what she was talking about, but I was hoping it was movie time. We'd watched *One Flew Over the Cuckoo's Nest* a few times now, but I could only remember seeing parts of it here and there. I hoped to remember enough of the parts so I'd technically remember the whole movie. The order of it didn't really matter to me.

"Want a pit cookie?" Harrison whispered, and dug into his nightgown. He pulled out three crumbled cookies. I didn't have to ask him why they were called *pit cookies*. I shook my head, and he smiled. "Good. More for me. Oh, they're so moist!"

I watched him as he put all three in his mouth and began to munch on them happily. He was my own hairy, balding Cookie Monster.

Was he a monster, like Cookie Monster? No, there was no way. Monsters weren't real. That's what the doctor told me. Those things were a delusion, something I made up to hide a bigger issue. I'd thought I hunted monsters because it made me feel special, important, and less afraid. The only monsters were Muppets, and the things in horror movies.

But if monsters weren't real, and I made it all up, was my girlfriend made up? Was she another delusion? And what about the other people I knew? The Jamaican guy I buy tools off, for one. Was he real? And why did I buy tools off him? Did I make repairs? If I didn't hunt monsters, what did I really do?

I wanted to cry. I felt so confused and lost, but the movie was about to start, so I sat back in my chair and watched as the credits began.

Then I was in the doctor's office again and I was mad. I didn't even make it five minutes into the movie before my world star wiped and faded back into the familiar room.

"How are you feeling today, Dillon?"

"Crappy," I told him, and was surprised to hear my own voice. It felt like so long since I'd spoken out loud, at least that I could remember. "But, I'm hanging in there, I guess."

"Well, that's something. You sound a lot better. We were worried about you after the fall a few days ago. Do you remember that?"

"Only that my knees hurt a lot." I reached down and winced as I touched them and felt the pain. I had forgotten what actual pain was. "What's going on?"

"I'm not sure I know what you mean."

"I felt that. And I can actually make sense of what's coming out of my mouth."

"Well, I thought it might be good to cut back your meds by a fair amount. You seemed to be turning inward a little too much, and there's no getting better without trying. Like I said many times before, the drugs only help so much. Especially these older ones that I personally feel are outdated. So I think if we do more sessions together, and you eventually join the group settings, you're bound to improve overall. But, I do want to try you on something new today. It's very exciting and I think it will do you a world of good. You will be there first person here to try it and

I think with that, and the two of us talking more often, things will turn around for you. I don't think they're the golden ticket, but along with our talks, I think you'll soon find your way out of here. Remember, it's our words that help us heal, grow, and learn. Now, why don't we start with how you're really feeling today?"

That night after an exciting dinner of chicken and rice, with Jell-O for dessert, we received our medication. I stood in line, waited for my nightly communion, and when it was my turn, I nearly expected the nurse to hold it out like the holy sacrament and gingerly place the pill on my tongue. Instead, I was handed a little paper cup with three pills in them. Two I knew as vitamins, and one was new to me. It was a big, purple thing that looked more like a horse pill than something a human should ever try and swallow.

"What's this?" I asked, and the nurse looked at me oddly.

"So, you can talk," he laughed. "It's a new drug. Doc says you're the lucky guinea pig in the group, so, swallow it and go sit and play pocket pool, Zippy."

I did as I was told. There seemed to be no fight left in me. I dry-swallowed the thing, as hard as that was, and went to walk away, but the nurse grabbed my arm and pulled me back. Of course, how could I forget? I opened my mouth and felt his invading sausage fingers swirl around to make sure it was gone. When he was satisfied I hadn't hamstered it in my cheeks, he pushed me back towards the games room and called out for the next in line.

I went into the rec room and sat down at a chair near the window. I was already tired from the day. It was the first time in so many days, days all blurred together, that I was able to string together coherent thoughts, but they weren't all straight. It was just the opposite, really. Most of the things bumping around in the old cranium were little more than a bunch of jumbled images, ideas and pictures that made no sense. I wasn't sure what was real, what was imagined, and what was caused by the medication. There was an idea there, of who I was, and what I did, but it wasn't solid enough for me to believe. I could pull up images of monsters, and creatures straight from nightmares, but I wasn't sure they were any more real that Santa Claus or Spider-Man. I looked at my hands, they looked real, familiar, and I hoped one day they were going to help me get a grip on reality. I needed to. I wanted nothing more than to fix myself, figure out what was broken, and find out where my problem ended and my real life started. I was broken, but at least I knew it. Most people here didn't seem so lucky.

"How's it going, Dill Pickle?"

I looked up and saw it was Harrison. He was digging his hands down the front of his pants and pulling them out to smell them. I hoped he just needed to check if a shower was required.

"Hey, Harrison."

"Wow! You're not a mute! That's so cool. So, were you just ignoring me before? If you were, it's okay. My dad's the same way. He got me an apartment, pays for it every month, but never visits. He's a dick, but if you were ignoring me, it's okay. You're not my dick... I mean, my dad, who is a dick. I'm not saying my dick is my dad. That'd be crazy."

"I think it was the meds they had me on," I explained, and he sat in a chair next to me. "Sorry. I could barely remember how to sit up, never mind speak."

"Oh, that's okay. I liked that you listened, even when you were all zombie zoned out. High as shit on the stuff they give you, but I like to think you listened to me. Most people just run away."

"Not sure I could've, even if I wanted to. But I didn't. It was nice to have someone other than the staff talking to me," I said, though I had a bit of trouble remembering much of what he talked about, other than a few rambles here and there.

"So, now you can tell me. Why'd they bring you here? It has to be good."

I shrugged. There were things I remembered: three guys with melting faces and a cold blackness touching me, but I didn't want those things in my head any more. They weren't real. I needed to focus on the truth of what happened, not the story my mind had told. The doctor told me to heal I need to push those lies away and embrace the reality of what happened. So thinking about monsters and faces drooling shadows wouldn't make me well. I needed to focus on wellness. "Why are *you* here?"

"Because people don't understand the things I do. In my building, the security guards are always on me. They tell me I can't walk around the halls in my underwear, but they don't understand. My place has bugs, and my cat, the one that had my friend hiding in it, died there. I couldn't stand to be in there long. So, I walked the halls."

"In your underwear?"

"Yeah. It's hot and I don't have any t-shirts — well, none clean. Plus, I have a killer Freddy tattoo on my chest. I like to show it off. So, I walk the halls to get exercise and to meet people. Physical health means better mental health, by the way. That's what they tell me, but I think it sounds crazy. Anyway, I was walking the halls, and this new woman moved in. She was so hot. She moved in just down the hall from me, and I wanted to give her a welcome gift. You know, like they'd do on TV? So, I went to her apartment, and her door was unlocked so I walked in and tried to give her my nicest butcher's knife. Apparently, she didn't want it."

"Were you in your underwear?"

"Of course. It was really hot that day. She screamed at me to get out, pulled her own knife out, which was way nicer than mine, and I left. A bit later I was standing in the lobby, and the cops showed up. They weren't very nice. I was told I was lucky I didn't have the knife any more, or I might've been shot. For what? Trying to be a good neighbor? What is this world coming to?"

What indeed?

I woke up in the middle of the night with a strange sensation. I slowly opened my eyes, trying to figure out what it was, and then I felt it again. Someone was sitting at the end of my bed.

I sat up, and I let my eyes adjust to the darkness. I could see someone there, their back was to me, but they looked all wrong. They didn't look solid.

I reached out, and my fingers slide through their shoulder. It was so cold.

"Hello?" I whispered with hesitation.

The person on the end of my bed turned and when they did, my heart sank.

No.

It couldn't be.

Something was wrong, it wasn't right. Maybe the meds they gave me were messing with my head, or I was having another episode. I closed my eyes and tried to lie back down. I told myself it wasn't real, I was dreaming, but they shifted on the bed and I could feel it. I sat back up and tried to touch them again.

"Can you not do that? It feels so weird," he said, and there was the smile I knew. I did know him. It was someone I'd seen before, so many times, but it was impossible. He was dead. Father Ted was dead and gone, and ghosts aren't real. The doctor told me those thoughts are part of my problem and when they arise I have to admit to myself how false they are. It was hard to think that way when Father Ted sat shimmering in the dark room. He looked very real, for a ghost.

"You know you're not real, right?" I whispered, and kept my hands to myself. "You need to go away."

"No, Dillon, you need to go away. You need to get out of this place. It's not good for you."

"You're not good for me. I want to get better, but how can I if you show up? I want to get the bad stuff out of my head. Monsters, demons and ghosts aren't real; which means you're not real. So if I'm seeing you, it means I'm not getting better. And if I'm not getting better, I can't get out of here and go home."

"And what would you go home to, Dillon? If everything you know is a lie, then what is the truth you so badly want to return to?"

I had no idea. I can admit, my mind hadn't even strayed to that way of thinking. The doctor had told me I was unwell, that my thoughts had led me to attacking three innocent people, so I needed to get better, let go of the delusions I thought of as real. But if they weren't real, I had no idea what was. Where did I live? Who did I live with? What did I do to make money? Who the hell was I, if not who I thought I was?

"You need to get out of here, Dillon. A lot of people count on you, but staying here is not helping them, and it's not helping you. You're a shell of the person I knew."

"You're dead! The dead can't come back to Earth. That means I'm crazy, and if I am, then I belong here."

"Crazy people don't know they're crazy, Dillon."

"But I know you're not real."

"What is real? It's true I may not be here, but if I'm not here, what am I? A visualization of your mental illness? Or am I a part of you that's trying to get you better, to let you know you're not as crazy as they're telling you? I'm not saying I'm a part of you, though. What I am telling you, Dillon, is that you need to pull yourself up by the bootstraps and get out of this place before everything you are is lost in these walls. Don't let them eat your soul."

Then, he stood up and vaporized into nothingness.

I wanted to cry.

I wanted to be better.

I wanted to be allowed to leave.

I wanted to find out what was real.

☀·☀

After a lunch of mac and cheese, hot dogs and Jell-O for dessert, I was taken down the hall to the doctor's office. He was in a sour mood, but asked how the medication was, if I felt better with the new pills.

"My heads a bit clearer today," I told him, and it was true. I kept my bedtime visitor a secret, but I hoped it was a one-off.

"Good. And did you notice anything unusual?"

Aside from my dead friend, you mean?

"Not really. I mean, my piss smelled pretty rank this morning," I said, offering another half-truth.

"Yes, that is one of the side effects. You may also notice green stool, but don't worry. That's from the pills as well. Any sensations in your hands or feet? Tingling, or numbness maybe?"

I shook my head and wondered if I should mention my visitor the previous night. I had hoped the vison of Father Ted on my bed telling me what he had was nothing more than a mix of new medication, stress, being overly tired, and coming down from the other drugs I'd been on. As someone who's not a frequent user of pharmaceuticals, I had no idea what kind of side effects coming off anti-psychotics were.

"Nothing at all?"

"Nope," I lied, and he moved on.

"Excellent," he said, and scribbled some notes down. "And how clear are your thoughts and memories these days?"

I shrugged. I wanted to say they seemed fine, but there was still too much in my head that didn't seem to make any sense. I could really visualize the monsters I'd fought off. I could smell their hot breath as I pushed strangely-shaped coins against skin made up of discarded items. I could feel them hit me with balled up fists of waste, and could taste the memories of satisfaction as I sent them back to where they came from. I could recall a life before this one, on an alien planet, where I was the last survivor of a race wiped out by demons, but I couldn't tell him this. I needed to be better, to be "cured" and allowed to leave so I could go out and find out what was real, and what I was imagining. Could it all be a lie, an elaborate illusion I'd created to hide scars from an abusive parent, or a terrible crime done to me? The doctor wanted me to believe it, and I really struggled with it. The reality in my brain and the one he tried to convince me of were in full brawl mode. I wasn't sure which one was going to win.

"You're not sure? Well, let's start with the day you were brought in here. That was something you've never been clear on. Can we go back to that day and see if you can recall the actual facts of what brought in with you here?"

I nodded. I knew what he wanted to hear, and spun off a story that made it sound as though I wasn't as confused as I was. I began with driving down to the lake to watch the storm, saying that I loved the way the waves looked when the winds were high. After that, I drove to the LCBO to pick up some rum and whiskey.

"For yourself?"

"Yes, I thought it was for someone named Godfrey, but I know now that I was just saying that to deflect that I have a drinking problem." It's amazing sometimes how easily lies roll off the tongue.

"And when you were there, something happened. You told me a story of monsters there with melting faces trying to attack you. Is that what you saw?"

I took a deep breath. I didn't want to think about that. Not them or anything that had happened since I got back from Niagara Falls, assuming I ever went there at all. I could feel it, the way the mist from the falls felt spattering my face when I walked down there with Rouge.

Rouge.

Her face hit me hard, something I had all but forgotten. I could see her soft skin, my hands going over it lightly to give her goosebumps. I could smell that soft rose perfume she loved to wear, and could hear her laughter as I told her some terrible joke. She was there, in my head, and remembering her fully, after such a long time, was the best feeling in the world. It had to be a real memory.

Please let it be real.

"Dillon? Are you okay?"

"Sorry," I said, coming out of the thought. "I was just remembering what really happened," I lied yet again. "It's starting to get clearer now."

"Good. That's very good. Tell me what you remember."

"I was in there, in the store picking up the booze," I began, but was holding onto the image of Rouge. I didn't want to let go of her. "I was over in the rum section, and these three guys came up to me. They kept trying to tell me they knew me from YouTube, but I told them they had the wrong guy. They wouldn't leave me alone. They just continued to say I was the monster guy they'd seen in a video and wouldn't drop it. Then, one of them grabbed me and I don't like that, so, I sort of lost control." It was an easy and believable lie, one that came without thought and as I said it, the doctor flipped through some pages, and then a few more. "I was arrested by a cop working in the store, and when another showed up, I was tasered and blacked out. My next memory is being here."

"You said one of them grabbed you?"

"Yes, the one I jumped on." And that was the truth as far as I knew it.

"Very good. It actually matches up with the video footage transcript, Dillon, so I want to tell you, that is some great progress."

"That's all I want. I just want to get better."

"But, what about the YouTube video they mentioned? Do you know what they were talking about?"

"I—"

There was a loud knock at the door, and then it flew open. One of the male nurses barged in, a bad look on his face.

"I'm in the middle of a session, Doug. What's this about?"

"We got a problem with one of the patients. It's bad. Real bad."

The doctor jumped up and ran out of the room, following the nurse. I left too, since there was no reason to stay behind. In the TV room, there was a horrible smell. Most of the on-duty staff were also in there, and just outside of it was a gaggle of patients looking on. I stepped up and saw the entire room had had been repainted poorly with what could only be shit. I could also hear someone screaming in there, but couldn't see who it was. I turned to one of the other patients, a woman some called Spacey Tracey, and asked her what was going on.

"It's Harrison. His dad came to visit today, and when he came from the meeting room, he went and started pooing in there. First he covered himself in it, and then the walls. Bobby was in there, pretending to watch reruns of Judge Judy, but the TV was off. That's when Harrison started. Bobby stayed until he started smearing it on the walls. He loves Judge Judy. I hope they clean it before movie night."

More screams from inside the TV room. The words were unintelligible, but once I knew it was Harrison, I could tell it was him. More nurses ran in, and before I knew it, the show was over. Someone must've already brought a gurney in there before I arrived, because when they all started to leave, they had him strapped to it. The smell hit me even worse as they began to wheel him out, and it was so bad that it almost made my eyes water.

"Everyone out of the way!" one of the nurses at the gurney barked, and we listened.

I took a few steps back and wished I'd backed up even further when I saw him. He was naked, dressed only in straps and a coating of light brown shit. I could tell he'd had corn the night before. He wriggled around, still screaming, but when I saw his face, the cries turned to something else. His voice turned down to the muffled echo of a scream as black sludge bled from his open mouth and his eyes wept black oil. He stared at me. His eyes had liquefied and dribbled down his turned face, pooled on the white sheets; I could still tell he was looking at me.

I turned from him, faced Spacey Tracey, but she only shook her head and looked mildly disgusted. She didn't react to Harrison's melting face.

What was wrong with me?

"Are you okay, Dillon?"

I turned, and the doctor was there. He looked at me with a face clearly full of concern. I bit back the terror I felt brimming within me, and tried my best to look normal.

As though *I* knew what normal was any more!

"Yeah. Fine. I just, you know, hate seeing him like that."

"Are you sure? You look very scared."

"Just worried about Harrison."

"You two are friends?"

"We talk. So, yeah, I guess we are."

"He'll be okay," he told me, placing what was supposed to be a reassuring hand on my shoulder. "He's just having a bad day. We all have them."

I nodded.

It seemed as though mine day had just turned down the same road.

I wanted this bad day to come to an end.

I wanted to get out of there.

Most of all, I wanted to stop seeing these things.

$$\bm{\H{o}}\cdot\bm{\H{o}}$$

That night, I took my pills and went to bed. I woke up a few hours later by the return of a man I knew to be dead.

"You're here again? Really?"

"I don't know, Dillon. Am I here, or is this all you?" he asked, crossing his hands on his lap.

"It must be the pills," I said, and closed my eyes. "These new pills are doing this. It has to be the damn drugs fucking with my head."

"That very well could be. I don't know, but I feel pretty real. Well, as real as someone with a body can feel, Dillon."

I sat up in bed and looked at him again. He appeared the same as I remembered him. I used to go to the church, and we'd sit for hours in his office. He loved tea, and telling me stories of his youth, and his quest to find faith. I'd tell him all about my latest exploits and he'd usually feel sorry for the creatures I dealt with. He'd explain to me the reason these things were drawn to Earth, that regardless of their origins, they were all God's creatures and should be allowed to be as they wished, as long as they didn't hurt anyone.

I miss those days. I knew they weren't imagined.

At least I hoped they weren't.

"Why are you here, Ted, assuming you are real?"

"Why are you here?"

"Are you going to keep doing that? Answering my questions with the same one aimed back at me?"

"No. I just want you to figure out what you're doing here. This isn't your place, Dillon. You belong out there in the world, doing what you do. You are someone who does good work, even if I didn't agree with all your methods. Even though you sometimes stray off your path, you keep people safe, and that's not being done while you're in this place. You need to get back out there and do what it is you do."

"What I do? I'm not even sure what I do any more," I confessed.

"That's the problem. This place has you mixed up, lost, and confused. You need to get back out there, Dillon. Something bad is coming. It always is. And if you're in here, there'll be no way to stop it."

"I can't just walk out," I said, a little louder than I should've, and my roomie mumbled for me to shut up. I lowered my voice. "And even if I could just walk out, I'm not sure I want to. I keep… seeing things, and I don't want to see them any more. I just want it to stop."

"I'm sure it will, when you figure it out."

"Figure what out? What's there to figure out? I keep seeing people melting, and it's a nightmare I want to wake up from. Nobody else sees it. Ever. I don't want it in my head any more. I don't want to feel it. You have no idea what it's like."

"You're right, I don't. But holing yourself up in here is not going to fix it, Dillon. You're starting to see it here too, aren't you?"

Harrison's face came into my head, and I tried to shut it out.

"Yeah, but that just shows you something is wrong with me. They had me on meds and as soon as they took me off them, I started seeing the melting faces again. And you."

"So you think the pills were helping you? Do you want those images blocked out?"

"Yeah, I do."

"You'd rather block them out and live in a waking coma rather than figure out why you're seeing them at all? Don't you think there's purpose to the visions you're having? Things happen for a reason, Dillon. You know that."

I did, but that didn't change the fact that I'd prefer never having to see, smell, or fear those melting faced things ever again.

"I'm so lost right now, Ted. I can't tell what's up or down, what's real and what's not."

"Maybe reality isn't something anyone really knows. Before I met you, I thought monsters were a thing adults told children about to keep them afraid to be out after dark and to go to bed when they're told to. Then, you came along and my world was turned upside down. I didn't run and hide from it, though. I accepted what I could and tried to understand what I couldn't. That's why I cherished our visits. I miss them, Dillon. You were a great friend and listener."

"Is this even real?"

"Do you want it to be?" he asked, and I nodded. "Then just let it be real. I promise, I won't tell anyone."

Two days passed. That was progress too. I was actually starting to be able to know one day from the next. I still didn't know what day of the week it was, or how long I'd been at CAMH, but at least there was something showing my improvement.

Over those two days, I didn't see the doctor or Harrison. I wondered what had been wrong with him, what made him freak out and cover the TV room and himself in the previous night's digested dinner. His stench lingered, even though cleaning crews had bleached and scrubbed every surface. I was sure there were going to be bits of shmear ingrained in the carpets and walls for the remainder of the time I was forced to stay there.

I steered clear of there for that reason, not to mention the fact that nothing was ever on the TV except for the few nights a week we were allowed to watch Jack Nicholson make the biggest mistake, pretending to be crazy until he was lobotomized. Spoiler alert!

The few times I did pass by the TV room, though, I was forced to think about Harrison. The smell brought him to mind, and I wondered again and again why he'd freaked out, and also what made him become one of the melted-face people. Since being locked up, I hadn't seen any of them, so what happened that made him change?

I tried to convince myself that it was the change of meds. I was taken off the anti-psychotics and started to revert to my clearly crazy ways. I fought myself over that very fact. It was as though there were two other me's in the room, arguing over my sanity.

Me One, I'll call him Pro-Medication Me, tried to convince the real me I was crazy and needed the medication I was on to stop believing in monsters, and seeing molten-faced people. Pro-Medication Me said that as soon as I had my next meeting with the doctor, I should tell him about what I believed I saw happen to Harrison's face, and about the nightly visits I'd been having with Father Ted. Since the time my meds were switched, the dead priest had come to see me every night. Usually, we talked just like we had before. We shot the shit about a lot of nothing, but in the end, he would keep telling me I needed to get out of the hospital. Pro-Medication Me explained how I was wrong. Ted had been simply another delusion, and not telling the doctor would just take me further down the rabbit hole. I didn't argue with that me. I didn't need to. That was Pro-Monster Me's job.

Pro-Monster Me was very vocal about getting the hell out of there. That version of my psyche made some good points, too. He said there was Rouge out in the real world waiting for me, and there was also my life. Not to mention all the people who counted on me to rid them of the things that went bump in the night.

"There's a reason you're seeing these people come apart the way you are. You need to find out why. Get to the source, and then it'll stop. Just like those headaches you had when there'd been a parasite attached to your brain. You didn't know about it, but you found out and dealt with it."

"The parasite wasn't real, idiot!" Pro-Medication Me cut in. "None of that was real."

"Of course it was. Are you really trying to convince us that the monsters we've spent years fighting aren't real?"

"Prove they were. Prove they're not part of a bigger issue: our mental health."

"Prove it? Are you kidding me? How about the tattoos we're covered in to ward off certain demons and spirits? How about the fact that there's a YouTube video of us fighting a monster, part of the reason we're here?"

"More delusions just piled upon other delusions. Can't you see you're rehashing the lies we've made up, spewing out the very falsehoods which brought us here? We need help and that's what we're getting here."

"What we're getting here is a mind fuck. We're being fed drugs meant for humans, and we aren't exactly human, are we?"

Pro-Medication Me turned to me and made a face to say *can you believe this guy?*, but I kind of did. After all, I was sitting in a room with two other versions of myself, listening to a debate over my own sanity and identity.

"Are you listening to yourself? *We're not exactly human?* Look at yourself in the mirror. Of course you are."

"Not really. Not down where it counts, and these drugs aren't meant for us."

"Of course not, you're so right. You're an alien who hunts monsters down, has a gorgeous girlfriend, and keeps the world safe. Sounds like delusions of grandeur to me."

I watched them argue back and forth; as though it was the worst tennis game I'd ever seen. Each of them made some good points, but I needed to eventually choose one or the other. The question was: which side did I need to true? I didn't want to stay in the hospital any more, but I also didn't want to keep seeing the things I had. It wasn't just like seeing a monster, or getting an adrenaline dump when put into a life or death situation, seeing the melting-faced things, and feeling their touch and their goop was like nothing I'd ever felt before. It made me feel as though I was dying, rotting away, ten times worse than when the shadow person entered me.

"Where's my son! Where is he?"

I heard the loud, gruff voice of a man yelling in the hallway, and the two Me's disappeared. They just went *POP!* and then they were gone; no decision made. I stood up from my chair in the rec room and went out to see what all the hubbub was about.

Over by the nurse's desk, there was a man in a red and black plaid jacket, wearing a black winter hat low on his head. His pants and boots were caked in white plaster and mud. He was husky and kept slamming ham-sized fists on the desk asking where his son was.

"Mr Manatalas, if you would just calm down, the on-call doctor is on his way to speak to you now," the male nurse behind the desk said. A second nurse, a woman who'd I'd only talked to twice, came around and tried to calm him down. She put her small, but no doubt strong hands on his shoulder and told him in a soft, gentle voice everything was going to be fine.

"Just take a deep breath and calm down," she said.

"Get your hands off me, and don't tell me to calm down! Tell me what the fuck is going on," he said, and pulled his arm away from the nurse, nearly knocking her over. "You people said he'd be fine here, that you'd take care of him because he couldn't live on his own. Then I get a call that there's been some sort of accident! Where the hell is my son?"

"Sir, if I could tell you, I would, but hospital policy—"

"Oh, Jesus… what happened to him? My other son was here once and overdosed. You people said the same thing when I got here. I was told they couldn't tell me anything, only the doctor could. Bullshit hospital policy."

"I'm sorry, Mr Manatalas."

"Just tell me, is he dead?"

She said nothing, but her head dropped and her body language told him everything he needed to know. He began to sob, no longer angry. His shoulders slumped and he looked as though he'd given up any fight he'd had in him. His son was dead.

Harrison was gone.

I felt weird.

What the hell was going on?

"You and Harrison were friends, weren't you, Dillon?"

I was sitting across from the doctor the next day in his office. I was still a bit numb after hearing about Harrison's death. I'd kept listening when the on-duty doctor had come to speak to Mr Manatalas. He'd refused to go to her office, so they stood near the nurse's desk and she'd told him how his son had somehow managed to break free from his restraints and used them to hang himself. Mr Manatalas had asked a lot of questions, most them about why his son was locked away and restrained in the first place, and why nobody had been watching him, but in the end, he left to prepare to bury his second child.

After that, I was left to ponder.

Even when Ted paid me a ghostly visit that night, he wasn't very helpful in pulling me out of my confused and disconnected state. My mind had become a multilane highway of thoughts and inner dialogues. I searched for answers in a world where everything was written in a language alien to me.

"Are you okay, Dillon?" The doctor asked, and I looked up for a second "You seem to keep drifting off."

"I'm just thinking. But yeah, Harrison was sort of a friend."

"I know this must be hard for you, Dillon. This is no place to deal with loss, on top of everything else. Especially since things have a way of not always being as they seem."

"It is hard. But I think the medication and these talks are helping me see what's real and what I've made up."

"I guess that's part of the problem now, isn't it?"

"What do you mean?" I was rightly confused.

"I'm at a real loss here, with how to start this, but I think we need to try. We need to work through some things that have been weighing on me a bit. In the last few days, I've been doing quite a bit of research, outside of my normal way of thinking. First thing I need to ask, though: have you had any issues with the new medication?"

"Not really," I lied, still not wanting to mention what I'd seen happen to Harrison, or my visits from Ted.

"Are you sure? You haven't been having nightmares? Nothing out of the ordinary?"

"No. Nothing out of the ordinary," I said, and that wasn't really a lie. Seeing the melted face and ghosts was once my normal life; or at least how I perceived it.

"And you never saw anything happen to Harrison lately? You didn't see his face melt the way you saw the boys change in the LCBO?"

I was shocked, and I couldn't make my own face do as I wanted it to, so he saw it. He leaned back in his chair and gave me a long, hard look. He was obviously concerned, and I was sure I was about to be put on the mind-numbing meds again.

"When did you see it?"

"I didn't see anything."

"Dillon, I need to know when you saw Harrison change. I saw the way you were looking at him when they wheeled him out of the TV room. Was that the first time you'd seen him like that?"

I shook my head. I didn't want to do this. I couldn't admit it to him, or to myself. I wanted it to be gone, for things just to go back to normal. I wanted to eat my dinner, ignore the disgusting Jell-O, talk to Ted, and sleep. I didn't want to look into the void. I didn't want to lose control of who I was again.

"I'm not going to put you back on the drugs, so you can stop worrying," he said, as though he'd read my mind. "Dillon, I need you to open up right now and stop worrying about what you think I'm going to say. I...I don't think you're crazy at all. I'm almost certain everything you think is real *is* real."

"What?" I'm sure he could see the shock on my face, but he clearly wanted to move forward.

"Just tell me when you saw Harrison change. How long ago did you first notice it?"

"It was when he was wheeled out of the TV room. His face started to melt and he had the stuff coming out of his mouth. What's going on? What are you trying to get at here?"

"Well, there's no sense to be made of the timeline. Were Harrison and those kids the only ones you saw change in that way?"

"No. There were three people in the shopping mall a few days before, and there was a police sergeant when I was arrested; the one who tasered me."

"I can look into the officer, just to make sure, but I think I already know what the answer to that is going to be. What are we talking about here, Dillon? I've been doing this a long time now, and never once have I been so sure something so impossible was actually true. How can anything you've told me be real?"

"I think we need to back up, Doctor. I'm still on medication, so I might be a little slow here. What is it you know?"

He took a deep breath and laughed to himself. "If I tell anyone this, I'm likely to be rooming with you. You know that, right?"

"Depends on what you're saying."

"I watched the video on YouTube, the one where you fought that monster. You mentioned it in a few of our sessions, and I hadn't yet seen it. After I saw the way you looked at Harrison, though, and then his passing, I was compelled to watch it. Turns out a lot of people have watched it."

"Oh Jesus! I just wish that was gone already."

"Well, it might be a good thing it's up. I had a hard time believing what I was watching, but if you were mentally ill, I can't see you going through all that, creating some very believable special effects, just to convince others of what you think is real. After I watched it I called Detective Garcia. You also mentioned him a few times in our sessions. He's wasn't in the office, off for a vacation, so I asked another detective I know to pass a message on to Garcia. I told the detective to let Garcia know I had some questions about you and where you were. He called me right away. How is this all true? Monsters? Demons? It's impossible, but Garcia said it's a hundred percent legit. I feel like everything I know is falling apart."

"Makes you wonder how many people in here are mentally ill and how many have just seen things the human mind isn't meant to," I said, feeling electricity run through me. Pro-Monster Me laughed somewhere in my head and stomped Pro-Medication Me to oblivion. It felt good. "There's something more though, isn't there?"

"Those three boys you saw in the LCBO… they died. It was maybe a week after you were arrested. They died in a car crash. You saw them melting, and then they died. You saw Harrison melting and he died. And I bet if I call the station and ask about the sergeant, she'll have passed, too. It has me thinking there's some connection there."

I was floored.

I never thought of that. I might never have added those things together. The people I'd seen melting died soon after. It made sense the second I heard it, but I immediately began to wonder why one led to the other. Was I somehow the cause? Did I infect them with something I picked up from Chance which led to their death, or was I seeing the fact that they were already marked for death? I remembered their melting faces. They were mirrors of their dead selves. Dead and in their grave, rotting, mouths full of dirt, their touch making me feel as though death and darkness was consuming me.

Oh my God!

"I think I know what this is!" I blurted out, and was floored by the idea of it.

"What is it?"

"I need to get out of here, to Niagara Falls."

"I'm not sure it's going to be that easy," he said, and I nearly laughed at that.

"How so? You know I'm not crazy. And if I'm right, there's something in Niagara Falls that will continue to kill innocent people if I don't stop it."

"You were charged with assault and with carrying weapons. They're not just going to let you walk out of this place. You're here for an assessment, and if they think you're good enough to be released, they'll lay charges on you."

"That's if they ever find out you let me out. You get me out of here, and I'll have Garcia fix the charges for me. You just let them think I'm still here for the time being."

"I could be fired and lose my license for this," he told me, not sounding convinced.

"You could. But you could also let me out and help stop more people from dying. There might be a gate opened just a crack, but eventually, it could fly wide open and start spilling out things that'll make you want to start medicating yourself."

He was quiet for a while, but I knew he'd see reason eventually. Admitting monsters are real is just the first step, but it's the most important one.

Wednesday

I stepped out and took a deep breath of chilly air, and it felt so good. Fresh air! After being stuck surrounded by the same walls and breathing recycled air that always smelled of stale piss, sweat, and some sort of medical ointment, it was wonderful to be outside. It was as amazing as if I'd been dying of thirst and been offered a drink, or starving and had a buffet laid before me. I closed my eyes, and enjoyed the moment, revelled in it before I finally had my fill and was ready to move forward.

Garcia was with me, and said nothing as I enjoyed myself. He'd managed to get me out, which he said hadn't been all that hard.

"I've gotten people out clean with deeper charges on them than you have, Dillon. You're free and clear, just try not to make this a habit."

I had no plans of that. As it turns out, I really enjoyed my clear-headed freedom more than I would've guessed. When you get everything taken away from you, even the simple joy of feeling the wind on your face makes you really appreciate all that you have.

As we walked away from the main doors into CAMH, I asked Garcia about my belongings.

"They're all in the trunk of your car. I got everything for you from holdings, and your car is right over there in the lot. Here's your keys." He tossed them to me and I would have kissed him if he wasn't the mean-looking, super masculine man he was. "I'll warn you though, your phone is toast."

"Shit. You have a spare one on you?" I asked with a laugh. Who had a spare phone on them?

"There's one with your stuff. I went into property where they hold lost and stolen phones. It's been there a while. It's a flip phone, even you can believe that. But you can switch your SIM card out for now and at least be able to make calls."

"You're a lifesaver. You didn't have to cut your vacation short for this, did you?"

"Yes and no. It's not like I was at Disneyland with my son. It was more of a staycation, so no worries." I thanked him for everything, and despite myself, hugged him. He didn't return it. "Unless you want me to take you back in there, you'll stop that, Dillon. Come on."

"Sorry," I said, and we headed to the parking lot.

"So, are you going to be okay now? I read the file before coming to get you, but I also spoke to the doctor in there. Sounds like some weird shit, but you have this, right?"

"I hope so," I told him, but my head was still a bit of a mess. There was a lot of fogginess upstairs. The doctor told me it would take a while to get the remains of the drugs out of my system, but I'd be fine after a few weeks. I would've loved to recover fully before getting back into my life, but there was no waiting around: I needed to get to work on the cause of all this misery. I wanted to deal with what was going on with me, and finish my job in Niagara Falls. My client might be dead, but since I'd been affected by the same thing, I'd have to do something about it. "I have to do a few things first, but then, I hope to end this madness and get on with my life."

"If you need any help, let me know. I still owe you for everything you did, Dillon."

"You want to help me with something? There is one thing that would make the next day or two easier."

"Name it, unless it's killing someone, then no."

"I don't need him dead, but I do need someone out of the way until I can get out to the Falls." I explained to Garcia all about Don Parks, who he really was and what he was doing on Earth. I held no details back, even telling him about how he'd been harassing Rouge before I ended up in CAMH. "So, I just need you, or one of your uniform guys to scoop him up on something and hold him for a day or two, tops. Try and make him a suspect in some stupid thing. It doesn't have to stick; it just has to get him out of the way."

"Easy enough. We pull people in all the time on bogus charges. You have his address?"

I gave it to him and he jotted it down. "You should call Rouge soon too. She was pretty freaked out, seeing as you've been gone for two weeks."

Two weeks!

It felt like so much longer, but it had also felt like one long, never-ending day at times. My plan had been to call her the second I got in my car. I could barely hold back the urge not to get into the car and drive right to her house. The way things were when I'd be arrested and locked away, my two weeks of silence must've made her terrified that I'd either abandoned her, or had been taken off the planet. I hoped she was okay, but felt nervous about letting her know everything that had happened.

"Have you talked to her since you found out where I was?"

"No. I only talked to her twice. She's really worried, but I told her she should trust you'd get word to her when you could. You think this Parks guy has been bugging her?"

"Not until you mentioned it. Damn it. Well, thanks for everything, Garcia. You ever need help with anything, let me know. I'll be there, and you'll get a nice discount."

"Cheap bastard. After this, you should take at least one case for free."

"That doesn't sound like something I'd do, but hey, you never know. I've been doing a lot of soul-searching in my therapy sessions. It could happen. I doubt it will, but you can dream."

I left him and went to my car. I took everything out of the trunk and was happy to see it was all there, especially my gloves and the Tincher. I took it all into the car, switched out my SIM card with quick, fumbling fingers, as I tried not to look at how decimated my old phone was. I saw my reflection in the spiderwebbed screen and didn't like how broken, shattered it made me look.

I tossed the useless one onto the back seat, then flipped open the old school monster cellphone and called Rouge. I was nervous, but excited too. I had no idea how much to tell her, but I want to tell her so much. I wanted to hear her voice, hoped she would be okay with me going to see her. Most of all, I wanted to know she was okay, and hoped hearing I was fine would bring some sort of relief to her.

She answered on the second ring.

"Dillon?! Jesus! Where are you?" Her voice was loud and frantic, and she sounded on the verge of crying.

"I got arrested."

"And you didn't think to call me?"

"I tried to, but something happened, and I wasn't taken to jail. They wouldn't let me near a phone."

"What are you talking about? Oh God, you're okay though, right? It wasn't that Parks guys, was it?"

"I'm fine. Really. I'd rather not do this on the phone, though. It would be easier face to face. I'd love to see you. And I really want to get away from here."

"I want to see you too, but we can't meet here. He's always driving by, checking up on me to see if you're around."

"Parks?"

"Yeah. He even came up to me in a coffee shop the other day when I was with Jill and Drew. He asked me where you were, when I talked to you last, he even asked to see my phone. I told him to take a long walk on a short pier. I would've said more, but I didn't want to have to explain things to my friends. Eventually he left. He's lucky we were in public or I would've knocked his perfect teeth out of his stupid face."

"I don't doubt it. You're more badass every day."

"I have to be. The world isn't getting any better. So, if he's smart, he'll keep his distance with me. By the way, he's been bugging Godfrey, too."

Of course he had. I hoped Garcia was already working on scooping him up so he wouldn't be a concern to any of us. He was such a pain in the ass, and Garcia was about to be my topical cream.

"Okay. Well, maybe you should take a cab somewhere and I can meet you there. I'll go ahead of time, and when you arrive, I can make sure he didn't follow. I have the cops going to arrest him, so he won't be in our hair for much longer."

"Arrest him for what?"

"Whatever they want. I need him out of the way for a little while. I need to finish that case I started in Niagara Falls."

"Does that have anything to do with why you were arrested?"

"It has everything to do with it. So, where should we meet?"

We decided to meet a little out of the way. At first, Rouge suggested we meet at the Eaton Centre, but the idea of getting there and losing my mind seeing more melted-face people ended that as a possibility. I though a more low-key place would be better. Even though I knew, or at least had an idea of what was causing the horrible visions, it didn't make it any easier to deal with. I figured it was best to just limit my exposure to crowds. When she asked about it, I told her I'd explain it all when we were together.

We agreed on meeting out by Bluffs in Scarborough. There was an old artists' hotel on Morningside Avenue, a place called the Guildwood Inn. She knew the place and would get ready and leave soon. I hung up, and sat back in the front seat of my car, looking down at myself.

I wished I could've gone home to change into something of my own. I guessed that since I'd fallen into the broken bottles at the LCBO, the things I'd been wearing, aside from my jacket, were tossed. Instead of what I'd normally wear, I'd been given bright red jogging pants, a Blue Jays T-shirt, and running shoes so neon the '80s were offended by how loud and obnoxious they were. At least I still had my lucky jacket, though the worn leather just didn't go very well with the free clothes the hospital had given me. I was sure it'd give Rouge quite a laugh when she saw me, so that was something.

Well, there was no way I was going to try and go back to my place. I had no idea where Parks was, or if he'd be watching my apartment, but I guessed he must swing by now and again. If he was checking up on Rouge, he was certainly doing the same to my place. And Godfrey's.

Damn.

I drove towards the Bluffs, and as I did, I called Godfrey's shop. I put him on speaker phone so I could keep both hands on the wheel. I was still not seeing quite as clear as I normally would, so better safe than sorry. It wouldn't do me any good to get into a wreck after everything it took to get me out of the hospital.

"Where the fuck have you been?!"Godfrey blared into the phone when he answered it.

I told him the whole story, from the lake, to the drive, to the LCBO, all the way to the adventures in mental breakdown lane. I gave him the whole rundown of events, even the visits from Father Ted; he didn't come on that last night there, which kind of proved his visits were drug-related visions.

"Well, I guess I can excuse you then. You had me freaking out."

"Sorry. I want to stop by there before the sun goes down, but I'm on my way to meet Rouge right now."

"Not a good idea."

"What part?"

"Either. That other hunter is out for blood, mon. He's here three or four times a day, saying I'm hiding you and if I don't give you up, then I'm going to be sent to some mining planet, or turned into a porter. He actually tore my store apart last week thinking I had some secret compartment where I hide assholes like you."

"He won't be a bother for long."

"Are you going to kill him? I'd pay to see that."

"Killing him won't do a thing except get me into more shit with the Collective. No. I have the cops looking for him. They're going to grab him and lock him up for a few days while I go and try to close whatever door is open, and end this. It might even

156

be enough to get the Collective to lighten up a little. That's my hope, at least."

"Well, if he's locked up, swing by, but not until then. I don't want him having any more reasons to fuck with me. You have an idea of what you'll need?"

I gave him a list. It was not a very long one, and I was glad to hear he had everything I required in stock. He also said he was going to throw in a few extra things, because if I was right about what we were dealing with, they might come in handy.

"They'll come in handier if you're wrong, too."

Thirty minutes later, I parked my car down the street from the Guildwood Inn, at the back of Sir Wilfrid Laurier school parking lot. I didn't want it anywhere near where Rouge was going to be, just in case Parks followed her and spotted it. From the road, nobody would see it, which worked perfectly.

I left my car, texted Rouge that I was there, which was no easy task. Having lost my smartphone and reverting to an old flip phone, I forgot how crappy it was to text people. I see why people used to use text speech with the old phones. It wasn't lazy; it was just easier than having to hit the buttons over and over to get the letter you needed, or counting on predictive text to figure out what you were trying to get across.

Still, I couldn't help feeling like Captain Kirk a little as I flipped it open. I almost asked Scottie to beam me up. It was the only good part about the ancient Razr.

I decide to cut through the woods to get to the Inn. I didn't know how close Rouge was to being there, but if she drove past and was being followed, I didn't want to bait myself out. The woods were nice, though. The leaves hadn't all fallen yet, and they were a rainbow of fiery fall colours. There were a few high school students hanging out close to the street. I could smell the acrid stench of weed before I saw them. They were all wearing the same style of clothes, almost a uniform, but one of their own choosing: skinny jeans, dark hoodies with *Hollister* written down the sleeves in obnoxiously bright white letters, and hats with flat brims that looked as though they were too small to fit on their heads. I went to walk by without a second glance, and then heard it.

"Holy shit! It's the Monster guy!"

"Sweet, hairy Jesus!"

"Monster man!"

"Nice kicks, dude!"

I turned and waved at them, pretending I didn't mind it at all, even though I did. They were just kids, and none of them were melting away at the moment, so I didn't see the need to be an ass. I had better things to worry about than a pack of stoners.

"Hey, can I take a selfie with you, man? My girl won't believe that I saw the monster killer himself."

"I'm in kind of a hurry, so no."

The kid made a sound and took a long drag on the smelliest weed I've ever had the displeasure of breathing in. Even in the great outdoors, it was pungent and eye-watering. The kid turned to his friends and whispered something I could barely catch, but I got the gist of it. I was an asshole, and a loser, more than likely a liar. I thought that was a good thing. Maybe if I pissed off enough people, they'd all just leave me alone and the video would die out.

Then again, that's not how the world worked since the invention of the internet. Once that came out, and social media took hold, well, everyone had a soap box and if you became the target, they wouldn't be happy until you were crippled.

"Man, this guy ain't shit. The whole thing was bullshit. Dude on *Real or Lies* showed how the whole video was done. CGI, bro! Good shit, like Star Wars, but fake as my sister's weave!"

"No way, it's real. I know someone who was there."

"Yeah, right. That's why buddy here is creeping through the woods next to a school. Maybe he's looking to battle the one-eyed serpent while he stares through the fence at girls running the mile."

"You worried he's gonna steal your job, Ty?"

"Fuck you, man. I don't need to spy to see some skin. That's why I got your mom's cell."

There was a sound of jeers and calls of major burns and I'd

just about had enough. If they wanted something I'd give them something. I didn't need them following me, anyway. Better to try and put something close to fear in them. I reach to my belt, pulled out my Tincher and went for it.

"Look, I'm on a case. I was told by a guy who hikes through here all the time that something *unnatural* has been seen in these woods," I began the lie, and saw their faces light up. Most of them were looking at the blade., not me. That was good. If I couldn't beat them, I might as well mess around with their heads. "Big, ugly thing, worse than the one you saw me fight on YouTube. It looks like it wears the skins of its victims."

"Oh, shit!" one of the group blurted out, and there was a nice twinge of terror in his eyes. "You mean there's something here? Like close?"

"I don't know how close," I continued. "I was told it's been seen between the school and the abandoned inn. I'm guessing that's where it's taking its victims to skin and eat." Man, this was easy, and it seemed to work.

"Yo, fuck the picture with this guy, we need to get the hell outta here, G!" yelled the one who'd said the video was fake. It was amazing how fast his opinion changed.

And with that, they all ran back to the realm of higher education, leaving a trail of their stench behind them. I walked through the dense cloud, heard their feet slip and slide over the path slick with leaves, and then, I could hear and smell them no more.

I moved quickly, hoped they wouldn't have a change of heart, and when I spotted the Inn through the foliage, I sent Rouge a text message letting her know I was there. She sent one back within a minute saying she was already in the parking lot. I wrote back for her to go around to the back of the forgotten hotel, to the stone stage and archway, I'd be there in a second.

When I saw her, my heart stopped for a moment.

I knew I'd missed her, I just didn't know it was that much. She looked stunning. She was dressed in jeans, a green knitted coat and had her hair in a simple ponytail with a green, tweed poor-boy hat. It was simpler than her onstage persona, but she was as breathtaking as always.

When she was close enough, I made a sound so she would see me. She gave a quick look over her shoulder, no doubt checking for Parks, then ran over to me and we wrapped our arms around each other. It was the best moment since we had left Niagara Falls. With all the stress aside, the mental hospital fading in the rear mirror, all there was in that moment was the two of us, engulfed in one another, not wanting to let go or lose the moment.

But moments like that can't last forever, and eventually we separated and she looked at me, her eyes shiny with tears. I'm sure mine looked the same.

"I played this moment over and over in my head on the drive over," she said, sniffling a bit. "Only I was one of those old movie star types, and before I hugged you, I slapped you in the face. I really wanted to do that."

"You still can if you want to," I laughed.

"I don't. Not any more. Plus, I think you having to wear that outfit's punishment enough," she said. She tried to smile, but her lips quivered. "I'm just… you have no idea how much of a wreck I've been."

"I think I do. I'm so sorry, Rouge. It's just—"

And the words died on my lips for a second. My heart sank, filled with the sudden urge to be back at the hospital, back in the dark void of drugs.

For a second—a blip, no more—Rouge's face changed. There was a moment, the blink of an eye, where it looked like she was melting, like before. Her mascara hadn't just started to run, it was the rot and coming-apart of death. She turned the way Harrison, the cop, the kids, the people in the mall had. I stepped back in that flash of disintegration. I'd been on the verge of screaming, but then it was gone. She was Rouge again. No melting. No muck coming from her mouth. It looked like there'd been a glitch, and then she was right back to her beautiful self.

I was worried. I didn't know if it meant anything, or if it was just the drugs still in my system. I hoped it was the latter, because the former meant something far worse.

Something fatal.

"Are you okay? You look like you just saw a ghost."

"Whatever it was, it's gone now."

"You saw something?"

"Sort of. But it won't make sense unless I tell you everything."

So, I did. I started from the start of it all; the beginning with Chance's case, what he'd seen and then what happened to me. I told her about all the people going on and on about the YouTube video, then meeting with Parks, before I'd ever started to see the same thing my client had. I explained how, when it started, I just put it down to stress, how everything piled high in a teetering Jenga tower. I went into great detail about the disaster at Sherway Gardens, and how that was the moment the tower first toppled.

"Then in the LCBO it happened again, and I couldn't even stop myself from attacking the kid, or the cop who'd shown up after I was arrested."

"You attacked a cop?" she asked, sounding mortified.

"Not my best moment. But that's what got me locked away in the hospital."

"What hospital?"

"CAMH," I said, and she gasped a little. Clearly she knew what it was.

"They put you in a mental hospital?"

"That's why I couldn't call you. They don't let patients do that. Not to mention they'd put me on so many drugs I was barely able to string two thoughts together. I had no idea what was up or down. They even had me thinking all this, my whole life, was just something I made up. From the monsters, to what I am, all the way to you. I was on some heavy drugs, and I was convinced that everything I'd thought was real was just an illusion. And then Father Ted showed up—"

"Your priest friend who died?"

"Yeah. I'm pretty sure it wasn't real, that it was because of a new drug they put me on, but I can't tell for sure. I'm still not sure what was real and what I imagined. One day seemed to last forever. I didn't even know I was gone as long as I was. I'd have random cuts on my knees, I'd be in the TV room, blink and then

I'd be in a room with other patients eating dinner, or in a room talking to my doctor. It was a nightmare, a life with every bit of colour and sanity drained from it. I'm just so glad it's over now."

"I have no idea how terrible it must've been for you. Now I feel like a jerk for being mad at you at all."

"Don't be."

"So, why'd they let you go? After two weeks, what made them think you were better?"

I told her how it all came together. I explained how the doctor heard me make mention of the YouTube video, and then searched for it. It was funny that the one thing I'd been spending so much time cursing turned out to be the thing that saved me from being kept in there any longer. She listened as I gave her a breakdown of how it led to us talking about the melting-face people, and how everyone I'd seen change ended up dead, at least the ones we were able to track down. I explained to her how Chance had had the same experience. All the people he'd seen melting ended up dead, including himself.

"He saw himself melting?"

"Yeah, when he looked in the mirror. That's one of the reasons he called me. He thought he was haunted by some sort of ghost bent on driving him crazy."

"Is that what it is? Is that why you're seeing it all too? Some ghost jumped from him to you?"

"No. It's not a ghost. I'm pretty sure it has nothing to do with—"

I stopped as her face did the glitch thing again. I turned away and took a deep breath. I knew it couldn't be real. After spending two weeks fighting to know what's real and what wasn't, I had to believe what I was seeing was just a reaction to the meds. To see if I was right, I looked back at her.

Thankfully, she'd gone back to normal.

"What's going on, Dill? You're kind of freaking me out."

"It's nothing," I lied. I knew my voice was giving me away.

"Wow. I guess this is going to be the time you start handing me a bag of horseshit? If that's the best you can do trying to keep poker-faced when you lie, don't ever try to organize a surprise party. You look like the pupper when I've caught her eating my socks. So, what is it?"

There was no point in lying, clearly, but the last thing I wanted to do was freak her out. She'd been through enough lately because of me. I didn't want her to think something bad was going to happen to her.

"I think it's the drugs they gave me," I began, trying to find an easy way to say it all. "They had me on sedatives—Clozapine— and then some new, experimental thing. I'm not sure they're out of my system. It's just freaking me out a bit."

"So, you're seeing things? Like pink elephants?"

"Sort of."

"Okay. I can see you're still trying to avoid it. You might as well spill the beans. I'm not just going to let this go. I can tell there's more to it than you're saying."

There was no way to beat around the bush. She wasn't going to let me off with a half-assed answer, so I'd just have to tell her.

"It's you," I began. "When I looked at you, for a split second, your face was melting." Her eyes opened wide, and I knew she was about to freak out. "But I don't want you to worry, darling. I've never seen anything like it before. It's more like a video game screen jumping for a second. Normally it's terrible, and I never see them go back to normal. This, it's just a flicker, and then you're right back to your gorgeous self. I'm sure it's nothing but me pushing all the drugs out of my body."

"How do you know it's not the drugs keeping you from seeing me melting all the time? Why do you think they might be making you see me only go on and off like that?" she asked. She sounded as though she was about to freak out.

"Because I was still on the drugs when I saw Harrison melt."

"Harrison?"

"He's one of the other patients in the hospital with me. I was on the meds and he still went into full melty-death mode. You're not. What I just saw has to be the drugs."

But did it? Was I really buying what I was saying? I know I wanted to believe it, because I didn't want to think anything bad could happen to her. I couldn't imagine seeing it, knowing it was real, and then waiting for death to come for her. For my own sanity, I needed to convince myself she was fine, that it was all my own issue.

"I hope you're right, but if you see something more, you tell me. Okay?"

"I'll do my best," I said, and we found our way back into each other's arms. I don't even know how long we stayed there like that, but I would've liked to never leave that moment. Her arms felt so good around me, made me feel like I was where I belonged. She smelt great and was so warm.

Eventually, of course, we had to get on with things.

"What do you do now? You said you knew what it was causing this."

"I think so. I need to back to Niagara Falls, where it all started. I think there's some sort of doorway open to a demon realm."

"Oh, that's what I want to hear. It's not going to be another Hellion, is it?"

"No. This is different. Someone, or something, has opened a gateway and it's caused a sort of infection. It's what's making me see what I am becoming, a beacon for death."

"That sounds lovely. Why are you seeing people who are going to die, though?" she asked. Her voice sounded a little shaky. No doubt she was still as worried as I was about seeing her glitch.

"I'm pretty sure the gate opened is the *Beelz* realm. The things that live there are a species of demons that are soul-suckers. They prefer to find souls about to leave a body to eat though, so they can see who is close to death in order to know where to be."

"You know this for sure?"

"No. Half the time I'm just winging it, Rouge, but it's the one thing that makes the most sense to me. If this is what I think it is, it could be enough to get Parks and the Collective off my back for a while. No guarantee, but it'll help. So, I need to throw caution to the wind a little, and head back to the Falls. Even if it doesn't get them right off me, I need to hope it is a gate, and that I can close it easily. It may be a guess, but it's all I got right now. There has to be a door opened and one of those bastards has managed to find a way to infect me. I might be wrong, but after all these years of doing this, I have to trust my gut."

"You've heard of this happening, though?"

I shrugged. I hadn't, but like I said, most of what I put together when I was doing my job involved gathering a few facts, and then winging it. I couldn't turn to Google to answer my questions or help me out. There were some books, sure, but they only knew so much about anything. This was a shot in the dark. All I could do was hope I wasn't aiming the gun at my own foot.

"Well, when do we leave?" she said matter-of-factly, and I couldn't help but let out a surprised laugh.

"What?" she asked, before realizing: "Oh, you think I'm letting you go there alone? You just finished telling me about all the drugs you still have in your system. It's not safe for you to try and handle this alone, and who else are you going to turn to? You can't take Godfrey with you. Not again. Not to mention I just lost you for two weeks. I have no plans on losing you for even more time. Like it or not, we're going to be partners on this one."

"I can't—"

"You will. I'm not letting this one slide, sunshine. Plus, keeping me close will ensure I'm safe, and not going to turn full melty-face on you."

"This doesn't feel good," I admitted, and it didn't. What if the reason I saw her go in and out of melting all came down to whether she stayed here or came with me? What if bringing her to Niagara Falls would make it go full because I was taking her straight into danger? I told her as much.

"Sooner or later, you're going to have to see that I'm a big girl, Dillon, and I don't need training wheels. I'm old enough to drink, vote and go to war. And I'd rather come along, make sure you're not going to go into some zoned-out drug state, than stay here and maybe get visited by your hunter buddy again."

Shit. I'd nearly forgotten about him. He'd be out of the picture for a couple of days, but when he was released by the police, he'd no doubt be on a tear for me. And one of the first places he'd go would be Rouge's house.

Damned if I do, damned if I don't.

"When do we leave?" she asked with a smile, clearly able to tell she was coming along.

"First, I need to get out of these terrible clothes," I laughed, looking down at myself. "Then, as soon as Garcia lets me know they picked Parks up, we'll go."

"Should I go pack a bag?"

Before we could go to her house to grab Rouge's things, including the puppy she'd need to drop off at her cousins house, I had to call Garcia, as I hadn't gotten a call or text from him yet. We still needed to lay low a little, and preferably not together, until Don Parks had been snatched up. The last thing I needed was for him to follow us to Niagara Falls. I told Rouge that if they still didn't have him, she'd have to go to her house alone to pack, and we'd meet up once the cops had done the deed.

"Oh, like you're not going to ditch me and run there all on your own. No way, mister. We're sticking together until all this is done."

"I'm not going to ditch you. We just need to be careful, keep our heads down, and my face off his radar. I promise I won't leave without you."

There was no answer at Garcia's end. I'd started to get worried he wasn't going to be able to do what I'd asked him to. He'd sounded as though it wouldn't be a problem, though, and I had to believe him. He'd managed not only to get me out of the mental hospital, but also got my weapons and car back for me, and had all the charges I'd faced dropped. I had nothing but confidence in him.

Five minutes later, I got a text saying he'd been right in the middle of arresting Parks when I'd called. How kismet was that?

The asshole put up quite a fight, the text read. *We had to knock him around a bit. He's a right prick, this one. We should be able to hold him for seventy-two hours now. Bloodied up the lip of one of the uniforms I brought with me.*

Perfect. I told Rouge the good news, and we drove straight

to her house to get done what she needed to. While she was in her room packing, I called Godfrey up to let him know we were going to swing by.

"What about the other hunter?"

"Detective Garcia arrested him for me. He should be away for a few days at least."

"Arrested for what?"

"At first as a favour to me, but then he assaulted a cop, so there's that."

"Remind me not to get on your bad side," he laughed.

"You've been on my bad side plenty of times, Godfrey. Unless you forget all those times you've sold me bad goods. When I nearly get killed because of you, it puts you on my shit list. But don't worry, that's water and something to do with a bridge. Bygones are bygones and all that crap."

After I hung up and Rouge was done packing, we dropped the puppy off. We made a quick stop at my house to change. I didn't need Godfrey ragging on me about my free hospital gear. Once I was back to my typical style of a hoodie, jeans, and my leather jacket, we drove to Godfrey's shop. He was sitting in the back room when we walked into the dark shop. He told me to lock the door, and when I did, he flicked on some lights. He seemed happy to see us, more so Rouge, but that's no surprise.

"How are you doing, beauty?" he asked, and hugged her. I had no idea they'd advanced to the hugging stage.

"Not too shabby. Trying to keep this one out of trouble again," she told him, thumbing at me. "He needs a chaperone to deal with this one."

"You joining the hunters now, Rouge?" he chuckled. "Best looking one I've ever seen."

"She's not going to be a hunter. I think I'm in enough trouble as it is, don't you?"

"Mon, she's already a hunter. Didn't she save your ass against the Hellion? Went face to face with one of those shadow thingies?"

"I didn't do anything with the shadow people," she corrected him before I could. "That was all Dill Pickle here. I just saved him from the biggest monster he's ever fought."

"Who said he was the biggest?" I asked, trying not to laugh. The Hellion, Rector, was by far the biggest, scariest demon I'd ever gone toe to toe with, and I'd die a happy man if I never saw another of his kind.

"You did," she said, and slapped me on the back. "You tell me all the time, bragging about how lucky you were to come out of it in one piece. You're welcome for that, by the way."

We all had a good laugh at that, a moment of levity, which was something I really needed. After that, I told Godfrey everything that had happened from Niagara Falls, until my release from CAMH. He listened carefully, especially attentive when I explained my theory that a door to Beelz had been opened and something from there had infected me.

"Sounds about right. You have any idea the location of the door, and who might've opened it?" he asked.

"Pretty sure the source of all of this is a church."

"It's always a church," Godfrey told Rouge. "They seem to be beacons for these things. Not because they're bad places or anything. Don't get me wrong. No, it's because the power they hold with their icons, the prayers of their faithful, and the sheer power of belief people that go there have. It's what calls demons to them."

"Well, this place wasn't a *real* church." I could see the confusion on both of their faces. "It was a weed church. The guy who ran it wasn't an actual priest. He was a guy who had an idea to find a legal, tax-free way to sell weed to people. Pastor Herb and two others—"

"His name was Pastor Herb?" Rouge asked, and when I nodded she began to laugh harder than I'd ever seen her laugh. "Clearly not his real name. Was he as Rasta? *Hey, mon, pass de 'erb!* No offence, Godfrey."

"None taken. You know I'm not really Jamaican, girl. This is just a façade."

"No," I told them, finally getting the joke. "That wasn't his real name. But he died in the church with two other people who lived there. Someone burned them: fire-bombed the place while they were sleeping. I'm thinking that might've been what opened the door."

"Like a trauma gate?" Godfrey asked.

"That's what I'm thinking, and hoping. I didn't notice it when I checked the place out, but there were a lot of symbols drawn on the walls, things I've never seen."

"Show me."

I didn't have my notepad on me. That was something that hadn't been returned yet. I was pretty sure the doctor still had it. I drew some of them from memory in the dust on the glass displays that held nothing of true value or magic properties. He looked them over when I was done and shook his head for a while, studied them again, and continued to shake his head.

"Looks like nothing. You sure that's all there was?"

"No, but this is what I remember."

"And you're sure this is the place?"

"Not a hundred percent, but it's all I have for now."

"Well, those things mean nothing to me," Godfrey said, looking down at them and shaking his head." If you think that's the key to anything, you won't get anywhere with it."

"I'm pretty sure that one right there is a band's logo," Rouge said, pointing at one of the shapes I'd drawn. "I used to see it on people's backpacks and books in school. I think Godfrey's right. Sorry, Dill."

"Godfrey's always right," the tool supplier said with an air of arrogance. "Now, I got the things you want. You two leaving soon?"

"As soon as we're done here."

"Give me a sec."

Godfrey went off to the backroom and Rouge turned to me.

"If it's not the church, where else do we look?" she asked me, and to be honest, I had no idea. Nothing else made sense. Every other place he held either had no history as strange or horrible as the church, and most of them had a lot of people in and out of there. Chance Anderson wouldn't have been the only one affected by the demons. It's not how these things worked. Somewhere I went into, a place I came in contact with, had demons that had either snuck through or been called to this world. It was a short list, and the church was suspect number one.

The other thing about this particular type of demon was their inability to use weak spots to enter the Earth realm. In order for demons from the Beelz realm to come here, there needed to be a gateway. Gateways from that world could only be opened with some sort of major traumatic issue, a porter, or by someone who'd deliberately called a doorway forth. Chance wouldn't have thought ghosts if he'd done the latter, so it had to be the church or a porter. I didn't want to think a porter, either. Someone using a porter—a body with a swirling gateway inside them—could open doors to anywhere. And the only way to close the gate was to kill the person who housed the doorway.

I'd done it before.

Well, Rouge kind of did too, but she didn't know the full details of that part of it.

"Okay, Dillon. Here you go," Godfrey announced as he walked back into the room. "Everything you asked for, but because of what you said, I decided to add a few other things. One of them is a bag of *Safferite Blue*."

"What's that?" Rouge asked, and Godfrey pulled the bag out.

"This is the dust made from an alien crystal. It can be rubbed on the skin to protect you from demon invasions, or put on the floor to keep out certain types of spirits. Very handy. So is this," he said, and pulled out a bronze rod with dark blotches on it. "This is *Azzeen Staff*. It can be used to kill some creatures, demons from Beelz fall into that category. It can also be used to close some gates. Trial and error for this one. I can't put any sort of guarantee on it as I've never seen one used before."

"I haven't seen one of them in ages," I said, happy to have it. I wouldn't have even thought to ask for one. I had never used it to close a gate, but once, a long time ago, I did kill a terrible demon with one. I lost it because it melted as it turned the monster to ash.

"It's been in the back room for a while, but I think it's as good a time as any to give it to you. I had to trade off a Boar Helm to get it, so you better be thankful."

"Oh, trust me, I am."

"The rest of the stuff you asked for is in there, plus an extra pair of spellbound gloves since you're bringing Rouge with you. Everything else you can show her what it's for. I think she'll make a great hunter," he said, and winked at her.

"She's not going to be a hunter, dude. Seriously."

"You say that now, but I can see her mind is already made up."

We left Godfrey's and started the drive to Niagara Falls. I didn't want to think about anything we were about to face. If I was alone, my mind would inevitably start to run through different scenarios. I'd imagine how things would go right and, of course, how they could go terribly wrong. The drive from Toronto to Niagara Falls can take anywhere from an hour and a half to two hours, so normally, it'd be quite a few scenarios I could run through.

Luckily, Rouge was there to keep me company and help distract my mind from wandering towards too many dark possibilities. Instead of thinking about being turned inside out, or being eaten alive by some monstrous bugs from a realm of dark and cold, I got to watch Rouge sing along to some CCR (the best driving music in my humble opinion), and when she wasn't doing that, we talked about other, more mundane things. Mainly about when I was going to finally move out of Casa de Dillon, and into her place.

"If all goes well here, and I get Parks off my back, I'd really start to consider it."

"Just consider it then? Really?" she chuckled. "It's not every day I invite someone to move in with me. You should consider yourself a lucky man to enjoy the house my grandfather built himself and my grandmother decorated with innumerable doilies of her own making. There are so many in there, I could open up a doily theme park or a museum."

"Now I'm sold," I said with a cup full of sarcasm, as we drove over the huge bridge in Hamilton. "I mean, you're a good selling point, but those lace bits are what really float my boat."

Not long after we were in Niagara Falls and I knew exactly where to go first. Coffee run. Caffeine would help me stay a little more clear-headed than I was feeling at the time. I found I was blinking more, struggling to make my eyes focus on things, and hoped coffee would help. Maybe some Timbits too.

We went through the drive-thru, got some food and drinks, and downed everything pretty quickly on the way to the former church of Pastor Herb.

"You're not going to ask me to stay in the car while you work, are you?" she asked as she sipped a steeped tea.

"Would you do it if I asked?"

"Did I last time?"

"Exactly. No, we'll do this one together. Just make sure to follow my lead and don't move too quickly. I'm not sure where the gate or doorway is, but when we find it, I don't want you falling into it."

"Falling into it? That can happen?" she asked, and looked rightly worried.

I nodded. "No matter how much you think you're ready to be involved in this, going into a demon realm, it's nothing like you'd expect. Iron Maiden and Slayer totally lied with those album covers."

She laughed, but I could hear nervousness in it. Not that I blamed her. This wasn't like starting a new job at Sam the Record Man or Honest Ed's. This was jumping into a world where the wrong move could mean not getting to see the next day. Especially for her. If I get injured, there is the magical bath I can take to heal me. If I get killed, only this body dies, but I can still take another. She couldn't, and when I drove and started to think about that more in depth, I couldn't avoid worrying more and more about this whole thing. The idea of her getting hurt, or worse, getting killed, wasn't something I even wanted to imagine. My time away from her in the hospital, losing all ideas that she was even real, was terrible enough. Actually losing her forever wasn't something I even wanted to allow to be a possibility.

I could feel her eyes on me as that began racing through my

head. I turned to look at her and saw her studying me. I wondered if she could sense my sudden apprehension.

"What's eating you, Dillon? And don't say *nothing*. You get a look on your face when something is getting under your skin, or you dirty little mind has taken a trip out of the gutter and into somewhere you shouldn't be visiting. So, what is it?"

I paused.

I wanted to think of how to put it without sounding like a dick. I didn't want to come off like I was some chauvinist who didn't believe women could do anything a man could do. The fact of it was, I wasn't an actual man, not in the sense of everyone else on Earth. I was comparing her not as man to woman, but alien to human, vast experience to not much at all. Still, I wanted to be gentle and yet truthful.

"I'm worried about you."

"Aw, that's sweet, but you don't need to worry about me. I want to be here. I want to do this, and help you too. It'll be fine."

"I know you say that, and I want to believe it will be. I mean, most times I do these things and walk away with little more than dirty hands, but we both know things can easily go sideways."

"But that's just life. Any time, on any day, something terrible can happen and boom, it's game over. I'm not going to live my life being afraid to do things just because there's a chance something bad may happen."

"But this isn't just living your life. You're deliberately going into something you don't really need to deal with."

"Okay, but what if I decided to give up the whole burlesque thing, which is going to happen, regardless of what you say, and decided to become a police officer or a fire fighter? There's the same or even more risk involved there. Would you tell me not to do that, even if I felt a draw to it?"

Would I? I wasn't even sure what the answer to that would be. When I met Rouge, she was a dancer and model, and that was how I saw her. Like most people, the jobs we do are part of what defines us. People see you as a seamstress, a librarian, or a teacher, and they can't see you doing anything else, especially if that something is the complete opposite of the life you project. Going from homeboy to adventure-seeker; from safe job to something you'd watch people do on one of those Discovery Channel shows that start off with the words *The Most Dangerous...* was hard for people to wrap their minds around.

"I can see you're having trouble with all that, Dillon, so let me help you a bit. It might keep you from saying the wrong thing, too. When I was younger, I did a lot to help people out. I would go from job to job, doing work that had meaning. This was when I was much younger. When I was the weirdo, the outcast, and I'd hide away in the things I did so I could forget all the bad things people would whisper about me, because when they saw how I helped out, it changed their view of what I was. Instead of seeing just this freak, they saw the good in me, and that felt great.

"Then, I get to this point where I put on this new look. My body changes to this ideal of what sexy is, and I go with it. At first, I didn't want to. I didn't want eyes on me, studying and critiquing my body as though I was putting it on display for them. But, eventually, I saw that I was helping people there, too. I told you before about how being on stage, I'm a distraction from the real world, from problems, and stress. I found that to be my own way of helping people. That's all changed now, so I want to do something with meaning instead of just fading away and being some homemaker, or your kept girl. I'm not that person. So, why not do this with you? It makes a difference, I get to experience something I've never done before, and I will actually be helping people in a way few get to. You can show me what to do, help me learn to do this with a good head on my shoulders, and one day, maybe you'll trust me enough to not worry any more. I still worry when you go out, though, so I won't get my hopes up on that.

"I just want you to trust that I'm not an idiot. I'm not going to go in all Leeroy Jenkins. I'll follow your lead. You just need to make sure you don't do anything stupid and teach me wrong. Sound good?"

I nodded.

How was I supposed to argue with any of what she'd said?

After that, we pulled up to the church and I reached to the back seat to grab the bag Godfrey had given me. First thing I pulled from it was a pair of gloves, similar to mine. They looked to be made out of soft leather, though I knew by the texture they were made of nothing from this planet, just as mine weren't. Usually, these spellbound gloves were made of the skins of a *Kern*, an *Atzii*, or a *Veek*. These were the most common creatures used, as they already held their own kinds of magic in them. The creatures didn't die when they gave their skins; they simply shed them as needed, a bit like molting.

I handed the gloves to Rouge and she inspected them.

"Are these like yours?"

"Yeah. They have spells cast into them, and contain different kinds of counter curses and magic. You use them to sort of freeze any spirit, monster, or demon you touch. It acts like a paralyzer of sorts."

"Wow. I have to admit, this is kind of cool. What else do I get?"

I passed her the Safferite Blue, a *Buern*; a circle of rope used to look through for monsters that devour light, and a *Klask*, a jar with a small, liquid-based bug inside it. I told her if she shook the jar a bit, the Klask inside would let out a high pitch sound that only demons can hear, and they don't like it.

"So it won't affect you, or anything other than a demon?" she asked and looked into the jar as the Klask moved from solid to a crystal blue water shaped bug.

"Want to try it out and see if I lose my marbles?"

She shook it, winced a bit as she did, but then looked at me and shrugged. "I guess you're right. I didn't hear a thing."

"Good thing you're not a demon," I laughed.

I took out a few more items, including the Azzeen Staff, more Firma Pitch, and my own gloves. My Tincher was already on my belt. I tossed the remaining items that I wasn't sure I'd need in the back seat, and then took a deep breath.

"Well, I guess this is it. You ready?" I asked her, and she looked more excited than I felt.

"I've never been more ready, Dillon! Let's get rambling!"

The church looked the same as it did the last time I'd been inside. We used the loose piece of plywood, pushed it aside and climbed in through the darkness. I pulled my small LED flashlight out to light my way; Rouge used her cellphone, having it out and lit before me.

"It stinks in here," she whispered, and it did. Same as before. There was the dust, the lingering remains of the fire, and just that smell an unlived-in, unaired space gets after a while. "Where should we check first?"

"The symbols I found are in the back area, where the offices and rectory of sorts were. The rest are in the basement."

"Yeah, but I already said some of those I know as band logos."

"I know, but it's a place to start. Come on. And keep your ears, eyes, and nose open."

"Nose?"

"You can smell these things, most times at least, especially if they're coming through a gate."

We moved to the back office area and I saw others had been in there since my last visit. Empty beer and liquor bottles were scattered about, and two boxes of pizza with pieces in them that had dried up and began to curl in on themselves. Probably kids from one of the local high schools broke in and had a little skid party here. Whenever I go into abandoned buildings, this kind of stuff is common. Urban explorers, teens wanting to feel rebellious, and on a rare occasion, an actual homeless person might be found squatting there. I hadn't found any signs of partiers the last time, but if they had just been cleaning up after themselves, or Chance was sending a caretaker in before he died, it made me question the graffiti even more than when Rouge had pointed out the fact that one of them was a logo.

"This looks like a romantic place to have a candlelight dinner. How come you never bring me to places like this?" Rouge asked sarcastically, and nudged one of the boxes of pizza with her foot.

When she did, she jumped back as something dark and wrapped in shadows sped across the room and disappeared out the door we'd just walked through. Bingo!

I pulled my Tincher out, and turned to pursue, but Rouge grabbed my arm and pulled me back with surprising strength.

"What are you doing?" I asked, and went to follow.

"It was a rat, Dill. Just a nasty-ass rodent."

Of course it was. Nothing was that easy, especially not as of late.

We walked through the office area and found nothing. We check the private and public washrooms, and other than some horrid smells, we found nothing. Our next stop was the basement. I warned her about the weak, water-damaged stairs. I explained that it must've been from the sprinklers when the fire happened, and helped her get down without an issue.

"That smoky smell is real strong here. Is this where the main fire happened?"

"As far as I can tell, yeah. Never read a police report, but that window there is missing," I said, pointing to the one I'd checked before. Then I showed here the remains of the beds and cots. "This must've been where they were sleeping when it came in. They wouldn't have had a chance to get out."

"This is so depressing. I've never been to anywhere like this before. I mean, I visited a place where someone died, but not where someone was murdered."

"Aside from all the stuff that happened in Innisfil," I corrected, surprised she'd forgotten all that mess.

"You know what I mean," she scoffed, but I didn't. "This is different. This was done by people. Not monsters, or demons, or ghosts; people killing people. I think it's different, even if you don't."

"I guess," I said, and began moving around the room. "Check for anything along the walls and on the floor. There are some symbols over there, but you might be right about that, so just look for something weird, or off. Something that doesn't seem like it should be there."

"Like a door or a gateway?"

"Yes, but not necessarily like you think. It might not look like a hole or some opening. Some of them might look like a puddle on the floor, or they can be an object brought here from another world. You'll be able to tell if you see it."

"I hope so."

We searched the room and by the end of it, found nothing out of the ordinary. I pulled out a golden, curved piece of metal from my jacket pocket, a *Zuuar*, which looks like a metal opener, and moved it along the walls and floor. The tool will glow brilliantly if it points at something non-human. Rouge asked what it was, and I told her. She came up behind and stayed with me as I followed the line of each of the walls, floor to ceiling.

Not even a flicker.

"You sure it works?" she asked, and I turned it towards us. It glowed more than I'd ever seen it, to the point it was almost blinding. The sheer darkness of the room must've made it seem even brighter than normal. "Okay, I get it. Wow! I can barely see now."

I tucked it back into my pocket and stood in the room, feeling as defeated as I had the first time. I was so sure it would be here. It had to be. It's always a church. Even when it's not, a lot of times it's in a place that used to be a church, or a graveyard. All that typical movie nonsense. It was based somewhere in reality.

"What now?" she asked, and wrapped her arms around me. "I'm guessing this is a bust?"

"It is. And really, I have no idea what to do now. I'm starting to question whether this is what I thought it was. If I'm wrong about this, maybe I'm equally wrong about it being a Beelz, too. But I was so sure it was here. To the point that—"

I stopped talking. There was noise above us in the main area of the church. I looked up and turned my light off, motioning for Rouge to do the same, but once again she was way ahead of me.

"You think the party squatters are back?" she whispered.

"Maybe," I said, but I wasn't sure. The footfalls were heavy, not like people sneaking about.

I moved towards the stairs leading up to the main floor, and when I got there, I could see flashlights moving around. I doubted squatters or the homeless would be doing that, which meant urban explorers, or something else.

Rouge took a step towards me, but I held up a finger, not wanting her to make a sound. Until we knew what it was up there, I didn't want to give ourselves away. I slowed my breathing down so I could hear better, hoping for voices. Usually urban explorers have phones on, or cameras, vlogging themselves to show the world how cool they are, how danger and adventure were their bread and butter. I wasn't hearing anything, though. Not a sound.

At least not until I was nearly blinded by a light in my eyes.

"Hands where I can see them, buddy!" called a voice behind the beam. I did as I was told, glad I'd tucked my Tincher away, because that sounded like a cop, certainly talked like one. "You alone down there?"

I thought about how to answer that pretty quickly. I could say no, hope Rouge would hide and then hope whoever it was up there would let me walk up on my own and not come down and search the place. But, if it was the police, or the building had security, there'd be little chance of that.

"No," I admitted, and looked over at Rouge, who gave me her best *what the fuck* face. I shrugged and tried to smile. "There's two of us here. You want us to come up?"

"You stay right there. Move, and I swear I'll put a hole through your head."

It had to be a cop. Security guards in Canada don't carry guns.

"Dispatch, this is unit 1120," he said and he sounded nervous. Why would he be nervous? He had the gun, not me. Then again, he was in a creepy, dark building where three people had been killed.

"Go ahead, unit 1120."

"I'm going to need additional units at 2340 Dunn Avenue. I have two suspects inside."

"Ten-four. Any info on them?"

"None at this time. Just send additional units ASAP."

Well, I seemed to be on a real roll with getting arrested these days.

W e were taken to the local police station and put in separate interrogation rooms. I'd told Rouge to keep her mouth shut for the time being. I figured the last thing I needed was for both of us to be locked up in a hospital that was Niagara Falls' answer to CAMH. I had an idea of what to do to get out of this, but it should be pretty obvious. When I get in trouble, I call for help. This time it would be a call for Detective Winger.

Ten minutes after being sat down in a room that smelled like onion-soaked armpits, the door opened and a man with a sad, long face walked in. He carried a coffee in one hand and a thin file in the other. This wasn't Winger, or her partner, Korkis. I had no idea who he was, but I was sure he was a cop, too. The cheap dress shirt that showed his undershirt through it, the stress lines on his face, and just the way he carried himself as he walked the short distance to the desk, screamed law enforcement.

He sat down, sipped his drink, and opened the file, scanning whatever was in there. I hoped it was a skin mag, or a comic book since there would be no way the cop who arrested me had already written a report, and I had never been arrested in the Falls. Even if they'd run a background check on me, they'd find nothing, but it would take a lot longer than ten minutes even if there was something to find.

This was Cop Games 101.

"We can save each other a lot of time if you just—" I began, but he slammed the file down, shaking the whole desk with the force of the strike, and his sad face transformed into one barely able to contain his rage. I hadn't been expecting that.

"You think this is about saving time, you junkie-piece-of-shit? You got nothing to tell me that I can't read in that file there. I know who you are, and I know what you were doing there, so cut the shit!"

Ah! This was bad cop. I knew that routine as well as I knew the rules to *Simon Says*.

"Detective," I tried to start again. "I'm sure you have an idea of—"

"You! You don't talk unless I'm asking you a question, nutbag! You and your junkie girlfriend are in a ton of shit. We know who the two of you are. We've been looking for you for a while."

"You have?"

"Oh, you're going to play dumb here?"

"No, I just have no idea what you're talking about."

He picked up the file again and smiled as he flipped through a few pages. "When was the last time you were in Niagara Falls?"

"A little over two weeks ago."

"Around the same time as Chance Anderson was murdered?"

"Yeah. I was working for him. When he died, I left. But if you could just—"

"And you came back here last week, right?"

Again he had a smile on his face as though he knew something I didn't. I wondered if I should just say *no*, or if I should try and tell him that I'd been in the hospital for the last two weeks. I had no idea if there was actually something in the file that could screw me over, so I decided against full disclosure.

"No, I just came back tonight."

"And went right back to the scene of your first crime?"

"My first crime?"

"When you burnt the church down, killing three people. Did Chance Anderson figure out what you'd done? Is that why you killed him?"

I sat back in my chair as though I'd been hit. Was this guy really trying to pin both of those crimes on me? Was he really trying to say I was the one who'd come here and burnt Pastor Herb and two of his followers to death, then killed Chance to cover it up? Where would he come up with that? How could he figure that?

"I have no idea what you're on about. I was never in Niagara Falls when the church was set on fire."

"Really? Because we have a witness that puts you there."

"Who?" I asked, unable to hide my shock.

"Yeah, wouldn't you like to know?"

"Can you call Detective Winger? She was there the day Chance was killed and knows I had nothing to do with any of this. I was helping to investigate the case. I'm not a suspect."

"Sure you're not," he said, and put the folder back down.

"You're as innocent as every single person we bring in here, asshole."

"Can you just get Winger?"

"She's not here. She's on a leave because of you."

"Because of me? What are you talking about?"

"Keep playing stupid, fuck face, but know this, your goose is cooked. You might've gotten away with it, but when you come after one of our own, you'll see what happens. You're lucky you're still in one piece."

I had no idea what was going on, but I was really starting to freak out quite a bit. Nothing he was saying added up, but it sounded pretty bad. If Winger was here, I was sure she would've helped, but he claimed she was on a leave of absence. Why? And what was with the jab about going after one of their own?

"Okay, I think I'd like to know what my charges are," I told him, worried about what he'd actually say, but I hid it well.

"You know what they are. Think of everything you did, and you tell me what you're being charged with."

"The only thing I did wrong was maybe break and enter, though I did have permission from Chance Anderson to go into all his properties before he died, so that won't stick. I have a contract and everything."

"As if we'd bring you in on something as simple as a fucking trespass charge. That's a fine, idiot. Keep going. You should clear your conscious and your soul. Just tell me what it is you did, and then, maybe we can talk about a deal for you and big red in the other room."

I hoped they weren't going at her the same way they were at me. I had no idea what she'd do or say under that kind of attack. I know people will say a lot of things under certain types of pressure, even admitting to things they didn't do. It wasn't weakness, or even fear; it was a way the brain tries to cope with stress by providing answers we think our accusers want to hear. I knew Rouge was stubborn, but since she'd never been in a situation like that—as far as I knew—I couldn't predict her reaction.

"Since I haven't done anything else close to illegal in your fine city, I can't imagine what the charges are. But I do know you have yet to tell me what I'm being held for, or even read me my rights. Or maybe I'm not under arrest at all, and I can just leave," I said, and looked at the handcuffs chaining me to the desk. "No, this looks like I'm under arrest. So, maybe due process, or Canada's version of it, is needed right now."

His face darkened and I guessed my lipping off wasn't helping my case.

Damn it.

"Okay, smart ass," he said, and pulled out his memo book. "It's my duty to inform you that you're under arrest for five counts of homicide, one count of arson, and one count of uttering a death threat. It's my duty to inform you that you have the right to..."

The rest of his words disintegrated into muffled shadows, words whispered over a vast void. He'd said *five* counts of murder, but I only knew of four dead. Who was number five? Was it Ms Mittz? Was there someone else I didn't even meet? And what was the uttering of death threats about? Where was this guy getting his information from? My guess was the same person who'd claimed I was in Niagara Falls the week of the fire at Pastor Herb's church. Someone or something was trying to turn me into a patsy.

"Do you want to call a lawyer?"

Maybe I did. If only I knew one to call.

The detective had been gone for nearly an hour and I'd started to feel sick to my stomach. My head spun. I'd become light headed, and there was more than one moment I thought I was going to actually faint or pass out at the very least. It'd already been a long day, and it felt as though it was being stretched out even more. How far could it be rolled, pulled, tugged, and yanked before something finally snapped and everything came undone? I was sure it was going to happen at any moment. Maybe when the detective finally returned and allowed me to make my phone call...

When he came back and asked again if I wanted to call a lawyer, I'd said yes, I did. I figured at the very least I could call legal aid, but he'd yet to come with a phone or to get me to take me to a phone. I tried not to let what he'd said run through my mind too much as I sat in the small room with nothing but my thoughts. It was hard not to, though. It was even harder not thinking about what they were putting Rouge through. She had nothing to do with any of this, and had no experience that I knew of dealing with cops, especially hard-nosed detectives who already had their minds made up of your guilt or innocence. I knew she was smart, and quick-thinking, even quicker witted, but this wasn't the type of thing you could be snarky and get out of. A murder charge was a weighty feeling on every inch of your body.

I felt impatient, and slightly anxious. One hour passed, and it was nearly halfway to the second hour being in there, and I was starting to need to piss. I would've gotten up and paced the room if I could, but I was still chained to the desk.

"Any time with that phone call!" I yelled, but the response was only the echo of my own voice.

This was just great.

It wasn't until a quarter past the second hour in the interrogation room that the door finally opened again. I let out a sigh of relief. By that time, I'd put myself into a full-on panic with all the possible outcomes that had played through my head. I'd be happy to say something to someone, even if it was the super-aggressive detective ready to accuse me with more crimes.

It wasn't him, though.

It was Detective Winger.

"Aren't you a sight for sore eyes," I said, as she shut the door. I smiled, figured she'd be my saviour, the one person who actually knew me here and had an idea of what I really did. No need to beat around the bush.

When she turned around, though, she didn't look like the same woman I'd known. There were circles as dark as coal under her eyes, and her skin was pale, nearly ashen. She had a look of someone who hadn't been sleeping much over the last little while, a feeling I knew all too well. "Are you okay?"

She sat down with a sigh, and looked at me. There was a deep sadness there, and a part of me wanted to try and console her, reach out and take her hands. But I was chained up and no doubt someone was behind the two-way mirror watching us.

"Why'd you do it, Dillon?" she asked. Her voice was low and coarse, like someone who'd just been woken up from a restless sleep.

"Do what? Are you talking about what he said? You know I had nothing to do with Chance."

"How do I know that? I don't really know you at all. And from what I've been told from an eye witness, you're the only one who's been at all the crime scenes."

"I wasn't anywhere near Niagara Falls when the church fire happened. I don't know the dates for that, but I can tell you, I hadn't been here in years before I got called by Chance. And yes, I was here when that happened, but I was nowhere near his office when he was killed."

"And what about last week? You going to tell me you weren't here last week? I'm sure you have some sort of alibi for that murder too?"

That murder? It must be the fifth homicide charge they were trying to pin on me. At least I had a good excuse for not been responsible for that. I'm pretty sure I hadn't been an outpatient at CAMH. I just had to hope that all traces of me being there hadn't been erased by Garcia and Dr Marshall.

"I do actually, a good alibi. I'd rather not talk about it here, but yeah, there was no way I was here."

"We have a witness, Dillon. The same one that puts you at the church on the day of the fire also puts you at the scene where Esho died."

"Esho? Who's that?"

"My partner. Detective Korkis," she said softly, but her teeth were gritted tightly and there was rage boiling in her eyes: rage aimed right at me.

"I'm so sorry, but I can tell you, I had nothing to do with that."

"I don't believe you."

"I can prove it." There was no way I was going to get out of this if I wasn't up front and told her everything that had happened. If they thought Rouge and I were involved in killing a police officer, we'd be in a world of hurt. No doubt one of us would end up in the hospital or morgue before we ever made it to court to be processed. Being transparent was the only we would walk away unscathed. "When I left here, things got pretty weird for me. The things Chance had be seeing, I started to see them too. I thought I was going nuts, and, well, I guess I did in a way. I was picked up and taken to the hospital. They thought I was nuts, so they put me in CAMH. I'm sure you know what that is."

She nodded. "How long where you there for?"

"Two weeks. It wasn't until I figured out the things I was seeing all had to do with *here*, and a doctor believed me, that I was let out."

"What were you seeing?"

"People with melting faces. Their eyes, noses and mouths bled this black oil full of insects. It's the same thing Chance Anderson saw. It's the reason he called me here to begin with."

"And Esho too," she said, and a tear leaked from the side of her right eye. She wiped it away and shook her head. "No. The two have nothing to do with one another."

"He was seeing the melted faces too? And did the people he saw melting eventually die?"

"How'd you know?"

"It's the same thing I figured out. Chance was seeing it too. He lost it even more when he looked in the mirror: he saw himself melting. That was a few days before he died."

Winger laughed and sat back down, still shaking her head though.

"None of this makes sense. You know that, right? What am I supposed to tell anyone when they ask me about this?"

"Is there nobody behind the mirror?" I asked, and she shook her head and told me the video camera was off. "You tell them what you can. But I had nothing to do with this, and I think a part of you knows it, too."

"Yeah, that's why I'm here. And why I turned the camera off. When you left, we started looking into everything, and none of it made a bit of sense. A few days later, Esho started seeing things, acting weird, and he started going off on his own. Then, he's dead, killed the exact same way Mr Anderson was."

"And someone puts me at the crime scene, also saying I was at the church?"

"Yeah. They said they never put two and two together, until Esho was found dead, but when his body was discovered, she pinned it all on you."

"She?" I asked, but I was starting to see where this was going.

"Yeah, Chance Anderson's secretary, Ms Mittz. She'd been clearing things out of Mr Anderson's office, and last week she showed up and found Esho dead in the same room where her boss had died. Right away she said she'd seen you driving down the street just as she arrived, as though you'd just left the office."

"Well, I was in the hospital, so we know that's a lie."

"But there's no way she did it. Look at her. I mean, she could have set the fire in the church, but there's no way she twisted the heads off two men that outweigh her by at least a hundred pounds each."

Oh, there was a way. I just didn't like the idea of what that way was.

"I need to get out of here," I told her, and lifted my hands up hoping to get her to take the cuffs off me. "I need to get to Ms Mittz and to Chance's office before anything else happens."

"No. You wait here and I'll go arrest her."

"That's not going to work. You have to know that."

"I'll take backup."

Since she'd come into the interrogation room and told me everything she had, I'd been adding it all together with what I already knew. I'd been piecing the whole mess together into a puzzle to try and make actual sense of it, create a picture that lined up. For so long I'd been missing crucial bits, but with the new information, I was able to unveil a truth that gave me one of those eureka moments.

"Backup isn't going to be able to help you, detective. Not with this. You're not facing a normal person guilty of murder, there's more to it than that. And if she touches you before I can end this, you'll end up going crazy like the rest of us."

"What are you talking about? I'll bring her in, get her to confess and then you can leave."

"It's not that easy," I said, and took a deep breath, getting ready to say things she might not be ready to hear. "This is not a woman guilty of murder and arson. There's something bigger at play here, and I think it's all focused at Chance's office."

"You're going to have to give me more than that."

"I know, for example, that some sort of gate to another realm has been opened, a place called Beelz. It's where some pretty nasty demons live."

Winger stood up abruptly and held her hand up. "No. None of that. I don't want to hear this, Dillon. There's no way I'm going to tell the higher-ups about demons and whatnot."

"You'll have to figure that out on your own, but if you go in there with backup, you're going to need to know what you're facing. There is a gateway open, and the only thing I can put together is that it's somewhere in Chance's building. That's why two people have died there. I could be wrong; it wouldn't be the first time, but what you've told me now about Ms Mittz, it has to be there. I'd stake my reputation on it at this point."

"So there's a gate opened. Why can't I arrest her?"

"Because she might not really be who we think she is. If she was there when the gate opened, or even opened it herself, then she may be the source of whatever has come through. That's why Esho, Chance, and I were seeing the things we were. She's the carrier of a demon from that world, and when she touched us, she infected us. Did she touch you at all?"

"No," she said, and sat back down. "But the day we met, Esho had been interviewing her and she kept taking his hand and hugging him."

"She did the same to me."

"So, we arrest her, and if she tries to touch me, I'll shoot her. Self defense."

"You can't. I don't know if this is even her fault. If the door was opened by someone or something else and she just happened to be there, she might've been nothing more than a convenient cab some demon has hopped in to take it where it wants to go. If you guys go after her, not knowing how to stop whatever is doing this, you'll all end up like Esho and Chance, or in a psych ward. This has to be done right. I need to go."

"I'm going to lose my job over this. I'm already suspended for not bringing you in when Chance died."

"If I don't stop this, more people will die, I can guarantee that. And there's going to be a lot more people going into this demon's belly than to the great beyond." I saw her look of confusion at that, but shook my head. "Never mind that. If you think all this is already crazy, you have no idea what else I could tell you."

"Well, how am I supposed to do this?" she asked, and looked back at the door. "It's not as though the station is empty and I can just sneak you out of here."

"What time is it?"

"Nearly eleven thirty."

"And when is shift change? Midnight?"

She nodded, and I told her what would happen.

Thursday

It was nearly two in the morning when the door to the interrogation room opened again. I was happier than ever to see not only Winger back, clear evidence bag with my belongings in hand, but she also had Rouge at her side. The detective looked nervous, but if she followed my instructions we'd all come out of the whole mess smelling like roses and saving lives.

"How'd it go?" I asked, and took the bag from her. I put my things in my pockets and attached my Tincher to my belt, then turned to Rouge and hugged her. "You okay?" I whispered in her ear, and she nodded.

"It went just like you said it would," Winger told me, but looked nervous.

"Staff is lower on the night shift, and when there's a call of someone breaking into a business, especially one like a Tim Hortons, the cops go running. The sleepier the town, the more cars show up. I'm sure it's all hands on deck there."

"Pretty much."

"And the video feeds?"

"All but the front end was turned offline."

"Are we getting out of here?" Rouge asked, and I handed her the items the police took from her when we were arrested.

"Yeah. This time I have no doubt where to go."

"You said that last time," Rouge snapped back, and I could see the look of concern on Winger's face.

"I didn't have the full picture then. Now I do. Let's go and get this over with."

We headed towards the back doors of the police station and when we stepped outside, there was no sign of my car. Great.

"Where's my car?" I asked Winger.

"There's nothing in the report about it. Maybe it's where you left it."

"And how far away is Pastor Herb's church?" I asked, wanting to make sure I had my car with me, in case I needed something from the bag Godfrey had given me. It would also be nice to get the hell out of Niagara Falls once the job was done.

"I can drive you there, but I thought you wanted to go to Chance's office."

"I might need things in my car first."

"Sure. Stay here and I'll pull my car around. We'll go get your car, and then we can drive over to the office."

"I\d appreciate the drive to my car, but you shouldn't come with me any further than that."

"This woman killed my partner, my friend. I'm coming, or you can go right back in that fucking room and wait to see what they do with you. With or without you, I'm going to go and deal with her."

I opened my mouth but Rouge put her hand on my arm and shook her head. She was right. There'd be no point in trying to argue the matter. It wasn't as if she was going to be stubborn or anything like that. The truth of the matter was, we needed her, and she needed to see what this was all about. She was going to have a hard time explaining everything to her superiors, but at least if she was there to witness it, to see that I wasn't lying or making up some weird story to save my ass, she'd at least be able to live with the decision she'd made.

☝ · ☝

We parked both cars a block away from the real estate office. The three of us stood on the deserted sidewalk, looked towards the unimposing building, and took a moment. I felt something close to fear stir in me. I wasn't really on my A game, thanks to the drugs still in my system, and I wasn't going into this alone like I normally would. Not only was I bringing a police officer with no experience in the supernatural, but I had the woman I loved at my side. Would I be worried about her safety the whole time, looking over my shoulder to ensure she wasn't in harm's way? That would be a good way to get us all killed, so I wanted to make sure I had my head screwed on right before we went in. I had to believe in them as much as I did myself. The problem was, I had little faith in my own skills at that moment, so my trust felt spread a little thin.

"You think she's in there?" Rouge asked as we started to make our way towards Chance's office.

"It's possible. If she's as bad off as I'm guessing, she might not be able to stray too far away from the gateway."

"Why not?"

"Some demons can only manage to be a certain distance from their home world. It's as though they're tethered slightly so they need to stay close to the breech. This is especially true if they need a human host or are more of a parasite with a symbiotic relationship to the host. They are only having a piggy back ride here inside a person. Others hide in the aura of a human and devour their souls before they move on to the next one."

"And a Beelz is one of those?"

"I don't know for sure. There are a lot of different demons living in that realm. Or it might not even be from Beelz at all. It could be any of them, or none of them. Until I see her, or the gate, I won't know what needs to be done. The only thing I know for certain is that one of these demons has infected Ms. Mittz, which is why she passed on these symptoms to me, Chance and your partner. How deep the grip of it is, I can't say for certain."

"You have done this before, right?" Winger asked. She sounded as though she expected it to be my first rodeo.

It kind of was.

"Not *this* exact situation, but something like it. I've never had a Beelz gate opened, but I know enough about them to know different ways to shut them down."

"I'm quickly losing faith in you." The detective's flat voice matched her emotionless face.

"That happens from time to time."

We got to the office front and the place was dark. I peered in through the window, thinking it might be possible Ms Mittz would be in there waiting for us, and we'd get it all done fast and easy. She wasn't anywhere in sight, but at least the front door was unlocked.

"That seems convenient," Rouge said, and I nodded. "I don't mean that in a good way, Dillon. You know it looks like a trap, right?"

"Of course," I said, which was only a small white lie. I didn't think it was a trap at first, I hoped it meant things were going our way. "Just follow me and stay on your toes."

"Do you think the door was unlocked like that when Esho came here?" Winger asked, and I really wished she hadn't, because the idea of Ms. Mittz drawing us in to her spider's web, only to twist our heads off, made me want to double back and just get the hell out of there. I liked our heads where they were.

"If you two want to wait outside, it might be better. You're kind of freaking me out, and I'm supposed to be the expert here."

"Don't worry Dill," Rouge tried to chuckle, no doubt looking to alleviate the stress. "If you get into any trouble, I'll save you again."

"You saved him? She saved you?"

"Sort of," I whispered, and heard the two of them high five behind me. Why weren't they as worried as I was?

It could be because by the time we'd walked through the whole office, we'd discovered there was nothing there. No sign of Ms Mittz and no sign of any doorway to another realm. I was well past self-doubting my experience and theories. It'd all seemed so right to me. The office had to be the key; it made sense in every way. There was Chance, the smell of staleness in his office, the head-twisting happening here in both cases, and Ms Mittz's claim of my involvement in all of it. The fact that the people she'd touched—myself included—saw the same melted-faced people, had to be more than just a mere coincidence. Add in that Esho and Chance both ended up dead in the exact same way, and in the exact same place led me to the office as the source of everything. So how could the gate not be there?

"Where does this lead?" Rouge asked, indicating the closet door in Chance's office.

"It's a closet," I told her, having seen Ms Mittz use it on my one and only visit.

"Are you sure? I can feel a breeze coming from the space at the bottom," she told me, and I rushed over.

You have to be kidding me! I thought.

I opened the door, and it looked like a closet, but there was no back wall there. When I'd seen it originally, there were coats and jackets hanging in there. With them pushed to the side now, I could see there was another door further back, and it was wide open to reveal a set of stairs going down. It was a secret room. I've always wanted to find a place with a secret room!

I pulled the Zuuar from my bag, aimed it down the stairs and watched as it glowed. There was something inhuman down there.

"Are you sure you two want to come down? This is the last chance to ditch," I said, and there might've been a part of me hoping they would, but both said no, and the three of us moved down into the space under Chance's office.

It was quiet below, and dark. Partway down the stairs, Rouge pulled her cellphone out and turned on the flashlight. There seemed to be no movement below, but I prepared myself for anything. I slowed my breath, listened as we descended and I readied for any sort of attack. We came to the last stair. I asked Rouge to shine the light around to try to find a light switch, and when she did, I flicked it and bright, fluorescent light lit the large, near-empty room. There were a few cardboard boxes stacked up near one wall, three file cabinets on another, and nothing else worth noting.

I lifted the Zuuar again, and it continued to shine, no matter what direction I turned it. Something was down there, but it didn't have a single source.

"We'll need to move some of the boxes," I said to the others. "Maybe check behind the file cabinets. Something has to be here."

"You sure that thing works?" Winger asked, as she looked down at the strange glowing metal in my hand. I really didn't want to take the time to explain it.

"It does. So there's something here, we just have to—"

My words weren't cut off so much as I'd just lost the ability to speak. I'd been shifting some of the boxes aside and turned my head to see Rouge move the file cabinets, and there it was. The sight was terrifying and glorious all at once. I'd never seen anything quite like it, but I knew what it was as soon as my eyes fell on it. We'd found the gateway, the door to the Beelz realm.

"You should step back," I called out to Rouge. She'd been standing in front of the rippling wall, but I didn't need to ask twice. She stepped away from it as I moved forward. It was mesmerizing.

"There's no way that's real," Winger gasped as I stepped past her to get a better look.

"It's real, alright. This is the gateway to Beelz."

"I've lost my mind, haven't I?"

"No more than the rest of us," I said, but then focused on the fissure.

The breach was about five feet tall. At the base, it was as wide as it was tall, but grew smaller until it ended at a point at the very top. There was a prism of light, rolling like waves on the beach, but shadows moved somewhere deep within it, indistinguishable shapes that looked as though they were coming towards the gate but never seemed to get there. This was it. This was the source of it all.

"Should we use the Firma Patch or the Azzeen Staff?" Rouge asked, and though I was impressed that she remembered the names so easily, it was too early for either of them.

"We can't do that yet, Rouge."

"Why not?"

"We need to find whatever demon or demons are already here and send them back first."

"Why not seal it and just use your Tincher?"

"If this is something from the Beelz realm, and it's somehow possessing or has attached itself to Ms Mittz, using the Tincher could kill her. I still have no idea how involved she is in all of it, but even if she somehow opened the gate herself, I can't kill her.

We need to split them apart, and then send it back through to save her. If we just kill the demon, she will die."

"But where is she?" Winger asked, and I turned to Rouge.

"You have the Klask?" I asked, and she nodded and pulled out the small glass jar with the partially liquid, partially solid bug in it. "Give it a go."

Rouge shook the jar a little harder than needed. The little blue guy inside flipped and flopped against the glass, and Winger watched in obvious, uncomprehending confusion. She opened her mouth to say something, but then there was a loud, ear-shattering scream that echoed around us, and she didn't need to ask anymore.

From the shadows under the stairs, Ms Mittz stumbled out. She held her hands to her ears and looked as though she was in extreme distress. I told Rouge to shake it again, and when she did, something flickered behind the secretary. It was fast, but when Rouge continued to shake it, the flickering made the shape more and more solid until it was in full view. It was the demon.

The creature was huge. It towered four feet over Ms Mittz. Its body was lean in the lower half and widened as it went upwards, and looked more like a shadow than anything solid. I could see its dark lower half was snaked around Ms Mittz's waist as the demon fought to hold on. Both the woman and her piggy backer both screamed: Rouge hadn't stopped shaking the jar, and I didn't tell her to stop when I noticed. Instead, I watched the scene before me, eyes stuck on the monster. There was no easy way to distinguish its features. It looked more like a living shadow with elongated arms that ended in dark hooks instead of hands. Its head was like a flame of shadows, listing to one side as it opened its mouth to scream and green, swamp-like light glowed from within.

This was the first time I'd come face to face with a demon from Beelz.

The screams stopped as the sound of breaking glass filled the room. I turned my head to see Rouge had dropped the jar and the bug inside evaporated as soon as the air got to it. That wasn't good. I looked back towards Ms Mittz, and she charged at me, the demon still in full view. Its hooked hands had disappeared back into the woman's shoulders, and as woman and demon came at me, I took several steps backwards.

"You!" Ms Mittz growled, but even though it was her mouth that moved, the voice was not hers or human at all. "You've been touched. Now your soul is mine!"

Well, I guess that's why it killed Chance and Esho. I'd never heard of demons from the Beelz realm claiming souls this way, but now I knew and would have to make a note of it so I could let the Collective and other hunters know. Always assuming I got out of it all in one piece.

The woman with the demon on her back continued to advance on me as I backed away. I fumbled with my bag. I needed to find something, and quick. My hands came out with a *Teed*, but that wouldn't help. Then I found a bottle of Refulgent, but using it would kill Ms Mittz. I was running out of time: the demon was almost on me.

My fingers touched something cold and metal and I went to pull it out, but as I moved back, my feet collided with something on the ground and I fell backwards. The bag dropped to the floor and my hands were empty.

I didn't really need it though, not to deal with the demon at least. My stumble sent me falling back and when I landed, I wasn't on Earth any more.

I've been to a few planets and realms in my very long life. I've seen colour that would drive a human mind to the brink of insanity. I've witnessed vistas the most drugged out hippie wouldn't even begin to imagine. I'd interacted with creatures that lived in more than one dimension at a time because their sheer size and magnitude didn't allow them to live on one plane of existence. I've heard sounds from beasts a human ear would never detect, and listened to alien oceans speak words in strange languages because they weren't just bodies of water, but living beings that could communicate with you.

Yet none of that compared me to the demon realm of Beelz.

I'd seen into gates to other demon realms, but I've never been unlucky enough to trip backwards through a door into a world I never wanted to be in.

What was worse was the doorway I'd come through wasn't on the ground level like it had been on Earth. Instead, it hung in the sky, twenty feet above where I'd fallen. I looked up at it, trying to see if Rouge or Winger were staring back at me, but the hole in the demon sky was just dim light, and even dimmer were the shadows of what could have been any of three people beyond it. If I hadn't known it was there, I would've missed it. I thought of calling out, hoping one of them would hear me and throw me a rope or something, but no doubt they were all busy with Ms Mittz and her monstrous passenger.

Not to mention I didn't want to bring any attention to myself in a place I didn't want to be.

Instead of yelling out to the people back in the world I'd fallen from, I looked around to see if there was something that would help me get back to Earth. My eyes could barely make sense of the scene they fell on.

I was on a hilltop of sorts. There was no dirt or grass under my feet, though. What I stood on looked more like lizard scales, as if the hill and the valley below was actually the body of some large monster I couldn't fully see. For all I knew I was right, but I didn't want to take time to find out if this terrible idea was real or not. Getting out of that realm—and fast—was my only concern.

A loud roar echoed through the air, followed by a vibration all around that nearly knocked me off my feet. I looked about, took the entire vista in, worried for a second it would be some indescribable beast with a curious palate, and a hankering for some Dillon tartar.

The red and blue sky was full of winged creatures that were less than solid, something that flowed and changed like quicksilver does on Earth. They moved around above like birds at times, but in the next second they'd turn into globs of liquid in a sky without gravity. They didn't look friendly in the slightest, but luckily they didn't seem to pay me any mind. They were all bigger than I was, but none seemed big enough to make the sound that had caused my teeth to rattle in my head. I turned my attention to the valley below, and to the horizon in the opposite direction of the gateway. That's where I saw what had made the sound, and my urgency to get out of the Beelz realm grew greater.

Huge creatures, ones that would put dinosaurs to shame, moved below. Their bodies were bloated, misshapen, with no sense of symmetry to them at all. One side was made of a nest of tentacles, or crab-like legs, while on the other side they had something that resembled human appendages. A little less than a third of the beasts had tattered wings made of what looked like silk, leather, or spider's webbing, while others moved across the valley floor on pools of crimson or deep violet, as though the liquid was their legs. And it might well be that way too. In places like Beelz, nothing made one hundred percent sense.

The good thing was, none of them seemed to notice me, which meant it was safe to try to get to the breach to get out of there. The last thing I wanted was one of those huge monsters following me out, and then I'd have to deal with the demon as well as them. If I was fast, I'd get back to Earth, find a way to detach the demon from Ms Mittz without hurting her, and then I could close the gateway for good. The faster I did that, the less likely one of these monsters would get out, or worse, another demon would find me and the breech. One demon was more than enough for me.

The question was how to get up and out of there. I didn't see a ladder. No trees close by to help out, and my bag was back on Earth. I knew it was going to be tricky. I had my gloves in my back pocket, my Tincher on my belt, and nothing else.

Well, that wasn't true.

I also had some gum in one pocket, my cell phone in another, and my wallet in my back pocket. If I was that guy from that show in the '80s, it would be enough to do the job. Alas, I'm not, and it wouldn't.

I had an idea then, and as stupid as it seemed, I thought I might as well try it. After all, I was on an alien planet, trapped in a demon realm with nothing but a few things from Earth. These creatures wouldn't have any idea what a cell phone was, and even better, the smell of the gum would be so foreign to them.

If I could somehow attract one of the flying creatures to where I was, I could try, somehow, to wrangle it and ride it up and out of here.

It sounded as good as any other choice I had, which was none. It was either that or nothing. I doubted there was a Home Depot close by so I could buy a ladder.

"Well," I whispered, "here goes nothing, I guess."

I took one of the hard-shelled gums out from the package and went to snap it in half when something hit me in the head. It didn't hurt, but I yelped and jumped, sure for a second that I was being attacked. I looked and saw a thin, yellow, nylon rope behind me. I followed it upwards and saw it lead to the breech, where the unmistakable shadow of Rouge hovered.

What was she doing? Had the demon gotten away?

Whatever it was, it would be better to just grab the rope and get the hell out of there. I took it, looped it around my waist and then gave it two sharp tugs. It tightened and I held on for dear life as I was slowly lifted over the alien landscape. The things flying above me were oblivious to my presence. They moved in circles and zigzags, some of them making sounds like cicadas as they flew, others sounded more like the crackling of electricity through an exposed cord. At least they weren't noticing me.

The things below, though, they did. I shouldn't have taken the gum out of the package. Next time, I'll be sure to remember.

I heard a roar, rumbling like an earthquake, and when I looked back down at the valley where the monsters had been, I saw most of them looking up at me. A terrible sound that made me think my ears were going to start to bleed echoed through the air as five or six of the creatures ran up to the top of the hill I'd just been standing on. The sight of their massive, hulking, malformed bodies coming at me like a high speed train caused panic to set in. I wasn't sure if they could fly up and follow me out, but if I wasn't raised faster, some of the huge beasts would have a chance at grabbing hold of me. I started to smack my hand against the rope, hoping they would get the messaged, feel the urgency, and then I heard a sound that nearly made me pee my pants.

It was so loud! Worse than sticking your head into one of those tall speakers at a concert, while Motorhead played Overkill. It was deafening, vibrating through my bones, and when I looked to my right, I saw the source. At least, I tried to make sense of it as best my mind could.

The ground had begun to rise. At least, most of the ground in my view had. There was something that resembled a face in what might've been the center of it. It was a wall of scaled meat and muscle with a huge, toothy hole that had to be a mouth. From that deep, dark orifice, a thousand tongues whipped wildly, and it all came straight at me. There was little doubt that the hill I'd been standing on was some monster after all, and it knew I was there. It was coming, but luckily something that big can't move that fast. As it shifted to get at me, the unwelcome tourist, the other, smaller monsters tumbled backwards off of it. I hit the rope over and over again as the red and pink tentacles got closer and closer. I screamed for them to hurry, getting to see way more of the inside of the mammoth's mouth than I wanted. I saw the end of Dillon right then and there, swallowed up by some unthinkable monster. I didn't want to wonder if there would be a way to get a new body if this one was devoured by that thing, but that couldn't keep the idea out. I closed my eyes as it inched closer and closer.

I was braced for some sort of attack; either from below, or from the giant beast. With my eyes shut tight, I didn't see the moment I was pulled from this version of Hell, and returned to Chance Anderson's office basement.

I was back on Earth.

It felt so good to breath in air that didn't smell of rot and sulfur, but there was no time to celebrate or rejoice. There was still a demon in the room and a gate that needed sealing before anything else could wiggle through there.

I jumped up off the ground, grabbed my Tincher from my belt and looked for the demon. Wingers and Rouge both stood in front of me. They were out of breath, but smiled. When I continued to take in the scene, I saw Ms Mittz unconscious on the ground, and there was no sign of the demon who'd been attached to her.

"So, what did I miss?"

"When I shook that jar and saw that thing, I was pretty freaked out. I can admit that. It's probably why I dropped the jar," Rouge began as we stood over Ms Mittz, who lay unmoving, but alive on the ground. "I looked down at the broken glass for a second and when I turned back to her and the demon, I saw she was coming at you. I could still see that black shadow wrapped around her waist and towering over her. For a second I froze, watching you as you stumbled back away from it. You were frantically going through your bag, but couldn't find what you were looking for. Then I saw your face change and I was sure you had just what you needed, but then you tripped on that thing there and went falling through the hole."

I looked back towards the hole and realized there was still something on the other side, coming at us, and I grabbed my bag.

"Where's the demon?" I asked hurriedly as I looked for the Azzeen Staff and the Firma Pitch.

"Your girl took care of it," Winger said, and put a hand on Rouge's shoulder. "This girl is pretty hardcore."

"You got rid of it? You're sure?"

Rouge nodded and started to explain how, but I stopped her.

"You can tell me after I do this. There are a few friends on the other side that are anxious to come over and see us. I'd rather they didn't."

I walked back over to the breech with the Azzeen Staff and tapped the edges of the hole. Two taps every half-foot would do enough to close the door. From inside the hell I'd just been in, I could see swirling shadows, growing larger as they got closer to where I was. I moved as fast as I could, and when I hit the final spot, nothing happened. The breech seemed completely unaffected by the action. I went through the routine again, felt urgency swell, but there was still no change.

"Shit."

"Why isn't it closing?" Rouge asked as she walked up beside me, looking into the void.

"I have no idea," I admitted, and looked at it again. There had to be a reason it wasn't working. I didn't want to think that Godfrey had given me something bogus again. Not now. There was little I'd be able to do to stop a full-on monster invasion if I couldn't shut the gate.

"Does that have anything to do with it? It's what you tripped over," Rouge said, pointing down at my feet. I followed her finger and saw the thing that had caused me to fall into the Beelz realm.

"You've got to be kidding me."

It was small, maybe three inches in height, fifteen in length and four in width, but there would be more to it than that. The rest would be buried deeper in the ground. What poked out was the same colour as the floor, a dull, concrete gray, possibly made of some alien stone, and carved with unearthly letters. It wasn't the first time I'd seen one, but usually they're a lot bigger, which meant there was more under the floor. I wouldn't doubt there would be some sort of cave system under this part of the city, which would be home to the rest of what I'd tripped over. What I stared down at was the top of an altar. These altars are part of a stone stairway into a demon realm, usual a one-way system. Someone had either tried to bury this when the building was built, or had uncovered it at some later date. Whatever the answer to that was, though, it didn't matter: it was the source of the gateway, and I knew what needed to be done.

"Stand back," I told them, and raised the staff high overhead. I whispered words I knew, spoke in an ancient tongue from a forgotten world, and then brought the bronze stick down as hard and as fast as I could. When it made contact with the stone, there was a blinding white light that rippled around us, followed by a high-pitched sound like metal scraping on metal. The ground under us shook like a mild earthquake, but it didn't last long. I heard Winger yelp as it happened, but then it stopped and the breech began to flicker and lose its substance. The stone on the floor had shattered, and I was quick to toss the staff down and grab the Firma Patch. I put it to work to seal any chance of the breach reopening.

The gate was closed, and everything would hopefully go back to normal.

"Now, you were saying..." I chuckled and, sat down on the floor.

"When you fell through the hole, the shadow thing began to laugh and was too busy looking at where you'd gone to worry much about me. I went into my pocket while its back was turned and pulled out this stone." She showed me what it was and I saw that it was a Swart Stone, a small black crystal that can be used to paralyze some monsters and demons. She was lucky it worked on the Beelz. "I remembered what you told me about it, so I ran over to the demon and her, and pressed it onto the demon's back. Only, I didn't know it wouldn't totally be solid, so my arm went through it and it touched her," she said, pointing to Ms Mittz. "She cried out, stumbled back and fell. The demon seemed unaffected by it, but she was out cold."

"It didn't affect the creature at all?" I asked, and made note of it. I'd have to remember to mark it down for others who might have a run in with something from the Beelz realm.

"Nothing, but it didn't come after either of us. It struggled, tried to pull away from Ms Mittz, but it seemed glued to her somehow; stuck in place."

That was strange. I held up my hand to try and take all that information in, to process it. Demons, monsters, and spirits have a few ways they can come to Earth. There are weak spots, places where one can pass through in its essence form, leaving its physical body behind in wherever it's from. Another way is to come through a breach, a portal, or a gateway. They're all the same, only slight differences, but it all comes down to the same thing. Whatever comes through one of them, they can bring their physical, more dangerous form along for the ride. They don't need to call forth or inhabit inanimate objects.

This seemed like neither of those.

This was the third, more uncommon way, and if I was right, it made sense why there was the top of an altar peeking out.

Centuries ago, long before the rules for visiting Earth were put into place by the Collective, some creatures came here freely. When humans found out about them, some viewed them as blights to the Gods they worshipped. Others looked at them as the real Gods. The latter created black churches and altars to these monsters, and the altars could be used to open doorways to demonic and alien worlds. Some of these gates were one-way streets: humans could go in, but nothing could come out unless called to do so. The ones that were called forward from one of these altars would be tied to that human, unable to roam the world freely. What the human didn't know, though, was when one of the demons became tethered to them the relationship wasn't as symbiotic as they might've hoped. The demon, if it was strong enough, would control the human and could even call forth more demons who could then roam freely, far away from the gate and the human.

I explained all this to Rouge and Winger.

"So why didn't we see it when we first met her?" Winger asked.

"I'm guessing the demon was able to hide within her when it wanted to, or she could've even willed it to stay hidden. It might've only become visible because you shook the Klask and it wasn't able to hide anymore," I said, just taking a stab in the dark. I had no real idea.

"And you didn't notice it or sense it at all?"

"That's not how it works. I wish it was, but no, I can't sense demons or monsters. I can sometimes smell them, or see signs they've left behind, but when I first got here, I had no idea what I was dealing with." I turned to Rouge then and asked her to tell me what had happened after Ms Mittz fell.

"I grabbed your bag and started pulling things out and using them." She held up three items: silver water, thistle glue, and a roll of Pagar (an elastic thread used to tether creatures in place). "None of them worked, so I ran back, worried the demon was either going to break free of Ms Mittz or she'd wake up. That's when I found this."

"That would work," I laughed, looking at the *Beegan* in her hand. A Beegan is an iron rod made of melted nails once used in crucifixions on Earth. These rods are then dipped in the blood of a Hellion—something not easy to come by, so you can guess how rare a Beegan is—but they are super-effective against a demon. The mix of Earthly relic and Hellion blood causes a demon to come apart, to be completely undone. It doesn't work on many other creatures outside of demons, but she made a good choice.

"When I brought it over to where the demon was, I could tell it was afraid, and it started to talk, to plead for its life."

"That wasn't fun," Winger said, sounding a little sad. "The thing was pathetic."

"It was," Rouge admitted. "But then I remembered it had already killed two people, so I didn't really care. I was going to do it. I wasn't sure how it worked, but figured I would try pressing it into the thing, like I did with the crystal. Even before it touched the thing, the shadowed colour began to turn white, ashy-looking, and then the demon became dust and evaporated. It was gone in seconds."

"You forgot a part," Winger said, and went on: "Before you touched it, it said that if we spared it, it would tell us what else had come through the gate. It said that even though the woman had called him forth, he'd helped others sneak out of there."

"Is it possible, Dillon?" Rouge asked, and I shrugged. I knew it was a possibility. The fact that there were no reports of a giant monster roaming around Niagara Falls made me doubt it. Then again, if it was a demon, similar to what had attached itself to Ms Mittz instead of one of those monsters that I'd seen, it might go unnoticed by people.

One problem at a time, I guess.

"So, that's it then? It's over?" Rouge asked and I nodded, but looked down at Ms Mittz. Winger was doing the same.

"How am I going to explain all this?" she asked, and I could only imagine how hard all this was for her. At least Rouge had an idea of what I did, had been part of this once already. For the detective, it was all so new and no doubt confusing. "What am I supposed to do with her?"

"Put everything on her. The only way that demon got here was because of her. She wasn't a victim in any of this."

"Why would she do it though, what was her motive?" Winger asked, and I admitted that I didn't know. Nor did I actually care. As far as I was concerned, I was done with the whole mess. "So I just book her on the murders and hope it sticks?"

"It's all you can do," I explained and hoped it would be enough. Of course, it wasn't.

"Nobody is going to buy that she did all this. They aren't going to believe she killed my partner, her boss, and burnt down a church, killing three more."

"I'm not saying she did the church. I think that has nothing to do with any of this, but she is responsible for the others. Somehow, she found that down here," I said, and pointed to the shattered remains of the top of the stone altar. "I have no idea how or why it was uncovered, and I don't know why she opened the gate and called the demon forth, but whatever the reason, she did it. That's why it was attached to her. She was the master of it, which means she needs to take the fall for all the shit she caused. And when you take her in and she no doubt starts to talk about demons and doorways to Hell, they will call her crazy and lock her up. Take it from me, it's easier for people to assume you're crazy than it is to accept monsters are real."

Friday

We decided to stay in Niagara Falls overnight. It was just a lot easier than driving back to Toronto after all that. We got a motel room; most of the bigger hotels were booked, but it was clean and bed bug free, so it was fine. Hours after we'd left the detective, she called me to let me know it had played out pretty well. Ms Mittz had gone on and on about monsters and demons, claiming she was some sort of witch who could call demons to Earth to take revenge on people who'd done her wrong. She warned them to release her, or they'd all be subject to the great culling. When they executed a warrant on her house, they found both Esho and Chance's heads. Both had been dipped in some sort of wax to seal them, and then they'd been placed on a bed of black sand in her bedroom. With everything she told the police and the heads found in her apartment, it was no wonder they figured she was mentally ill. She'd be lucky to see the sun ever again.

It worked for me.

"So, you're in the clear again?" Rouge asked when I hung up.

"Looks that way," I said and grabbed her around the waist and pulled her to me. "I'm pretty impressed how you did out there. You might not have known what you were actually doing, but you saved the day."

"Yet again. You still worried about me joining you?"

"Only as far as the Collective goes. You know this was big, closing the gate and stopping this demon, but they may not go for a human hunter. That guy Parks seems to be gunning for me

209

and us as a couple. I know the Collective sent him, but I think if they want, they could call him off. I'm hoping they will. They can't afford to lose me."

"Or me," she laughed. "I seem to have a knack for slaying demons."

That she did.

We arrived back in Toronto close to six in the evening. We stopped by to pick up the puppy and then decided to head to Rouge's house. I called Garcia to see if there was any word on Don Parks, but just got his machine. I left a message and hoped all was as it was when we left.

"You hungry?" Rouge asked as we walked into her house. "I'm famished."

"I could go for some pizza. Want me to order?"

"Does this girl like rhinestones? Damn right I do."

I laughed and placed an order for our usual. Pizza was one of our go-to meals, so it was easy to just use the automated line and repeat the last order we'd had. While we waited, we changed into some lounging clothes, turned on Netflix and started watching TV. For weeks she's been trying to get me to watch Gilmore Girls, so I decided that, since she'd impressed me so much in Niagara Falls, I owed it to her.

We were almost done the first episode when the doorbell rang. Rouge went to go to it, but I stopped her.

"You sit, demon slayer. I got this one."

I grabbed the food, tipped the driver and locked the door. The pizza smelled so good, I wanted to bury my face in it. I opened the box to take a look at it, and as my gaze was downwards, I noticed someone on the other side of the open pizza box. I closed the lid, a smile on my lips, expecting it to be Rouge.

It wasn't.

It was Don Parks.

"Hey, Dillon," he said, his face partially engulfed in shadows. "Miss me?"

"What are you—"

He didn't wait for the question. Instead, he charged at me, his own spellbound blade in hand, and knocked me over. We fell backwards, the pizza, pop, and dipping sauces flying. My back smashed hard into the ground and he was on top of me. I grabbed his wrists as he did his very best to turn my body into his blade's sheath. He grunted and used everything he had in him to stab me.

"You thought you were so slick, didn't you? You got me arrested, as though that was going to save you." He growled the words through gritted teeth as he grunted and pushed the blade closer and closer to my chest. I wanted to let go of his wrist for a second, so I could reach down and grab the Tincher from my belt. Would I be fast enough, or would I get gutted like a fish? I knew I was quick, but my Tincher was—

Shit!

I realized I didn't have my Tincher on my anyway. I was already in pajama pants, my chill gear.

Well, that certainly sucked.

"Look," I tried to say easily, but struggled to get the words out. "It's not... what you... think. There was... a... demon..."

"You think I care, Dillon? I don't give a rat's ass. You're going back, and the Collective is going to have your ass."

The blade moved closer to me.

I was losing the fight.

He had leverage and started to lean in harder and harder on the blade.

There was only an inch between me and the tip of the steel, a small void keeping me in this world. I couldn't let him win. I didn't want to go.

"I think this is it, Dillon. Any last words?"

I smiled and he didn't like that at all, but it made him stop pressing so hard, just for that moment.

"Yeah," I said, out of breath. "Rouge's an amazing hunter."

He must've heard or sensed her behind him, because for a moment he tried to turn his head. If he had managed, he would've seen Rouge standing over him, my Tincher in her hand. If he'd been faster, he would've seen a flash of steel before she buried it right into the back of his head, the point coming out his cheek.

But he didn't see any of it, because she didn't wait until he could turn around. He was dead and gone before he knew what hit him. The blade dropped from his hand and clattered to the floor.

The body Don Parks had come to Earth in soon followed.

"Are you okay?" Rouge asked, and helped me up. I was amazed by how cool and calm she sounded.

"I think so. Are you okay?"

"Of course, although, I think saving your ass is starting to get a little too common." At that, she laughed, but there was a bit of uneasiness in her voice. It might have been because she was looking down at Parks' body, and the gravity of what she'd just done to save me had hit her.

It did the same to me.

I'd already been in trouble for a laundry list of things. Now the Collective would add dispatching another hunter to the list of my offences. Not the best thing, but there was no real choice. He'd been about to do the same to me. He would've if Rouge hadn't stopped him. The big problem was trying to figure out what happened next. There were a lot of possibilities, most of them on the side of things I'd like to avoid.

Time would tell.

"Hey, Dillon?"

"What?"

"Can I keep his knife?"

I had no idea what to say. I looked from her to the lifeless body of Don Parks.

Once upon a time, things used to be so much simpler.